The Cardinal

& The Crow

D0943232

Alice Kanaka

ISBN: 979-8-9863105-1-0
First printing June 2022
Cover art by Neutronboar
Edited by Teresa Grabs

Table of Contents

Chapter 1

J ack entered the small town of Santo Milagro in a plume of red dust. His shiny new Ferrari was not meant for dirt roads and was so covered by dust it was indistinguishable from every other car in town unless you spied the fancy wheels or the logo on the trunk. He drove slowly down the three blocks of Main street, shaking his head at the potholes and lack of pavement. Slowing to a stop in front of the only saloon in town, he checked his instructions again. Yes, he knew about GPS capabilities, but he had been warned about the absence of a signal out here. Sitting back in his seat, he gaped as a tumbleweed rolled down the street. *Why would anyone choose to live here?* He didn't see any signs of life other than an old man with some dogs a block down.

Jack read the sideways-hanging sign creaking loudly as it swung back and forth. *'uck Horn loon'... close enough.* He pulled into one of the diagonal parking spots and looked sadly at the reflection of his not-so-shiny car in the darkened windows. The sounds of playful barking and shutters clacking in the breeze joined the creaking sign, reminding him of the movie *Tap*.

When he opened the car door and put a shiny, black shoe down, he was rewarded with another cloud of dust. The dogs he'd seen on the corner came running over, kicking up more dust as they vied for attention. Jack sighed and decided to let it go; there was no way he was leaving here without everything he owned being covered in dust. He took a shallow breath through his nose, squinting and trying not to breathe, as he ventured inside.

Greeted by a dark, beer-scented interior, it took a minute for Jack's eyes to adjust. When they did, he was greeted by a plump, gregarious waitress wearing a bright, pink dress. "Hello," she said, smiling. "Welcome to the Buck Horn Saloon! I'm Alley. Is there anywhere, in particular, you'd like to sit?"

There were no other customers in the saloon, so Jack indicated a corner booth. The floor was old, scuffed, wooden planks but clean, a jukebox sat in the back next to a small dance floor, and bare bulbs hung from the ceiling served as lighting. "Are all of these photos local?"

"Yes! This saloon has been here since the 1800s. The photographs and memorabilia all have historical significance. If you'd like a guided tour around town, you should ask Randy, at the hotel. His brain is plumb full of knowledge."

"That sounds interesting," he fibbed, "but first, I have a meeting with someone named Sam." Jack sat in the padded green booth and wiped at the sticky table with his handkerchief. He looked up as the doors swung open with a thwack, and in walked the most striking woman he had ever seen. Tall and slender with spiky, fire-engine red hair, she exuded understated confidence.

Alley elbowed him and giggled. "Seems like you have good timing, mister. There she is now!" She moved aside and said, "Hey, Sam!"

Sam smiled at Alley as she strode over and stuck out her hand. "You must be Jack."

He stood and took her deeply tanned hand, his eyes quickly running up her trim, muscular arm to her beautiful face and unusual hair.

"What?!"

"I apologize." The hard, uncompromising look in her green eyes surprised him, and he found himself sweating. "I expected to meet with an elderly man. My father instructed me on his deathbed to repay an old debt."

Her eyes softened. "I was named after my dad. He passed away last year."

"I'm sorry to hear that. My father left me a letter to read once I was with your father. It seems they were both a little too late. Why don't we order a drink and see what he had to say?"

Sam narrowed her eyes and seemed to consider before nodding.

Alley hovered nearby. "Are you ready to order?"

"Modelo Negra, please, Alley." Sam slid into the booth across from Jack"

"Hey! That's my favorite! I'll have one too." Jack watched Alley leave. "She's like a candle in a squalid cave."

"She might not appreciate your description of her saloon, but she does add some cheer."

Jack pulled out an envelope. "Would you like to read the letter, or shall I?"

"You read it." Sam's voice wavered.

Jack grew concerned about what might be in the letter. His father could be singularly tactless. "Do you want me to read it to myself first?"

"No, just read it aloud."

He took his butter knife and slowly opened the envelope, pausing while Alley delivered their beers. The letter was hand-written on the same rich-looking parchment as the envelope.

Son, if you have followed my instructions, you are now sitting with your uncle, my brother, Samuel Olivares. Several years ago, I was in financial difficulties, and he lent me some money to keep my business afloat. I know that he put himself in a difficult situation to help me out, and I have worked hard to live up to the faith he had in me.

So, Sam, I have instructed Jack to return your money ten-fold upon my death. More than anything, I wish I could be there to return it to you in person. I wish I could give you one last hug and tell you how sorry I am and how much I love you.

I love you, brother, and I hope you can get reacquainted with your nephew, Jack, and find joy in your extended family.

Jack glanced up and found Sam staring at him. He took a drink and remained silent as he watched her process the letter's contents.

"Wow. All this time, I thought my dad had been swindled. I thought someone had taken advantage of him and caused him to work too hard and have a heart attack. I didn't even know he had a brother."

"I didn't know either. I wonder why they didn't tell us."

Sam and Jack stared at each other. Cousins. Jack had grown up with a father who didn't seem to love him. Most of his life, he had tried to make him proud. He had thought he was alone in the world, but he wasn't, and neither was Sam.

"Sam... I thought I was just coming here to repay a debt and was planning to leave right away, but you're the only family I have, and I'm on vacation. I think it would be nice to get to know each other."

"You should stay a while if you have time."

They looked at each other, searching for some family resemblance.

The western-style saloon doors swung open again with such force the capacity sign fell off the wall and shattered. "Who's the joker off-roadin' in the flash-mobile?" a man bellowed, rolling his eyes and giving a booming, fake-sounding laugh.

Sam's lips formed a thin line, and her eyes glinted dangerously.

"You get out of here right now, Peter!" Alley lost some of her composure and poked him in the chest. "I don't want any trouble from *you* today."

"Aw, come on, sugar. You know you still love me." He smirked.

Sam stood, knocking over her drink.

"You sit back down, cowgirl. This is none of your concern."

Jack took Sam's hand and nodded toward where she had been sitting. She jerked her hand away but slowly sat back down.

Jack got out of the booth and strode over to Peter, extending his hand. He was a good head taller and twenty years younger, causing Peter to lose a little of his bluster, but not much. "I hear you don't think much of my ride." Jack smiled without mirth. "How about you and I take a little stroll?"

Despite Sam not wanting Jack to feel like he had to fight her battles, she was impressed by his assuredness. He reminded her of a jaguar, tall and lithe, with wavy black hair. He managed to command respect with the utmost restraint. Peter, on the other hand, was all 'sound and fury, signifying nothing,' as Faulkner would say.

"I've got business right here."

"No, you don't, you snake! You stole my land and my house. There's nothing more you can do." Alley crossed her arms and stepped back defensively.

Peter's evil chuckle gave Sam goosebumps. "You a little behind on the mortgage, sugar? 'Cause I've got a banker owes me a favor." He looked her in the eye until she looked away, then gave Jack a shove on the way out. "You mind your own business, pretty boy!"

Sam rushed to Alley, hugged her, and led her to the booth.

"I don't know why he has to be so mean." Alley's hands shook.

"I don't know either, but we're not going to let him take the saloon. I wonder what he's got on Mark."

"Who's Mark?"

Both women stared at Jack with surprise.

"I forgot you were here. Jack, this is Alley Carruthers. She owns the saloon. Mark's her brother. Alley, this is my cousin, Jack."

"Your cousin! How exciting!" Alley exclaimed with her usual enthusiasm. "I didn't realize you had a cousin!"

"I didn't either. We just found out."

"Here we should be celebrating, not worrying about Peter and his plans. Let me bring another round."

As she bustled off, Sam squinted at Jack. "How much money did you bring for my dad? Would it be enough to pay off a smallish loan?"

"I'm not sure. I haven't opened it. Here, take a look." He passed her an envelope.

Sam ripped it open and grew very still.

"What is it? Are you okay?"

She took a deep breath. "It's more than enough. Did your dad leave you anything? Do you need some of this? It's a lot."

Jack smiled. "My dad left me plenty, and I have my own career. That is all yours to do with what you like."

She stared at the cashier's check and wondered what she should do with it. She certainly didn't want Mark to get his hands on it.

"Sam, why would Mark foreclose on his own sister? Don't they get along?"

"No, it's not that; it's Peter. He seems to have a little dirt on everyone, and he has a way of making people do what he wants."

"Even you?"

"Yes, he has some photos, but when he tried to get to me, I told him to do his worst."

"Not a terrible secret, then?" Jack raised his eyebrows.

"I suppose it depends on who you ask." She grinned.

Alley set their drinks down. "What are you two smiling about?"

"Well... it just so happens my uncle left me a little money," Sam explained. "Just enough to get us both out from under a certain banker's thumb."

Alley's eyes went wide and a little teary. "You would do that for me? I would pay you back. I promise." She paused. "Mark's not a bad person, and I know he loves me."

"I know." Sam put her slim hand on Alley's. "This will take the pressure off Mark too."

Alley nodded and began to cry in earnest."

"Why don't you close up and take the afternoon off? I'll sort things out with Mark once the check clears."

Alley nodded and sniffed before shuffling over to the door and turning off the Open sign. "I don't know how I can ever repay you. You've been my only real friend in this town, and I just..."

"We've all been through a lot, Alley. We'll get through it together." Sam gave her a kind smile and nudged Jack. "Come with me, cuz. I'll show you to the hotel and introduce you."

Sam gave Alley another hug. "Why don't you try to get some rest."

They walked three doors down to the Los Milagros Inn. Jack hadn't even noticed it because all the storefronts blended together, giving the street an "old west" feel. Although the exterior wasn't much to look at, the interior was ornate. Sam introduced Jack to Randy, the proprietor, then said, "I have some errands to run, Jack, but I'll come back, and we can have dinner if you like?"

"That sounds great."

Randy handed Jack a large brass skeleton key on a metal ring and smiled. "I'll give you the grand tour on the way to Room 5." As they went up the grand, central staircase, he said, "The elevator works sometimes, but my general rule of thumb is don't take it unless you have to."

Jack wasn't sure if he was expected to laugh, so he coughed politely into his fist.

"There are toilets and a shower room on either end of the hall," Randy continued. "If you have an emergency, like after Edna's jalapeño surprise, there is a chamber pot out on your balcony."

Jack's eyes got wide.

"All I ask is that you don't use it inside the room and make sure you clean it before checkout. There is a fifty-dollar charge if you don't."

Jack started to sputter.

"Edna makes the surprise but expects reparations if someone tries to return it."

Unable to hold it in any longer, Jack doubled over with laughter. "I'm sorry if that wasn't a joke." He gasped.

Randy looked at him with a twinkle in his eye. "I wondered how long it would take you to crack."

"I was trying so hard to be polite," Jack said, regaining his breath.

"I could see that. Just don't laugh when you see Edna." Randy chuckled.

"Is Edna your wife?"

"Lord, no, but she might as well be. She's been giving me hell for thirty years."

Outside Room 5, Randy said, "If the key doesn't work, just jiggle it. If there's a fire, you can either brave the fire escape or slide down the banister. I find they are equally effective."

Jack laughed and entered his room. When he turned to thank Randy, he wasn't there. He peeked out the door, but his host had completely disappeared. Shrugging, he closed the door and looked around. The room was sparsely furnished with an old-fashioned bed with giant, squeaky springs, a sink, a wardrobe, a chair, and a lamp. *I won't be in here much anyway, but maybe I should have brought a book... and a toothbrush.*

Sam had lived in Santo Milagro her entire life, except for college. It was home. She walked by Melissa's shop, incense wafting through the open door. Tia waved from her nursery window across the street and motioned toward her new floral window display. Sam reminded herself to pay Tia a visit. The air was filled with the tantalizing aroma of grilled beef and onions as she passed The Ugly Orange Cafe. Her destination, Our Lady of Milagros, was not as tiny as might be expected.

Built in the 1800s, in southwestern adobe style, the community kept their place of worship in good condition. Sam entered through the heavy, wooden doors and saw Father Garcia sweeping the stone floor in front of the altar. Behind him, a handcrafted crucifix hung backlit on the wall, striking because of its size and relative simplicity.

Two tall sconces stood on either side of the stone altar, and kneeling rails lined the front of the platform.

Father Garcia was an older gentleman, but it was impossible to guess his age. He wore a plain, black cassock, and his curly, gray hair was tousled by the wind. "Good afternoon, Samantha. It's so good to see you." He smiled and set the broom aside. "Have you come for confession?"

Sam glanced toward an unfamiliar middle-aged woman with long blond hair lighting a candle on the far side of the sanctuary, then shook her head. "No, I've just come to pray, Father."

"You don't have to be here to pray, you know. God hears you wherever you are."

"It just feels more official when I'm here." She smiled.

"You know, your abuela used to come here and pray. She was the most extraordinary woman I've ever met. She had a powerful faith. She even pulled me back from the brink once."

Sam raised her eyebrows.

Father Garcia lowered his voice. "I sank into a deep depression, and my mind began to stray toward suicidal thoughts. I couldn't hear God and thought he had abandoned me."

"What happened?"

"Somehow, your abuela knew. She counseled me and prayed with me, then took me to the hospital."

Sam stayed quiet.

"It took medication and therapy. I don't know what caused the depression, but we are only human. All of us. And God will always take care of us and forgive us. He sent your abuela to help me in my darkest hour."

"Forgive me, Father, but why are you telling me this?"

"I have seen you struggling, and I wanted you to know that I see a lot of her in you. God has a plan for you, and he will provide what you need."

Sam lowered her head. "Thank you, Father. I needed to hear that."

He smiled and retrieved his broom before moving away to give her privacy.

Kneeling in one of the wooden pews, Sam bowed her head. She didn't pray aloud, but she knew God could hear her.

> *Dear heavenly father, I think you have answered my prayer. My cousin Jack came to town today. He's not really what I meant when I prayed for someone I could love and trust, but maybe family is what I need right now. I feel surprised and grateful, Lord. Thank you for answering my my prayer. Please help me to find common ground with him and to allow myself to trust again. In the name of the Father, the Son, and the Holy Ghost, Amen.*

She crossed herself and stood, blinking away unshed tears.

When Jack arrived downstairs at the hotel restaurant, across from the reception desk, he saw a large A-frame chalkboard at the entrance. 'Special: Edna's jalapeño surprise' was written in beautiful, cursive letters that reminded him of his grandmother. Looking through the doors, he saw that it wasn't very busy, and most of the customers already had their food. He waited for Sam to arrive and wondered how brave he was after Randy's colorful jokes.

He could sense Sam's arrival before he saw her. He didn't know why, but she exuded a pleasant, almost palpable energy. Once they were seated at one of the gleaming wooden tables, he said, "What exactly is the jalapeño surprise?"

"No idea," Sam said, wrinkling her nose. "I think that's why it's a surprise."

"Let's order one just to see."

"If you order something that starts with 'Edna's' and you don't eat it, she will come stomping out here to ask you why and then stand, tapping her foot while you do."

"Come on. We have to order it now. It sounds like an experience I don't want to miss!"

10

"You've been warned."

A pretty, young server named Sally took their order. They decided on a steak dinner, a salad to share, and Edna's surprise.

When the food arrived, Jack ate his salad and a piece of the steak and tasted the jalapeno surprise. He grinned at Sam, put his fork down, and waited.

"Why are you doing that?"

"After Randy's jokes and your warning, I just have to meet this lady."

There was a ruckus in the kitchen, after which the doors flew open, and a tiny, white-haired woman flew out of the kitchen, wearing a white apron and a pair of pince-nez glasses.

Jack smiled as she marched toward their table.

Hands on her hips, she asked, "Why are you smiling, young man?"

"I told my cousin, Sam, that I wanted to meet the incredible chef who made my dinner, and she told me the only way I could meet you was to not eat it. And here you are, just as she told me. Would you like to join us while we eat?"

Edna's eyes sparkled, and she smiled so wide Jack thought her face might crack. "I would love to join you. But first, let me get you a warm plate and some dessert for Ms. Smarty Pants." She whisked his plate away and headed for the kitchen.

Out she came with a piping hot plate, followed by a waitress carrying three pieces of pie and a bartender with three shots of apricot liqueur. She sat at the table and watched Jack enjoy his jalapeño surprise, answered his culinary questions without giving away her secrets, and surreptitiously watched him interact with Sam. Jack even shared a bite with Sam, who agreed it was delicious.

After they had finished dessert, they thanked her graciously and moved to the bar area so the waitresses could clean up.

"That rascal Randy told me all kinds of tales."

"He always does; that's why I wanted you to meet him."

"Speak of the devil."

"Hi, Randy."

"Hello, my dear." He turned toward Jack. "You have made our Edna very happy this evening. I have a special present for you." He smiled as a bartender brought over a large fruit bowl-sized glass filled with frozen, green liquid and two straws. "It's our new specialty, reserved only for customers who aren't driving. Give it a try, and tell me what you think."

They each took a sip and looked surprised. "That's really good! I was expecting a margarita taste, but it's very delicate, not overly sweet."

"Fruity. It doesn't taste like alcohol at all." Sam nodded.

"Yeah, be careful about that. There's quite a bit in there." He gave them a grin as he wandered over to another table.

"You're sure good at making friends," Sam said a little enviously.

"What are you talking about? They all love you."

"They've known me my whole life. If I walked in here as a complete stranger, no one would even talk to me."

"They are only talking to me because I'm with you." He smiled. "Now, help me drink this behemoth."

"What is there to do around here?" Jack asked.

"We could go riding tomorrow."

"ATVs?"

"Horses. Do you have any other clothes with you?"

"No." He glanced down at his expensive business clothes. "I wasn't planning to stay."

"I have some you can use."

He looked her up and down. "Even though we both seem to be of the long, narrow variety, I don't think they'll fit."

Sam laughed. "Not my personal clothes. Clothes that will fit you."

"Whew! I thought you were really underestimating my size."

They started talking about the ranch, had another fruit bowl of drink, and the time flew.

At closing time, Jack said, "You'd better stay here tonight. I'd hate to lose my favorite cousin to a drunk driving accident."

"I'm your only cousin."

"Yes, I know. Steady there. Do you need a hand?"

"Nope." She shook his hand off.

Once in Jack's room, he pulled her over next to him in front of the mirror, almost causing both of them to land on the floor. "When I look at you, I don't see myself, but we must have some similarities since our fathers were brothers."

"The shapes of our eyes are the same." Sam studied their reflections in the mirror. "It's just hard to tell because there are four of us."

"Our smiles are the same too."

"Your nose is smaller, and your face is more oval."

"My mom was Japanese, but there's definitely some family resemblance."

"Peter called you pretty boy." Sam laughed. "I need to sleep," she mumbled, falling across the bed.

Jack grabbed a blanket and made himself comfortable in the reading chair.

Chapter 2

The next morning, the ice broken, Sam said, "Why don't you just stay at the ranch while you're here. There's plenty of room."

"I don't want to cause you any inconvenience."

"It's more inconvenient having to drive to town every day." She laughed. "We should stop by the restaurant on our way out. They have a breakfast buffet, and I could use some coffee."

"Sounds like a good idea. I am starving for some reason."

Down at the restaurant, the chalkboard read 'All You Can Eat Breakfast Buffet.' Jack watched Sam as she worked her way through bacon, fried eggs, hash browns, toast, pancakes, yogurt, cereal, mixed fruit, and coffee. "You eat like a trucker. Where do you put it all?"

She squinted at him. "Look at your own plate, troublemaker."

"You have a point, but still, most women I meet don't seem to eat at all."

"Everyone has to eat. Maybe they just do it when you're not looking. Are you ready to go?"

"Sure. How far is your ranch?"

"About seven miles. That could take five to twenty minutes depending on the weather and the vehicle." Once outside, Sam took one look at Jack's blue-green Portofino and laughed. "You'd better not leave that here. Why don't you follow me, and we'll put it somewhere safe."

She leaped aboard her tractor, and it roared to life while Jack gingerly got into his precious car.

Once they arrived, Jack looked around in awe. He didn't know how much of the land belonged to Sam, but it stretched in every direction as far as the eye could see. The red cinder driveway spread between the house and three barns in the shape of a large speech bubble; not quite round, but not square either.

The large, white three-story wooden house and three barns reminded him of Goldilocks and the Three Bears. Papa bear was enormous. Jack imagined Sam kept equipment in there, like her tractor. The mama bear housed stables, and the baby bear, well, he wasn't quite sure. Wooden post fences with gates separated the driveway from the fields, where field fencing crisscrossed and encircled the pasture. Pasture was not quite the word he was looking for. Yes, cows were grazing, but scraggly-looking plants, juniper trees, and boulders grew wild in red, clay-filled dirt. The sky seemed to stretch forever, with mountains in the distance. *It's beautiful in a wild way.*

"Let's get your car stowed, and I'll give you a tour." Sam hopped from the tractor. "The small barn will do, I think. We can give it a wash tomorrow if you want." She grinned, then guided him into the barn and helped him get his things from the trunk. Sam kept talking as she moved from one location to another, and Jack missed most of it because he was too busy looking around.

At the house, Sam said, "Just leave everything here in the mudroom, and we can put it away later. My friend Melissa's coming over tonight, but I'm sure she'll be glad to meet you. We don't have too much time, so we'd better get a move on. You do ride, right?"

"I have been on a horse once or twice, but not since I was a kid."

"Great! It's like riding a bicycle. You never forget!" She turned and shouted, "Roger! Bring out Ghost and Parsnip for us, will you?"

"Sure thing, boss!"

"It'll be easier to get around on the horses. Oh! I forgot about your clothes. Come on!"

Sam took him back into the house and into a spare room behind the stairs. On the way, he noticed that they were being followed by a white cat with half a black mustache. His tail was pointing straight up, and he looked like he was keeping an eye on them.

"Someone is following us."

Sam looked around and smiled. "That's Chiquito. I named him 'little boy' because he has that half mustache. He's my buddy, but he usually hides when I have visitors. He seems pretty interested in you. Do you have a cat?"

"No, I've never had a pet."

Her eyebrows rose in surprise. "Not even a goldfish?"

"My father didn't want the hassle. I learned to stop asking after a while."

They entered a nondescript room. There was a bed and a dresser, but no pictures or knick-knacks. The large walk-in closet, however, was full of men's clothing and shoes in different sizes.

"See if you can find something that fits. There are underwear and socks in the dresser. I'll be outside with the horses."

She closed the door, and he could hear her footsteps on the stairs as he turned his attention to the closet. T-shirts, flannel shirts, hoodies, and all types of jeans hung neatly, arranged by size. Athletic shoes and boots lined the floor, also by size. Jack's mind spun, but he easily found everything he needed and quickly changed.

"Ooh, look at you!" Sam said when he joined her by the horses. "You look like a proper cowboy! This is Parsnip. She's pretty easygoing, so you shouldn't have any trouble with her." She stuck an overturned five-gallon bucket by the left stirrup and held the reins while he mounted. "She's been trained to turn using the reins together, so just hold them in one hand and use them to guide her."

Parsnip pulled at the reins, bobbing and shaking her head. She moved forward and back, swishing her tail while Sam called to her horse, Ghost.

Sam leaped aboard her horse much like she leaped onto her tractor, holding onto Ghost's mane.

"Where's your saddle?" Jack asked, admiring her skill and athleticism.

"Oh, no need. Ghost and I are buds." She leaned forward and wrapped her arms around the horse's neck. "Right. Let's go!"

She pressed her legs against the sides of her horse and took off at a canter. Roger had opened the gate, so she flew right through, into a large field dotted with cows and juniper trees. Jack didn't have to do anything except hold on because Parsnip didn't want to be left behind. He did have to hold on, though. He almost came off his saddle when they began to move.

At the far end of the field, Ghost slowed to a walk. Sam pointed beyond the fence. "The creek and the land on the other side are all part of the ranch. We have guest cottages, stables, and a mess hall over there. People come here on vacation for fishing, riding, and water sports."

"Is that why you have the field fenced off?"

"Partly. But there are also certain plants growing along the river bed that can make the cows sick. I'd rather not take any chances."

Jack nodded and followed her to another fence. She leaned so far over he thought she might fall off her horse, but she got it unlatched and latched it back up behind them.

The entire tour lasted two hours and ended with Sam pointing out another ranch.

"The property line is just beyond this field. That's Peter's ranch. He bullied my dad, trying to get him to sell, and pressured Mark to call in his loan after he lent your dad that money. Dad worked hard alongside the ranch hands, trying to make enough to get it up to date by the deadline. He did it but then had a heart attack and ended up in the hospital. When he came home, I thought he was gonna be okay, but he died two weeks later of a second one."

Jack could see her fighting not to cry.

"I blamed his death on anyone and everyone, including your father." She looked at him with shame. "The anger kept me going, but it's been poisoning me. It's time I try to let it go."

This cousin of his was really amazing. Love and admiration welled up in him like nothing he had ever felt before. And the funny thing was, it wasn't a romantic love; it was brotherly… cousinly? He caught himself before he laughed.

"Am I amusing you?" Sam demanded.

"No! I was just thinking about how amazing you are and how it seems like I somehow know you. It's like my heart knows you're family and loves you already. Does that make sense?"

"Grandma always told me love is our greatest treasure. She said without it, we aren't really living. I thought I found it once…" She looked sad and angry, then her face took on the stoicism he had seen when he met her. "Let's get back. We should clean up before Melissa comes." She nudged Ghost and went flying across the field toward the house. Jack hoped they could both find grandma's treasure someday. Maybe it could heal some of Sam's pain.

Roger was waiting for them when they got back. He helped Jack dismount and stuck out his hand. "I'm Roger, the head ranch hand."

"I'm sorry, Roger. This is my cousin, Jack. He'll be staying here for a while. I should have introduced you before we left."

"Glad to meet you, Roger. Is that your dog?" He pointed at a medium-sized red and white dog.

"Yes, that's Red. He likes to help herd the cows."

"How old is he?"

Roger scratched the light stubble on his chin and frowned. "About four, I guess. I'd better get a move on. It was nice meeting you, Jack."

Jack nodded and smiled.

They entered the kitchen through the mudroom at the side of the house. The kitchen was the heart of the house, large and comfortable, with lots of counter space and seating for guests.

"May I use your phone?"

"Of course." Sam led him around the corner to her office. "Make yourself at home."

Glancing around at her messy desk and file cabinets exploding with paper as he dialed, he didn't know how she could work in there. "Hello, Penny. I know I said I was taking a week, but it's going to be longer. Could you let Dr. Charles know and give him this number in case he needs to reach me? Cell phone coverage is very spotty up here."

Sam walked in as he was hanging up. "Everything okay?"

"Yes, just extending my leave."

"You can do that?"

"I haven't ever taken a proper vacation. My staff might be doing cartwheels."

Sam gave a little snort and said, "I doubt that very much. Why don't we get cleaned up? I have spare everything, so I'll give you a little tour first and show you where to find things."

As usual, Chiquito followed them from room to room. Jack could see the living room just past the kitchen and the office. Small, cream-colored sofas and recliners surrounded a coffee table. A flat-screen tv sat on a stand in front the far wall, which mostly consisted of floor to ceiling windows. Bookshelves lined the wall near the office and the other side opened up into a family room.

"This is the fun room," Sam said as she walked through and flipped a light switch. Jack stared in wonder. Video games, a karaoke machine, a ping pong table, and a baby grand piano stood out. "We need fun stuff to keep us occupied when we're stuck indoors. You can come back and play later." She laughed.

The room with the magic closet was behind the staircase, along with a second bedroom, the laundry room, and an extra bathroom.

"There's a laundry shoot upstairs and it comes out here." They went back around and up the stairs. "My room is next to my father's bedroom on that end.

I haven't been through his room yet, so I keep it locked. Not sure what I'm waiting for."

Jack noticed a bright red painting behind her. "Did you know that painting is the same color as your hair?"

"Is it? Grandma Olivares painted it. She told me that cardinals represent the visiting spirits of loved ones who've passed on. I always think of her and my father when I see it."

"Maybe we should call you the cardinal." Jack smiled. "Some of my colleagues call me the crow. We can be birds of a feather."

"Why do they call you a crow?"

"Because my eyes are so dark, and I like to solve puzzles."

"That makes sense, I guess. I like the idea of being birds of a feather. But onward. You can take the room at the other end of the hall. They all have their own bathrooms. Towels are in this cupboard." She showed him the cupboard in the hall and the laundry chute, then she led him to his room. "Put anything you like from the clothing closet in here and there are soaps, shampoos, toothbrushes, everything you might need in the bathroom drawers. Any questions?"

"No, I think I'm up to speed. I don't think I've ever visited anyone who was so prepared for guests. Thank you very much."

"You're welcome. Go ahead and take a shower, and I'll meet you downstairs."

Sam paced in the kitchen, looking out the window with each pass. She paused when Jack entered. "I'm surprised Melissa isn't here yet. She's usually early."

"Why don't we grab a couple beers and figure out what we want to eat?"

"She'll feel bad if we decide without her."

The phone rang, and Sam snatched the receiver on the first ring.

"Melissa?" Her brow furrowed as she listened. "You can come over later if you want." More pacing. "Ok. Well, have a nice evening." She slowly placed the receiver back in its cradle and stood there for a few seconds. "Well, I guess we're on our own."

"She's not coming?"

"She said she forgot she had plans with Peter, but she didn't sound very happy about it."

"Why is she dating him?"

Sam shook her head. "I have no idea."

"Well, here's that beer. I'll make dinner. How's that?"

"Are you sure? I could make some burgers or order a pizza."

"I'm sure. Do you have a rice cooker?"

Forty minutes later, Jack placed two plates on the table—rosemary lemon chicken with sliced onions and red peppers, wild rice, and salad artistically arranged on each plate.

"Wow! This is beautiful, Jack! I'm impressed."

"I love to cook for an enthusiastic audience."

"Let's eat! I'm starving!" She took a bite of tender chicken and another of wild rice and rolled her eyes. "Mmmm. Where did you get that rice? And what did you put on it?"

"You know when you left me at the hotel yesterday?"

She nodded.

"I wandered around a little and found a small grocery store across the street, so I picked up a few things."

"Did you think I'd let you starve? And how did you think you'd cook it?"

"We hadn't decided I'd be staying here, so I was thinking ahead. And I also bought a small rice cooker."

"I'm glad you were thinking ahead because this is delicious. Thank you."

Jack smiled. "So what's on the agenda for tomorrow? I don't want to get in the way if you have things to do."

"I've tried to get ahead with the books because we have a big event coming up."

"What kind of event?"

"Every year, my father hosted a big charity ball in the large barn. All of the proceeds go to a charity called Sleep in Heavenly Peace. They make bunk beds for kids who don't have their own beds. Last year, my father passed away just before the ball, and it was canceled, so this year I want to have the best one yet, in his honor."

"It sounds very important to you."

Sam swallowed hard and nodded.

"I'll do whatever I can to help."

"Thank you, Jack. I've been planning for months, but it's crunch time. Hundreds of people come, and it's the event of the year for some country folk. It also makes a huge difference to SHP and the kids they help."

"That's a lot of pressure."

"I guess it is, but it's a labor of love, and I want to make my father proud."

Jack smiled. "You will."

He paused and said, "You know, I knew I had an uncle. I just hadn't heard anything about him for so long that I forgot. My father didn't tell me who I was visiting. He just said 'an old debt,' and I assumed it was a friend of his."

"I'm glad he sent you here."

"Me too."

They washed up the dishes together and went upstairs, heading in opposite directions at the landing.

"Goodnight, Jack."

"Goodnight, Sam. Thanks for inviting me to stay."

He went into his room and heard the bolt on her door click. *Smart lady and not blindly trusting after all.*

Chapter 3

Melissa gave Sam a big hug when she answered the door the following morning. Sam was smiling and animated instead of grumpy about the night before. Melissa's eyebrows rose when a man's voice wafted from the kitchen. She looked narrowly at Sam. "A man?"

Sam beamed. "Yes. A cousin! He's in there talking to Chiquito."

"Wha-a-at? Where did you find a cousin? And Chiquito likes him?"

"Come on in, and I will tell all." Sam moved to the side and motioned for Melissa to follow.

Chiquito was climbing on Jack's shoulder, rubbing his face against Jack's stubble, and purring like a little engine. Both women stopped and stared in amazement.

Finally, Melissa remembered her manners and extended a slim, pale hand. "Hi, I'm Melissa. I can't believe Chiquito likes you. He never likes anyone but Sam!"

"Glad to meet you." Jack shook her hand and flashed a slight smile that didn't reach his eyes, making Melissa feel unwelcome.

"Unbelievably, I've found someone in my family who can cook. Would you like some breakfast?"

Melissa nodded and sat at the table while Sam dished out pancakes, eggs, bacon, and hash browns. "It looks delicious, but I don't know how many people you think you're feeding. There's no way I can eat all that!"

"Just do your best." Sam smiled.

She told Melissa all about meeting Jack the day before while Melissa ate, oblivious to her discomfort. "How's your business going?"

"It's starting to really take off. Especially the online store. That was a great idea! Do you want to go gathering with me tomorrow?"

"I wish I could! I always learn so much when we go together. With Jack here and the charity ball coming up, I just don't have time. After breakfast, I'm dragging Jack to mass. Would you like to come with us?"

"No, I need to open the shop." Melissa thought about the things Peter made her do and the secrets she kept from Sam. *I would probably burst into flames if I stepped through the doors. I should just tell her. Would she forgive me?*

"I need to get some supplies, too. Maybe I can bring Jack by to see your shop after mass."

"Sounds great!" Melissa lied. Jack made her feel paranoid, as if his black eyes could see right through her, like he could read her thoughts. She ate as much as her tiny frame could hold and pushed her plate away. "I'm gonna explode if I eat another bite! That was delicious, Jack!"

"Well, let's get a move on," Sam said. "We don't want to be late!"

After mass, Sam and Jack walked the block to Melissa's shop. The shop, like all the others on Main Street, had the same exterior, but Melissa's had a lot of windows. Jack didn't know much about crystals, but he liked how they shone in the sunlight, sending rays of color through the store. When they entered 'Mel's Healing,' Jack barely noticed the unobtrusive lighting, rather noting that the cheerful sunlight from the windows gradually decreased toward the back into a darker and more mysterious ambiance. One customer browsed the eclectic jewelry and tarot cards. She had a long blonde braid and tight jeans, but when she turned around, Jack noticed that she wasn't nearly as young as she looked from behind. She glanced at him with interest as she left the store.

Two shelves of books captured Jack's attention as he watched the woman leave. Unfortunately, a wall of scent; intensely fragrant incense, burning sage, scented candles, and unidentified herbs engulfed him. His eyes stung, and his nose itched. "Perhaps I could wait outside. Your shop looks fascinating, but I seem to be allergic to something." He sneezed again.

"Sure. It's not for everyone," Melissa said, smiling sweetly.

As he walked outside, he heard her whisper, "Are you sure he's who he says he is?"

Jack sat on a bench outside the shop, thinking about Melissa and Sam and their friendship. He was so lost in thought that he didn't notice someone sitting beside him.

"Hey, man, I'm Steven. I hear you're Sam's cousin."

"News travels fast." Jack nodded. "I'm Jack." Steven was tall and slender, with long, wavy blonde hair. His brand-name hoodie, knee-length board shorts, and Vans screamed 'surfer.' Jack didn't want to be rude, but he was curious. "Are you from around here?"

"I didn't grow up here, but I have family in the area. Where are you from?

"Albuquerque."

"Cool. I've never been there, but it sounds like a happening place. You going to the big dance?"

"I can't guarantee it, but since it's at Sam's ranch, I'm guessing I am."

Steven nodded. "Well, see you around then." He rose and left.

Jack watched him walk away. *I wonder what that was all about. Santo Milagro sure seems to have a lot going on for such a small place.*

By the time Sam came out of Melissa's shop, Jack had all kinds of questions about Santo Milagro. Several people had spoken to him about nothing at all, and no one seemed surprised that he was sitting there. Sam was on a mission, though. She dragged him through every shop in town, about twelve if he counted correctly.

He saw someone watching them through a window full of plants and nodded in their direction. "Who's that?"

"Oh, that's Tia. She and Melissa are the resident plant experts. Tia can grow anything, and both of them can identify any kind of herb."

They got back to Sam's truck, and Jack helped her load her purchases in the back. "Thanks for helping me with the shopping. I like to combine trips instead of driving back and forth all the time. What would you like to do now?"

"Do you really want to know?"

"Of course. I wouldn't have asked otherwise."

"I'd like to get a couple of six-packs and go swimming. I am so hot and thirsty, I could drink a river while I'm soaking in it!"

"Is that a saying?"

"Probably not."

"Well, then, first stop, Cindy's Market."

"Who's Cindy?"

"No idea, but she sells beer."

"Good enough. Where are we going swimming?"

"There's a pool at the ranch. Didn't I show you that?"

"No. That's not something I would've forgotten."

"Hmm. Well, I have a pool. I just keep it covered because I'd rather not swim in mud."

Jack nodded. He would rather not swim in mud either, but he would if it was the only thing available. "I now understand pigs a little better."

Sam looked at him curiously but said nothing.

Once back at the ranch, Jack found some trunks in the magic closet, and the two of them met on the patio to uncover the pool.

"What's with all the men's clothing?"

"That's something my dad started. When we had guests or temporary ranch hands, sometimes they didn't have anything appropriate to wear. When they left, they could return it or not if they needed it. Sometimes, we get donations."

"Do you have women's clothes too?"

"Not really. Not many female ranch hands show up, and if they do, they can either borrow some of mine, or we can go into town. Women can be more difficult to size."

Sam and Jack had discovered they both liked Metallica, so the Black album was blaring on Sam's CD player as they drifted around on floats, sipping their beer., when Steven paid them a surprise visit.

Steven suddenly rounded the corner, beaming and holding up grocery bags. "Bros! I brought ribs and slaw!"

Jack immediately got out of the pool, while Sam gawked in disbelief. They grabbed a couple of towels and sat at a wrought-iron picnic table to eat.

"Want a beer?" Jack asked.

"Yeah, thanks, bro. I brought another 6-pack too."

"Cheers." They clinked their bottles.

"Why are you here?" Sam asked finally. Jack and Steven stared at her until she grew angry. "Seriously. You've never visited before, even when you were dating Melissa. You never even say hello. Why did you suddenly decide to come over?"

"I don't know." He shrugged. "I met Jack in town, and he seemed cool. I thought it'd be fun to hang out."

"It was nice of him to bring food, don't you think?" Jack asked.

"Well, yeah." She looked at Steven. "So you came over to hang out with Jack?"

"Um... yeah. And you."

Sam nodded and decided to let it go and after that initial bout of awkwardness, they had a great time. They drank, played in the pool, and danced to whatever crazy songs came up on Steven's playlist. Sam realized she hadn't enjoyed herself so much since her father died.

It grew late, and Steven said, "Let's watch a movie."

"I think I need to get to bed." Sam wondered if he planned to stay indefinitely. "It's going to be pretty busy around here tomorrow. You guys go ahead if you want."

Steven seemed oblivious to Sam's hint. "How about Deadpool!"

Jack shook his head. "I suppose I'd better make it an early night too. I have breakfast duty. Maybe we can do it another time."

"Cool. Thanks for letting me hang out with you guys."

Chapter 4

The next couple of days were a whirlwind of activity. So many people came and went that Jack couldn't remember most of them. Melissa came over to help Sam make garlands, so he went out to help Roger build a temporary stage in the big barn.

"I'm sorry I'm not better at this," he said. "I grew up in the city, and my father didn't have much time to teach me basic skills."

"I hear you can cook."

"True, but I taught myself out of necessity." Jack smiled. "I didn't need to build a house, but I needed to eat!"

"It's a handy skill. Stick around here, and you can learn all you want. That's what Ms. Sam's dad told me a long time ago."

"I don't know how long I'll be here, but I'm always up for learning life skills."

Roger studied Jack for a moment. "We're getting together to play cards tomorrow night. You wanna join us?"

"Yes. I'd like that."

"I'll come get you around six then. We usually bring our own beer and order pizza."

"Thanks, Roger!"

Sam and Melissa worked on the garlands for hours. Chiquito had made himself scarce. Every once in a while, Sam got up and looked out the kitchen window. "Is it weird if my house guest is friends with the ranch hands?"

Melissa shrugged. "I don't see why it would be. How long is he going to stay?"

"I don't really know. We haven't talked about it."

Melissa opened her mouth to say something, but Jack swung into the kitchen

"Guess what?" he asked.

"What?" Sam asked.

"I just got invited to the guys' poker game."

"That's great!"

Melissa stood. "I have to get home, Sam. Let me know if you need more help tomorrow."

"Okay. Thanks, Mel."

Jack watched her leave. "Is everything okay between you two?"

"Yes, of course."

"Would you like to come too?"

"No, it's a guys' night out. I would make everyone uncomfortable. I can make plans with a girlfriend." She smiled.

Jack cocked his head and searched Sam's face. "What's bothering you then?"

Surprised by his perceptiveness, Sam said, "I've just been a little worried about Melissa. I'm sure it's nothing."

Jack nodded and gave her a hug.

For the first time, she didn't push him away. She hugged him back and felt a flood of kindness and warmth that she hadn't felt in a long time. "Why don't we order pizza, and I'll challenge you to a ping pong tournament."

"Ohh, you are in big trouble, missy. I am the king of ping pong."

"Not for long!"

They spent hours playing ping pong, trying to sing ABBA in Spanish, and eating pizza, until they both flopped down on the sofa for a rest.

"Let's get to bed. I want to take you on a hike in the morning, and we have to be back before the volunteers show up."

"Sounds good. But first, you have to dub me the king of karaoke."

"I don't think so. I'd call you a wannabe."

The playful argument turned into a pillow fight, and Sam ran away upstairs. "Goodnight, Jack!"

Jack laughed. "Party pooper!"

Sam and Jack left the ranch at dawn. Sam was wearing her usual jeans and tank top but had swapped her cowboy boots for high-topped hiking boots. She recommended them to Jack as well. She carried a backpack, and he wondered what was inside.

"Why are we walking instead of riding?"

"When you ride, you don't see the little things. I thought you might like to really see the land. For example, what did this range look like when you were riding?"

"Mostly, dirt. It was whizzing by as I tried to stay in the saddle."

"And now?"

"Well, there's still a lot of dirt, but it's beautiful, in a wild, unkempt way."

Sam laughed. "There have to be a lot of plants too, so the cows can eat. They're pretty good at finding food, but we have to be sure we know what's growing on the range, so they don't eat anything that will make them sick."

"What's that?" Jack pointed to a grayish bush.

"That's a fourwing saltbush. And that's blue grama. You can recognize it because it grows in clumps and the seeds grow sideways like little brushes. The trees are mostly piñon pine and juniper. Deer like juniper berries, so they keep the deer from mowing down the pasture in the fall."

Jack looked around with interest and saw a tiny cactus with a beautiful orange flower. He squatted down and reached out his hand before Sam stopped him.

"It looks like you could just touch the flower, but those needles are like finger magnets. And they hurt!"

"With the cactus and the boulders, I guess walking at night would be a bad idea."

31

"Not the best. There are coyotes too, but the fences usually keep them out."

"This is Molly." Sam walked up to one of the cows and gave her some blue grama grass she had pulled.

"I had no idea how big cows are up close. She's huge!"

Sam nodded. "She's a sweetheart, but it would be dangerous to spook the herd, especially during calving season."

They continued down to the river. "You said the fence here is to protect the cows, right?"

"Yes, there are several herbs and poisonous plants that like the water."

"But wouldn't it be much easier to allow them access to the water? Couldn't you just remove those plants?"

Sam thought about how to reply. "It would be a pretty high-stakes gamble, plus there are other dangers. The cows could drown when the water is high, and there are predators like coyotes. The fence keeps them relatively safe."

"How would I know if a plant is poisonous?"

"Melissa tells me not to touch anything if I don't know what it is. I learn a lot from her when she takes me out to collect medicinal plants. She is like an encyclopedia."

"How did she learn so much about them?"

"I'm not really sure. She reads a lot, and I know she's taken some classes. When we were young, she thought she was a witch. She would read up on how to make natural remedies and cook them in a little cauldron. She had to test them on herself because no one else would touch them." Sam smiled at the memory. "We can go through the gate if you'd like to give your feet a soak and have a snack."

"That sounds good. I'm getting thirsty too."

Sam led him to the riverside and sat on a boulder beneath a juniper tree.

"Look," Jack whispered. "There's a cardinal in that tree behind you."

Sam turned her head and looked up into the tree. "I wonder if it's Grandmother," she whispered.

"I bet it is." He smiled, and they watched as it flew away. "What do you have in the backpack?"

"All kinds of things, but most importantly, I have water and lunch." She handed him a water bottle, a tuna sandwich, and a banana.

"When did you put this together? I didn't even smell the tuna."

"I did it last night. I wanted to surprise you."

"You did! And this is the perfect spot for a picnic. What did you put in the tuna?"

"Oh, goodness. You should probably ask me what I didn't put in it. There's miracle whip, mustard, relish, green onions, red onions, tomatoes, dill pickles, jalapeños, and cheese."

"It doesn't even taste like tuna. I love it!"

"Tuna tastes a little fishy. I like to disguise it. The green onions help a lot. We should probably head back when we're done. Was that enough food? I have some crackers too."

"It was plenty. Thank you for lunch and for sharing all of this." Jack gestured at the space around them.

"Thanks for coming with me. Ready?"

Jack nodded, so she repacked her pack. "Need any more water before I put it away?"

"No, I'm good."

"Oh, look, Jack!" Sam pointed across the river where an antelope watched them curiously. Jack had never seen one in the wild, and he was mesmerized by its big, black eyes. Then he looked at Sam briefly, and it was gone.

As they started back, Jack concentrated on looking for animals. He didn't see many, possibly because of all the noise he was making, but he saw a couple of rabbits and a squirrel. Sam pointed out a snake hole and some deer scat. They walked to the road and followed it back, making a large loop.

"Thank you, Sam," Jack said again.

"You were right. The land and the sky are so big. It's easy to miss all the little things."

Sam smiled and gazed at the sky. "Whenever I leave, even for a short time, I miss this place. It's very special."

When they got back to the house, people were already arriving. Volunteers were decorating the barn and stringing lights outside. They marked off parking spots and set up tables. Women from town were baking in Sam's kitchen. A seamstress brought a rental tux for Jack and a few dresses for Sam to try on.

"Why did she bring them here?" Jack asked.

"We don't have a rental shop in town, so people place orders at a shop in Las Rodillas. Then they bring the rentals around to everyone the day before the event. I am difficult to size, so they bring several for me to try. Do you want to help me choose?"

"Sure. Will they alter the tux if it doesn't fit right?"

"Yes; you'll want to try it on."

They went upstairs, and Jack put on the tux. The seamstress pinned it where it needed narrowing, and then Jack went to find Sam. She was wearing a flowing white gown that looked lovely on her, despite being too large.

"This is ok, but I want to try on the red one. It matches my hair." She went to change, then reappeared wearing the red dress.

"You look like a phoenix," his voice sounded almost reverent.

She studied herself in the mirror, and Jack studied her. The dress was bright red and sleeveless. Covered in orange and gold sequins, it hugged her body to the floor, with a slit up the side so she could move. Her height and slender figure made the simple dress stunning. Her hair and the sequins gave a fiery effect. "I think this might be the most beautiful dress I've ever seen."

It's not the dress. "It's perfect."

She twirled around in front of the mirror and gave him a hug. "Thanks for your help."

"I didn't do anything."

Sam chuckled. "True, but you were here. If it was shorter with fringes, I would look like a flapper. Go see if the seamstress needs you, and I'll change back into my ranch duds."

Roger knocked on the kitchen door at six, as promised. Jack was waiting with Sam at the kitchen table and jumped up to answer. Giving Sam a little wave, he grabbed his beer, followed Roger out to his beat-up Jeep Wrangler, and got in. Roger drove farther into the countryside and stopped at a brightly-lit, triple-wide manufactured home. Jack looked around curiously. The yard looked landscaped and well-kept. Roger knocked twice and walked right in.

Once inside, he introduced Jack to his friends. "You all know who Jack is. Jack, this is Ben, the saloon's chef. This is his house. That's Carlos. He works at Peter's ranch."

"Should be Alley's," Carlos mumbled.

"You've met Father Garcia, I think."

Jack's eyebrows rose a little.

"My winnings go to charity." He smiled. "So they don't mind too much if I win."

"Here's our special guest, Dr. Moe. He doesn't come out much because he's busy patching up people's pets."

"Nice to meet you," Dr. Moe said politely. He was a kind-looking man with straight, sandy hair and black-framed glasses. Jack thought he looked more like an accountant than a veterinarian.

"And finally, this knucklehead is my racing partner, Steven."

Steven smiled. "Hello, Jack."

"So I only have to remember three new names. That makes it much easier. Thank you all for inviting me this evening."

"I see you brought your beer," Ben said. "I ordered the pizza a few minutes ago, and you can choose a seat." Ben gestured at a big, round dining table covered by a plastic tablecloth.

The pizza arrived, all six boxes. Ben placed them on the counter between the kitchen and the dining room and invited everyone to use the refrigerator if they wanted their beer to stay cold. He also set out a stack of paper plates, napkins, red pepper flakes, parmesan cheese, and a bottle of mustard.

"What's the mustard for?" Jack asked.

Steven rolled his eyes. "Ben thinks pizza crust with mustard tastes like a hot pretzel. It's his house, so we have to humor him."

"It's delicious. You should try it," Ben told Jack with a smile. He was a large man, almost as tall as Jack and certainly heavier, but his easy smile and jovial attitude made everyone feel at home.

Once everyone had a plate of pizza and a beer, they sat at the table and got ready to play. "What'll it be tonight?" Ben asked. "Poker or Blackjack?"

They decided on seven-card stud, and Ben dealt the first hand. Most of the conversation was lighthearted banter about the game until they'd all had several bottles of beer.

"What's it like living with the ice princess?" Steven asked Jack.

"Why you so rude?" Carlos asked. "Maybe you tell us why Melissa dumped your dumb ass?"

Steven turned an ugly shade of purple

Father Garcia cleared his throat. "Let's remember we're all friends here."

"We are all a little curious about Sam," Ben said. "She's always kind to Alley when she stops by the saloon, but she seems like a very private person."

"I don't really know what you're asking. She's been very welcoming. I don't think I could have asked for a better cousin." He looked at Moe as he dealt the next hand. "Do you have family around here?"

"Sort of. It's a long story."

Jack nodded, accepting that Moe didn't want to talk about it.

Carlos asked, "What kind of work do you do?"

"I'm a forensic medical examiner.""

"What's that?"

"He does autopsies on people who die of unnatural causes," Moe said. "To find out what happened to them."

No one said anything, but Carlos looked at Jack with round eyes and crossed himself.

"Tell Jack about the racing," Ben told Steven, who'd remained silent since his unfortunate question.

"There's a track east of town," Roger said enthusiastically. "Steven's like royalty there. He even races out of state."

Steven finally smiled at that. "Royalty, huh?"

"You should come watch sometime," Roger said.

"I'd love to." Jack smiled.

Four hours later, Jack was the big winner. He donated his winnings to Father Garcia.

"This is very generous of you, Jack."

"If you had won, the money would have gone to the church. This way, it still goes to the church, and everyone's a winner."

Father Garcia nodded happily, and everyone took their leave, toting little packages of leftover pizza.

Back in Roger's Jeep, Jack thanked him again for inviting him.

"I'm sorry about Steven. Sometimes he doesn't have much of a filter."

"It's okay. I was just a little surprised. He seemed interested in her when he came to the ranch, so that *ice princess* comment was unexpected."

"He usually gets whatever he wants, and Sam ignores him. It drives him nuts."

When they got back to the ranch, Roger parked the Jeep, and they got out. Red ran to greet his master and jumped around, wagging his tail.

"Do you live here?"

"Yes. I have a small apartment in the barn. Ms. Sam's father built it for me when I first came here. I hope you had a good time tonight."

"I did. Thanks!"

He headed a little unsteadily for the house and found Sam watching tv. Chiquito jumped off her lap and wound around Jack's legs before resuming his position. "Did you call it an early night?"

"No, she didn't show up. I tried to call her, but she didn't answer. It's okay, though; Chiquito and I binge-watched Midsomer Murders."

Poor Sam. "Heading for bed soon?"

"Yes, might as well. Tomorrow's the big day."

Chapter 5

The following morning, Sam found Jack in the kitchen working his culinary magic. He placed stacks of french toast with fresh berries and whipped cream on the table, along with strong, delicious smelling coffee.

"Wow. This smells incredible. How long have you been up?"

"A while. I thought it was a french toast day. Do we have any plans other than the dance this evening?"

"No, but there's still quite a bit to do. Did you have a nice time last night?"

"I did. Roger's friends surprised me. Ben, Carlos, Dr. Moe, Father Garcia, and Steven were there."

"What? Father Garcia was playing cards?"

"For charity." Jack laughed. "I gave him my winnings."

"You won?"

"Yes. I think the other guys were surprised. I hope they'll invite me again."

"I'm sure they will!"

After breakfast, Alley arrived at the ranch with a kitten.

Jack answered the door and invited her to have some leftovers and coffee. He peeked in the towel she had wrapped around the kitten. "It's so tiny!"

"I still have to feed her with a bottle. Her mother lived outside the saloon and got hit last night."

"Was this the only kitten?"

"No, but the others got adopted. Did you want one?"

"I don't know anything about cats, and I'm not sure Chiquito would forgive me."

"I don't know much about them, either. I was hoping Sam could help me out."

Sam and Chiquito entered the kitchen just then. "Hello, Alley. Who do we have here?" she asked, looking at the kitten.

Alley repeated her story and handed Sam the black kitten.

"You are just adorable," Sam said before setting her down for Chiquito to check out. He sniffed it, gave it a lick, and left the room. Sam picked her back up and handed her to Jack.

He inspected the kitten before holding her close to his chest. "What's her name?"

"She doesn't have one yet."

"She's precious," Sam said. "Maybe you should call her Milagro, your little miracle." Sam put her face right up to the kitten, against Jack's chest.

"Wait your turn, woman! Your hair is going right up my nose."

Sam laughed. "Give her here then, you cat hog!"

"You two are like siblings, fighting over that kitten," Alley said. "You can visit her any time you like."

"I never had a pet, but I've really enjoyed getting to know Chiquito."

"Would you like to name her?" Alley looked at Jack with brown eyes that seemed to warm him from the inside out.

"How about Preciosa? She really is precious."

"That's perfect, Jack." She smiled at him. "Could you help me figure out how to take care of her, Sam?"

"Of course! What supplies do you have so far?"

"Nothing. I don't know where to start."

"I think I have some things you can use while she's small. Let me see what I have."

She left to look, and Jack sat with the kitten.

40

Sam came back with her arms full. "I have a kitten-sized bed, litter box, scooper, and bowl, and I can give you some litter and a couple of toys, but you should buy some kitten food once you wean her off the dropper. Maybe have Dr. Moe take a look at her and give you some advice."

"Thank you so much, Sam! I really appreciate your help."

"My pleasure. Will you be at the ball this evening?"

"For a little while. I don't want to leave Preciosa alone for too long."

Alley took her leave, and Sam waved after her.

"Kittens are so stinking cute," she said.

"I've never held one before, but now I want one!" Jack agreed.

"Good to know. Now I know to keep you away from the pet store." Sam smiled.

That evening, Jack and Steven admired the barn. "It looks great," Jack said.

"I think this is the best one ever."

"Sam told me people come for miles to attend. She seems really proud to carry on the tradition."

"Yeah, her dad started it. It all goes to that cool charity that makes beds for kids."

They stood in silence, taking in the thousands of twinkling lights outlining the barn. Jack cringed a little at the cacophony created by the local band as they warmed up for the evening. The caterers artfully placed food, beverages, and decorative centerpieces on long tables covered in white cloth, and Jack laughed when Steven reached for an hors d'oeuvre, only to have one of the caterers smack his hand with a plastic spatula.

"Whatever they are, they smell so good, bro. I just can't resist them." Steven looked longingly at the table as he rubbed the back of his hand.

Jack gave him a sympathetic look. His stomach rumbled loudly. "The guests will arrive shortly, and you can pile up a plate."

Ranch hands volunteered as parking attendants, and Jack, dressed in his rented tuxedo, waited out front for the first guests to arrive.

Sam put glitter on her cheekbones and shoulders. The final touch. Ordinarily, she was no-frills. She didn't wear makeup and opted for jeans and tank tops. Tonight, though, she had gone all out. She wanted to be the best hostess she could be in memory of her father. And she wanted to do her dress justice. She scrunched up her long, narrow dress and knelt next to her bed.

Lord, Father Garcia told me you can hear me from anywhere. If you can hear me, I hope you'll let my dad know how hard I worked on his charity gig. I hope he's proud of me. I miss him so much. I know he's there in heaven with you and mamma and that they are happy and at peace. Tell them I love them, Lord. Amen.

She stood, straightened her dress, and put on some low heels. She didn't want to tower over all of her guests, but a little heel was necessary with the dress. When she finally made her way downstairs, she found Jack waiting for her at the entrance to the barn. He caught sight of her and froze.

"Sam. You look so beautiful tonight."

"You look very handsome too," she said, taking in his wavy, dark hair and those bottomless black eyes. She blushed and turned away. *Yikes. Where did that come from?*

Once they reached the barn, Sam sent Jack ahead while she remained at the entryway, greeting guests as they arrived. She knew most of them, even those from out of town, either through business or previous events. When the line dwindled to a trickle, she turned to see Jack, headed her way with a plate of food.

"It's going fast," he said. "I thought I'd better get you some. Come join us at the table."

She sat with Jack, Roger, Edna, and Randy and picked at her food as she observed the festivities.

"The food is great," Roger said.

"It is," Edna agreed. "Not as good as mine, of course."

Everyone good-naturedly agreed with her, no matter their opinions. Sam thought Ben had really pulled out the stops with his new catering venture but didn't mention that.

Her eyes drifted across the large dance floor, packed with happy party-goers dressed in their finery. It warmed her heart to see so many smiles all around her. The band played everything from rock ballads to square dancing music. When they started playing a rousing country song, Jack proffered his hand and raised an eyebrow. "How about it, cowgirl?"

"You know how to line dance?"

"Of course. It's popular in Albuquerque too."

They joined the crowd on the dance floor, and Sam was breathless by the end of the song. A slow song started, and Sam excused herself to get some water. Jack started to follow her but stopped at a table where Alley was sitting by herself, then led her to the dance floor. Sam watched them for a moment; Jack's tall frame hunched over Alley's much shorter one brought an errant tear to her eye. They looked so sweet together.

Ben said hello, and she congratulated him on the catering. "I've heard nothing but rave reviews," she told him.

"Thank you for giving me a chance. I know how important this event is for you."

"Do you want to take a little break and square dance with me?"

"I don't think I should, but Roger's sitting over there like a hermit. I bet he'd like to dance."

"Okay. But do take a break when you get the chance. You deserve it."

Ben smiled and headed back to the dessert table.

Sam danced with Roger and a dozen other men before she heard a commotion near the entrance and went to investigate.

As she approached, Steven swung at Peter, knocking him into the nearest table. Peter charged at him, and they both landed on the floor, kicking and punching, knocking over anything in their way.

Melissa stood nearby, wringing her hands. Tears trickled down her cheeks. Sam went to her and put an arm around her, but Melissa shrugged her off and turned away.

Jack rushed over, followed by Sergeant Mickelson from the local Sheriff's office. "Stop!" Jack commanded." This is a charity event. Have some respect!"

Peter looked like he might start swinging at Jack, but he saw Sergeant Mickelson and changed his mind. He walked up to Steven and poked him in the chest. "She's mine! You keep your hands off of her." Then he grabbed Melissa's wrist and started dragging her to his truck.

"I'm sorry, Peter, but I'll need a word with Melissa before you go," the sergeant said.

He guided Melissa to the side and spoke with her for a couple of minutes. Sam could see her shaking her head, and then she returned to Peter's side and got into his truck.

Steven scowled but got another drink and sat at one of the empty tables. Sam stood looking out at the parking lot, worrying about Melissa. Something was going on with her, but Sam didn't know how to help.

Jack saw a middle-aged woman talking to Steven at a table near the entrance. It took him a moment to place her in Melissa's shop. She was slender, with a weathered-looking face and blonde hair pulled up in a bun. She wore a simple black dress and flat shoes. Her expression was intense, and Steven slouched and hung his head while she spoke. Finally, she rose from the table and put her hand on his shoulder before heading for the exit.

Jack wandered over to the table and sat down with Steven. "Who was that?"

Steven glanced up at him and frowned.

"Do you want to talk about it?"

"What are you? The resident shrink?" Steven growled.

"Right. I guess not." Jack stood and collided with Alley in his haste. "I'm sorry, Alley. Are you alright?"

"Hi, Jack," she said, looking a little pink. "I'm fine. I was wondering if you'd like to dance again."

"I would..." He smiled gently. "But I need to find Sam and make sure she's okay. Maybe later?" He saw her smile droop, and he felt guilty, but he had seen Sam's interaction with Melissa and was worried about her.

The crowd was thinning out, and the band was starting to pack up when he finally found her, sitting in a folding chair at the back of the stage. "Hey, cuz. What's going on?"

She looked up at him. "I don't know. I've never seen Melissa like that before. We used to tell each other everything. We have always been there for each other. But when I tried to comfort her tonight, she pushed me away like she didn't even know me. I think something bad is going on, but I don't know what it is."

"It'll be alright. You've had a big day, and she was in the middle of a traumatic situation. Let me help you back to the house, and you can check in with Melissa in the morning when you have both gotten some rest."

He helped her up and put his arm around her shoulders so she could lean on him. He helped her up the stairs and went back down to make a cup of tea. Chiquito was staring at him. "What do you want, old man? Are you hungry?" Chiquito walked over to his bowl and sat looking at it. "Are you psychic? Sometimes I think you are better at communicating than most people." Jack got him some food and watched his tail flip back and forth as he ate.

Chapter 6

Sam and Jack were having breakfast the next morning when someone tapped on the backdoor. Sam found Melissa standing outside the door, still wearing her dress from the night before.

"Oh, Sam. I've made the biggest mistake of my life." Melissa was crying, causing mascara rivers to flow down her cheeks. Her hair had flown the coop.

"What happened?"

"I talked to Steven last night and realized we belong together. I told Peter it wasn't working out, and I still love Steven. He hit me." She gestured to her black eye. "He locked me in the bedroom and sat in the living room with the shotgun all night." She took a deep breath. "This morning, once he fell asleep, I picked the lock with a bobby pin and snuck out. I'm afraid to stay at home, Sam. Can I stay here for a few days?"

Sam hugged Melissa and was relieved when she didn't push her away again. "Of course, you can stay! For as long as you like. Would you like some breakfast?"

"No, thanks." She eyed the bacon. "Well, maybe a little. And some coffee."

Sam felt happy to be doing something to help, even something small. She loaded up a plate, poured some coffee, and took the extra bacon to the table. She saw Jack heading for the door and said, "I'll be right back." She grabbed the keys to the truck off the hook and ran to catch up with him. "Jack! Here. Take the truck."

"Thanks, Sam. You guys need to talk, and I have some errands. I'll get some gas while I'm out."

"Thank you." She smiled and waved as he pulled out, then went back inside. Melissa's breakfast and the bacon were gone. "Where'd you put all that food?"

Melissa glanced at her plate. "I don't know. It must be in the hollow leg." She smiled slightly.

"Would you like some more? Have you been eating?"

"I think so. Sometimes time flies by, and I forget things."

Sam grew concerned. "Maybe you should see a doctor."

"I don't like doctors. Do you want to go gathering with me?"

"Sure. Are you looking for anything in particular?"

"Not really. I'm running low on everything, but I'd really like to find yarrow, snakeweed, and valerian because I have orders I need to fill."

Do you want to take the horses? It will save some time."

"Sure. It's been a while."

Roger brought out Parsnip and Ghost, and Sam suggested they stop by Melissa's house to grab some boots, but Melissa shook her head. "My sneakers are fine. I don't want to go there."

She's really spooked. "Shouldn't we call the Sheriff and report Peter's assault?"

"No, I'm not ready to do that."

Why won't you report him? If he was arrested, you could feel safe again.

The trip went well at first, with Melissa picking handfuls of various plants and digging up roots, but she grew irritable as the afternoon progressed and defensive whenever Sam gently inquired about her situation. By the time they returned to the ranch, she was furious. She dismounted, threw the reins at Roger, and stomped into the house.

Roger looked at Sam, and she shrugged sadly. She didn't know what to do. Melissa seemed like a different person. She walked into the kitchen where Melissa was busy banging bowls on the counter .

"I'm sorry, Melissa. I just wanted to help."

"Then leave me alone. You can help by minding your own business."

"Okay, but I'm here if you need me," Sam said quietly. She went into her office and closed the door before the first tear fell.

Jack had driven into town and bought gas as he'd promised. Parked outside the Sheriff's, he saw Peter arguing with a man in a suit across the street. Before he could intervene, the Sergeant from the dance approached the station, so he flagged him down. "Hello, Sergeant. I thought I should stop by and introduce myself. I'm Doctor Jack Olivares, the Chief Medical Examiner for New Mexico. I'm on vacation but thought I'd let you know I'm in the district."

"It's an honor to have you here, Dr. Olivares. I'm Dennis Mickelson. Everyone calls me Mick." They shook hands. "You're Sam's cousin, right?"

"Yes."

"Come on inside. The Captain's on vacation this week, and this is a small office, but I can introduce you to Deputy Flores."

"Anita, this is Dr. Olivares, Sam's cousin."

"Just call me Jack."

Deputy Flores was a petite young woman with dark hair pinned in a bun. She glanced up and smiled as she spoke on the phone, her fingers flying across her keyboard. After she hung up, she said, "Mucho gusto," and picked up the ringing phone again.

Mick led Jack to his desk. "Would you like some coffee? It's always good when Flores is working."

"That sounds great."

Mick got up and went around the corner, returning with two mugs of aromatic coffee.

"Thank you. This smells great. Who is the Medical Examiner for this district? I didn't think to look before I left because I thought it was a day trip."

"The position is empty at the moment. Usually, the ME works at the morgue in Las Rodillas."

"Let me know if you need a hand. I can probably get you some temporary help."

"Thank you, sir!"

"I also wanted to let you know that Melissa showed up at the ranch with a black eye this morning. She said Peter hit her and locked her in the bedroom overnight. She's staying with Sam and is safe for the moment, but I thought you might like to have a word with Peter."

"I will. Thank you for letting me know."

They talked about their jobs and the challenges inherent to a rural district for about an hour, then Jack took his leave.

After he left the station, Jack saw the saloon across the street and decided to check on Alley. Entering the saloon was a deja vu that seemed years ago, not days.

"Jack! What a sight for sore eyes. I swear you are the most handsome man I've ever seen! Do you know you and Sam look so much alike I could have guessed you were related, well, except for your coloring." Alley stopped and blushed.

Jack smiled. "Why don't you pour us each a drink and sit down with me. I'll explain that mystery."

Alley giggled her way to the bar and shouted over the music, "What would you like?"

"Modelo Negra if you have it."

She came back with two tall black cans and two glasses on a tray. She poured and handed one to Jack. After a long drink, he wiped the foam off his lip and let out an ahh of contentment. "So?" Alley prompted. "The mystery?"

Jack laughed. "It's not really much of a mystery. Our fathers were brothers and looked very much alike, if the pictures are any indication."

"So handsome, just like you," Alley said coyly.

"Well, beauty is in the eye of the beholder, they say." He winked.

"So you and Sam are both very tall and slender and have the same smile."

"Yes. But my mother was a dark-haired, dark-eyed Japanese beauty. Sam's mother was a light-skinned, green-eyed, Nordic goddess. Sam showed me pictures."

"She sure is beautiful." Alley sighed wistfully. "She's taller than most men in town and has a figure most of us would die for." She looked down at the table.

Jack took her hand. "Looks are something you inherit from your parents. They don't say anything about who you are."

Alley looked up at him.

"Also"— he glanced down— "not everyone has the same definition of beauty." His heart beat faster and his stomach felt quivery when he said, "I happen to think you're very beautiful." She snatched her hand from his. "I love the golden halo your hair makes around your sweet face."

She blushed three shades of red.

"I love the mirth in your sparkling blue eyes and the dimples in your cheeks when you laugh."

Alley stared at him in disbelief. No one had ever spoken to her like that, and he had clearly given this some thought.

"I love your effervescent personality, your optimistic energy, and your kindness." He took her hand back and kissed her knuckles. "Don't sell yourself short, Ms. Alley. You are exquisite. Would you like to have dinner with me tomorrow evening?"

"Of course!" Alley giggled. "You have just earned so many brownie points; I don't even know what the prize is!"

"Good. I'll be here to pick you up at six. I should go now." He kissed her hand and disappeared out onto the street.

After Jack had left the station, Sergeant Mickelson decided to pay Peter a visit.

He parked on the road in front of a beat-up pickup truck that might have been green at some point but now looked mostly rusty.

The white farmhouse that had previously belonged to Alley's family sat facing the road, but everyone used the side door to keep down the amount of dust tracked inside. As Mick approached, he overheard Peter speaking with a woman at the door."

"You're not married anymore. You could at least meet them," she said.

"I've told you no."

"Is it because of that little floozy you're seeing?"

Mick was close enough to see Peter's face turn purple. "Get off my property, and don't come back!"

"You're going to regret this. She won't stick around, and you'll end up old and alone, with no one to blame but yourself."

"Get!" Peter pointed to the road, and the woman stomped down the steps toward Mick.

He didn't know her, but he recognized her from around town. After she passed him, Mick approached Peter. "Good afternoon, Peter. Everything okay?"

"What do you want?"

"I came here to speak with you about Melissa."

"Women! What about her?"

"She showed up with a black eye and claimed you gave it to her."

"Now, why would I go and give my girlfriend a black eye?"

"Jealousy? There was that altercation last night."

"She came home with me, didn't she. I had no reason to be jealous. She's probably covering for that animal. Steven."

"If it happens again, I'll bring you in for assault, whether she presses charges or not. You need to keep your fists to yourself."

Peter glared at Mick. When it was clear Mick was not intimidated, Peter said, "Message received, loud and clear." He walked back into the house and slammed the door in Mick's face.

Alice Kanaka

Chapter 7

J ack returned to the ranch, and the air was filled with tension. Melissa frowned at him from the kitchen table. Chiquito sat on top of the refrigerator watching her, his tail twitching back and forth. "What's up?"

"I'm just sorting my gatherings. Sam's in her office." She nodded but ignored him.

He continued into the office and shut the door.

Sam looked up from her laptop. "Take a load off, cuz."

"Has it been like this all day?"

"No. We went gathering earlier and had a nice time, but then she got angry with me for prying." She hung her head.

Jack remained silent. He squeezed her shoulder.

Sam patted his hand. "It'll be okay. Why don't you take a dip in the pool or watch TV? I'll be done in about an hour."

"I'd make dinner, but she doesn't want me in there."

"She's suspicious of you, for some reason."

"Yes... it makes me wonder."

"Wonder what?"

"I don't know. Maybe she just needs some space." He gave her a half hug. "I'll go watch TV, then make dinner when you're done." He walked into the living room and sprawled on the loveseat. Chiquito jumped up on his lap. As he was sitting there, he heard a knock on the door and turned the sound off.

"What are you doing here?"

"I'm avoiding Peter like you told me to. Why are you here?"

"I'm here to see Jack."

"Why? You should be checking if I'm okay and asking me about my bruise."

"Is Jack here?"

"No. Just go away!"

Jack silently entered the kitchen behind her, and Steven smiled.

Whipping around, Melissa said, "You! I've never trusted you."

Jack was puzzled by her reaction and watched her stomp off before greeting his visitor. "How're you doing, Steven?"

"Traitor!" she shouted before slamming the door behind them.

"Bro, everyone seems mad at me today, and I don't even know why."

"Everyone? Who's mad at you?"

"Well, Melissa, for one."

"Did you talk to her after the ball?"

"No." Steven scratched his head and frowned.

"You're not concerned about her?"

"She chose to leave with that guy. What am I supposed to do?"

Something is off. Jack's brow furrowed. "Did you need something?"

Steven stared at Jack with a blank look on his face. "No, I guess not. I didn't realize you had company. Maybe we can hang out again sometime."

"Sure. See you later." Jack closed the door and wondered what that was all about.

Sam wondered about the racket but stayed in her office until she finished. *Jack and Melissa can work it out.* When she put her things away and walked into the kitchen, it was empty. There was a mess, but no people. Jack was watching TV with Chiquito. "Where's Melissa?"

"I'm not really sure. I'm trying to keep my distance because I seem to agitate her for some reason. She might be in her room."

"She sure left a mess. Let me see if I can get her to clean it up so we can make dinner." Sam knocked on Melissa's door before entering. Melissa had her suitcase open and all of her things strewn on the bed. "What are you doing? Are you leaving?"

Melissa paused. "I don't know why, but your cousin hates me. He watches me all the time. It's creepy. I think I'd feel safer at home." She went back to packing.

"Jack doesn't hate you. I'm sorry you think that. I'm here, though, and there's a deadbolt on your door, so you're perfectly safe."

Melissa started crying.

Sam hugged her. "Everything will be fine."

"I'm sorry, Sam. I've just been so afraid. I'll try harder to make friends with Jack."

Sam smiled and hugged her tighter, then she went back downstairs to the mess in the kitchen. She put on a pair of rubber gloves and began putting the herbs or weeds or whatever they were back in Melissa's basket.

Jack walked into the kitchen. "Are you allergic?"

"Not necessarily, but Melissa always tells me to wear gloves if I don't know what something is. She pulls up clumps, and just about anything could be mixed in."

Jack nodded and stayed back. After Sam had cleaned up the mess, they worked together on making dinner.

"You are so creative in the kitchen, Jack. Do you think you could teach me how to cook that way?"

"I'm not really a recipe follower. but if you have a cookbook, we could start there."

"What is this called?"

"Um… Jack's leftover surprise? I just take leftovers and layer them in a casserole pan with whatever sounds good. So tonight we have leftover rice in the bottom, then I cut up the chicken and vegetables from the night before last and simmered in some cream of chicken soup, sour cream, a little milk, and some pepper.

That goes over the rice. Then on the top, we put the cheese you grated."

Sam's mouth made an oh and she bent over to take a closer look.

"You can use pasta, potatoes, or rice on the bottom, along with whatever sounds good. Sometimes it's great, but not always. It'll be ready in about twenty minutes if you want to call Melissa."

Sam went upstairs and gently opened Melissa's door. She was sleeping, and Sam didn't want to disturb her, so she returned downstairs. "I think she's worn out from a very emotional day. She can eat when she wakes."

They had a nice dinner, filled with laughter and good food. It was a relief to forget about everything that had gone wrong and just enjoy each other's company.

"I think I'll call it a night," Sam said after they cleaned up.

"I'll watch a little TV, and then I'll head up too."

Melissa peeked over the banister, found Jack sleeping on the sofa, and retreated into her room. She really wanted to see Steven, but he had given her strict instructions to stay put. Jack was a pain, and she couldn't wait to go home. She poured her glass of bedtime bourbon and changed into her pajamas, sighing.

In the morning, she found Jack and Sam at the stove.

"Good morning!" Sam sang out. "Jack's teaching me how to be more creative in the kitchen.

"Morning." Melissa sat down heavily.

Sam brought her a cup of coffee and sat. "What's going on?"

"I don't know. I feel like we're kind of drifting apart." Her eyes shifted to Jack and then down again.

Without turning around, Jack said, "Maybe you two need a girls' night. I have a date with Alley tonight, so I'll be out of your hair."

Melissa's face brightened and Sam said, "A date?"

Jack chuckled and shrugged.

Chapter 8

That evening, Jack picked Alley up at exactly six in his recently washed Ferrari. He dressed in the clothes he wore when they met and went around to her apartment on the second floor. She answered the door in a beautiful, bright yellow A-line dress and sandals with sunflowers in them. Jack handed her a single yellow rose. "You look beautiful, sunshine."

Alley blushed and giggled. "You, kind sir, are as charming as you are dashing."

Jack beamed and offered her his arm. "Your chariot awaits."

Alley gasped when she saw his car, and he was glad he bought it after all. He opened the door for her, and she might have fallen into it rather than slide, but she laughed good-naturedly.

"Might take a little getting used to," he said. "I have to fold myself in half to get in."

He drove to Ristorante Scalinetto in Las Rodillas. Although the restaurant was an hour away, Jack and Alley chatted comfortably during the drive. She wanted to know all about his life in Albuquerque, asking him about his family and job. Jack felt like Alley was the first person he had met in a long time who really wanted to know the man inside the suit.

"Do you know," she said when they pulled up, "I haven't been to a really nice restaurant in forever. I almost never get to Las Rodillas. This restaurant looks so fancy."

"It does," Jack agreed as he got out of the car and walked around to open Alley's door. "It's not often you see a stone building around here."

Alice Kanaka

"I love the fountains," Alley said, "and the plants. It's almost like finding an enchanted house in the middle of the forest."

Jack took her hand and helped her up from the low-slung seat, then they walked inside. The hostess, who stood in front of the entrance, took Jack's name. There wasn't a waiting area because Ristorante Scalinetto was reservation only. She picked up two menus and led them through the restaurant to their table.

The restaurant, reminiscent of an Italian plaza, was built around a central fountain and boasted travertine floors. The mural-covered walls depicted ancient storefronts, furthering the plaza motif. Vines and small twinkling lights hung from the rafters. Soft music played and candles glowed on the table tops, lending an air of old-world elegance.

Alley looked around with wide eyes. "Oh, Jack! This is beautiful! I feel like I'm actually in Italy."

"I'm pretty impressed too. They've really outdone themselves."

"Your server will be with you shortly," the hostess said, handing them their menus as they sat. She returned shortly with a warm baguette, olive oil, and balsamic vinaigrette.

"I don't know what any of this stuff is," Alley whispered, scanning the menu. "And there are no prices."

Jack glanced at the prices on his menu, surprised at the restaurant's assumptions. *What if the woman was paying for dinner?* "Since the menu is so complicated, why don't we get the five-course set meal for two? Then we can try a lot of things without having to choose."

"That sounds perfect! A little bit of everything."

"The wine menu is pretty long too. Should we ask the waiter what he recommends? Or do you have a favorite?"

"Oh, no. I don't know much about wine. Whatever he recommends is fine."

The waiter appeared with a flourish. "Good evening. May I take your order?"

"We'd like the meal for two."

"Very good. Would you like to order wine with that?"

"Yes, what would you recommend?"

"Perhaps a red to go with the steak?"

"Do you have a good Shiraz?"

"Yes, sir. I'll be back in a moment."

The waiter brought Jack a sample to try, which he passed to Alley. "What do you think of this one?"

"That is the best wine I have ever tasted! I should get some for the saloon."

Jack smiled at her enthusiasm, then turned to the waiter. "You can bring the bottle."

"Is it expensive?" she whispered, once the waiter had left.

"Yes," he whispered back. "But it's my favorite."

"You have excellent taste."

"As long as you like it, I'm happy."

The waiter brought their first course, the antipasto, and Jack said, "Five courses is a lot. Don't forget to save room for dessert." He winked, and she smiled.

The salad came next, with a fresh baguette. "Just these two courses would probably be enough," Alley said.

"We should remember that for next time, but we can always get a doggy bag."

"Do you ever eat what you take home in a doggy bag? It never seems to taste as good the next day."

"No, you're right. I almost never end up eating it, but I have a hard time leaving it on my plate if it's really good."

"So you take it home just to keep yourself from overeating?" She scrunched her nose up.

"I guess I do." He reached for the baguette the same time she did, so his hand brushed against hers, and he wished they were sitting on the same side of the booth.

"That fountain makes me want to go for a swim. Have you ever gone swimming in a fountain?"

Jack paused while the waiter cleared their salads and brought steak and vegetables. "I don't think I have," he said finally. "Have you?"

"I did once. My parents took me to Oregon one summer, and it was so hot. Not hot and dry like here, more sticky hot. There was a park with a fountain; I don't even know how to describe it. It looked like terraced boxes, filled with water that spilled over like a waterfall. People were playing in the water, so I got in too. I'm sure I have pictures somewhere." She smiled at the memory.

"I think it would be fun to travel and experience new places with you."

"Why? I don't really know about anything outside of New Mexico."

"You help me see things in a new way."

The waiter brought out pasta with marinara sauce when they were about halfway done with their steak.

Jack was bemused by Alley's lack of pretense. The women he had dated in Albuquerque had feigned sophistication and picked at their food. Alley was so open and genuine, he felt almost shy with her.

"I am going to burst."

"You don't have to eat it all. I'm leaving my broccoli," Jack said jokingly.

"Poor broccoli. I'm leaving mine too. Do you have some kind of hobby, Jack, or do you work all the time?"

"I go out with my colleagues quite a bit when I'm home. I do play the piano, and I like to read."

"I play the drums." Alley blushed. "Really? That is so cool. Will you play for me sometime?" "Maybe," she said coyly.

The waiter brought them each a slice of tiramisu for dessert. "Can I get you anything else? Some coffee, perhaps?"

"Perhaps you could bring us two snifters of O'Porto."

"Yes, sir," he replied, returning to the bar and returning quickly with two rather large snifters.

It was very good Port; Jack could tell by its fragrance.

"Smell your Shiraz first, and take a taste," he told Alley. "Then do the same with the Port."

She did as instructed and raised her eyebrows.

"What do you think?"

"Well, first, this is not the same Port they sell in the supermarket. That stuff is crap compared to this."

Jack laughed.

"Seriously."

"Yes, I know. The Port is delicious. I like it a lot, but it's sweet. When I drink the Shiraz, I can taste that same woody flavor but without the sweet."

"Yes, I see what you mean."

"Which do you prefer?"

"You chose perfectly. The dry wine with dinner and sweet with dessert." Alley didn't look like she was quite sure what he was talking about, but she looked happy.

Once they had finished dinner and Jack had taken care of the bill, they left the restaurant. Jack took Alley's hand. "Would you like to take a walk?"

"That sounds lovely."

They strolled down Main Street, looking in the shop windows, then returned to the car.

Alley slept most of the way home. When they arrived at the saloon, she asked if he'd like to come up.

"I'd like to come in the door to give you a goodnight kiss in private," he said. "But then I'd like to take things slow with you. I want to linger and savor every step, so we have a million memories."

Alley felt a little light-headed, but she said, "I'd like that too." She let him in the side door, and they shared their first sweet kiss. It heated up until Jack almost changed his mind. But Jack knew that Alley was different, and he wanted to do things right. So he reigned himself in and bid her goodnight.

Chapter 9

The next day, Jack was up early. He made coffee and breakfast, then sat to look at the newspaper while he waited for Sam and Melissa. He figured they might get up late since they had still been having a rousing girls' night when he got home.

Sam was the first downstairs, lured by the smell of coffee.

"Good morning, sleepyhead." Jack put down the paper. "Looking for coffee?"

"My hero! Hand it over."

"You looked like you were having a good time last night."

"We did! How did your date go?"

"It was great. Have you been to Ristorante Scalinetto?"

"No, but I've seen it."

"I'll have to take you there sometime."

"Did Alley have a good time?"

"I believe she did."

Melissa came downstairs, and Jack poured her some coffee. "I made pancake batter but thought I'd cook them fresh when you came down." He poured some oil in a pan and measured out six dollar-sized pancakes. He was just flipping them when he heard a loud banging on the door. Sam went to get it and stepped back in surprise when Sergeant Mickelson came barreling in. "Doc... Jack! Can you come with me?" Mick asked breathlessly. "I have an emergency."

"Sure. Just let me get my things." Jack handed the spatula to Sam. "Don't let them burn." He winked. Taking the stairs two at a time, he raced to his room, grabbed a large leather bag, then headed for the door.

Once they were in the patrol car, Mick said, "Peter Sloan is dead. I think it might be murder. My Captain's on vacation, and right now we don't have a medical examiner. I don't know what to do!" "Okay. Breathe. That's why I went up to get my bag. I have everything we need for a mobile lab."

"I was hoping you'd say that!"

"No one has entered the crime scene?"

"No, sir! I put up crime scene tape and posted two deputized civilians out front."

It might have been better for him to stay and send one of the deputies."

Mick drove out of Sam's driveway onto the road, then took the next driveway to the neighboring ranch. It might have been funny if not for the circumstances. Mick parked the car. "This is Peter's house. He's inside."

Jack looked around as he followed Mick toward the side door of a single-story farmhouse. The house was old, but in good repair; the light blue paint looked new, and the windows glistened in the sun. Peter's red truck sat in the cinder-covered driveway.

Mick nodded at the two deputized civilians near the door. "Have you had any company?"

"Nah," Julio answered. "It's kind of creepy knowing he's in there. And the smell." His face got a little green, and he swallowed hard.

"You can stay out here but stick around. We might need your help. This is Dr. Olivares, the Chief Medical Examiner, so anything he needs... he knows what he's doing."

"Good afternoon. Has anyone entered the crime scene?"

"We haven't been past the bedroom door," Sully said.

"Good. Let's take a look, Sergeant." Jack pulled some disposable scrubs out of his bag, putting them on over his clothes. Then he pulled on a pair of gloves, handing a second pair to Mick before stepping under the crime scene tape and walking into the house.

He wandered around the living room and kitchen, noticing the cleanliness and lack of clutter. When he got to the bedroom door, he stopped outside another strip of crime scene tape.

The room looked neat and clean, like the rest of the house, except for the messy body between the bed and the door. The victim was wearing a white, fuzzy robe, but it wasn't done up. He was laying on his back as if he had fallen there, but his arms and legs were flung out in different directions. Bodily fluids were sprayed on the floor, bed, and walls, but there was no blood.

Jack turned to Mick and raised an eyebrow. "This is a first. I've never been at a crime scene without a team of detectives and techs collecting evidence and asking questions. We'll need to make sure we follow protocol and document everything. Do you have a camera?"

Mick shook his head apologetically, so Jack pulled his camera out of his bag and handed it to him. "Take pictures of the scene from every angle, then closeups of the bodily fluids." Jack pointed to the feces and emesis around the body. After Mick photographed them, Jack spoke into a small recorder and collected samples.

They focused on the face next. Mick took photographs, and Jack noted swelling, as well as maggots and postmortem purging in the nose and mouth. A visual check of the body showed no wounds other than an abrasion on the victim's right arm and a severe case of dermatitis. The victim's skin had a greenish tint, and his abdomen was distended.

After taking more photographs, Mick helped Jack carefully turn the body to one side, so he could see the severe postmortem staining on the victim's back. Jack used the blanching test, pressing his thumb in the discolored area for one minute, to make sure the staining was fixed and noted no shifting of postmortem lividity.

When they were finished with the preliminary check, Jack said, "Has anyone looked around for possible evidence? Pill bottles, syringes, recently eaten food, cups?"

Mick had been very quiet while they were working, and Jack's question made him jump.

"No, it's just us, Jack." He looked at the body. "Do you have any idea how long he's been dead?"

"I need to do some more testing, but I saw him in town when I stopped in at the station on Monday, around noon. He probably didn't go home immediately, and right now, it has been forty-eight hours since I saw him. Looking at the body's level of deterioration, I would estimate at least twenty-four hours because maggots are present. The marbling of the skin and bloating usually occur between eighteen and thirty-six hours. I will be able to narrow it down once I open him up."

Jack glanced up to find Mick staring at him. "There are so many variables; it's hard to be exact."

"Television shows make it look so easy. I came over to speak with Peter after you left at two. He was standing in the doorway, having a disagreement with an older lady. I didn't recognize her, and she left when I approached."

"We should try to find her. Are there any next of kin?"

"I'll find out, but I don't think so."

"Since this whole situation is pretty unorthodox, I'm going to go out on a limb and suggest this might have been a poisoning. I won't know for sure until I do a lot more testing, but there are no visible, life-threatening wounds, and I've seen similar symptoms: projectile vomiting, diarrhea, and severe dermatitis, in other cases of poisoning. The rather quick onset of putrefaction could indicate that one or more seizures quickened the march of rigor."

"He was poisoned?"

"I'm not able to give an official verdict. But because there are just two of us here, and it's a possibility, I'd like to collect anything we can find that might have been a conduit: plates, cups, food, liquid soap, creams."

Mick nodded his understanding and went to ask Julio and Sully for assistance. They were still collecting evidence when Jack heard the crunch of the ambulance tires from outside.

65

He met the EMTs at the door and helped them carefully wrap and move the body onto the gurney.

"I'll ride to the morgue with the body. See if you can get someone from Las Rodillas to help out here and meet me there," he told Mick.

Chapter 10

Sam paced back and forth. "I'm really worried," she said for the umpteenth time. "Maybe we should try the station again," Melissa suggested. "Or take a walk?" Sam shook her head and stared at the phone.

"What does Jack do for a living?"

"I don't know. It never came up. I never asked. He seems to be good at everything. The first day we met, he told me he had his own career, but I didn't ask what it was. I am the worst cousin ever."

The phone rang, and Sam snatched it up. "Jack?"

"Hey, Sam. Is Melissa there with you?"

"Yes, we've been waiting here for hours! What happened?"

"It's kind of a long story, but could you bring Melissa to the morgue in Las Rodillas?"

"Then you'll explain everything?"

"Yeah. Could you bring some food, too? I'm starving."

"Will do, cuz! See you soon." Sam hung up quite relieved. "Come on, Melissa. We're on a mission!"

Melissa rolled her eyes and sighed. "Why do you jump every time he needs something?"

"I want to find out what's going on. We need to take Jack some food, and he'll explain everything."

"I guess that's a fair trade. What should we get him?"

"I'll just pack up a bunch of leftovers, and we can have lunch together." Sam started digging in the fridge. "We have plenty of food in here."

It took Sam half an hour to get the food ready, and then they went out to her truck. The hour-long trip to Las Rodillas went by quickly because Sam asked Melissa what she had been working on lately, and that led to a lively monologue about a new type of salve she was experimenting with.

When they arrived at the morgue, Jack greeted them at the front desk wearing scrubs. Sam stared at him in confusion. She had seen city-slicker Jack and cowboy Jack, but how did he end up in scrubs in a morgue in Las Rodillas? He was supposed to be on vacation.

Jack, completely unfazed, said, "Hello, ladies. Before I take a break, could I ask a very big favor?"

Sam and Melissa nodded reluctantly. "Why are we here?" Sam asked.

"Come with me," he said as he ushered them toward the pneumatic doors.

Before the doors opened, an officer posted at the reception desk called out, "Samantha Olivares?"

Sam felt a little alarmed as she turned toward the desk.

"Could you fill out this visitor's form, please?"

Sam hesitated and looked at Jack, wondering why she felt like he was singling her out on purpose.

"It's fine. You can meet us inside." Jack led Melissa through the doors, leaving Sam in the lobby.

Jack and Melissa walked down a long, sterile-looking hall. The light green walls and fluorescent lights made her feel like she was in a science fiction movie, and she started to sweat. Her claustrophobia and paranoia began to rise as she lost sight of the entry. "Where are we going?" she asked in a high-pitched voice. "Who are you anyway? Why isn't Sam with us?"

Jack opened a door on their left and proceeded inside. "There was a homicide this morning, and I would like you to provide the official identification of the body."

"Why me?"

Jack stood next to her and gently pulled the sheet back from Peter's head.

Melissa gasped when she saw Peter. His body was partially covered, but his eyes were wide open, and he seemed to be staring at her. He was just as frightening in death as he had been in life. "P-Peter!" She sobbed and stepped back. She didn't know if she should grieve or celebrate. "I wasn't prepared for this," she said shakily. "I loved him, and I hated him. He was very cruel." She touched his cold cheek and began to cry.

"Thank you. I'm sorry I had to ask you to do this. We can go now."

When they left the lab, Jack removed his scrubs, hung them up, and then motioned to the hand-washing station where they thoroughly washed their hands. Melissa was very quiet as they returned to reception. She was thinking about the fragility and impermanence of life. She wished she had her purple crystal. It always helped her stay calm.

Sam stood abruptly and rushed over to Melissa, pulling her into a hug. "What happened?"

"Come," Jack said. "Let's go have our picnic, and I'll explain."

They sat at a table in the shade, and Sam unpacked her basket. "I never asked you about your work. I feel ashamed but also confused. Why are we here?"

"I'm on vacation. No one asked what I do, and it's not something I just bring up. I'm a forensic medical examiner. I stopped in at the Sheriff's office to introduce myself, so Sergeant Mickelson knew I was staying in Santo Milagro."

"Why did he come get you?"

"His Captain is on vacation, and the Medical Examiner's position is currently vacant. He needed help."

"Who died?" Her eyes widened as she glanced between him and Melissa. "Peter?"

Melissa nodded.

"Why are you crying? I thought you'd be relieved. Happy even." Little wrinkles appeared between her brows.

"He was mean sometimes, and I wanted to break up, but in a way, I loved him. It's hard to see someone you cared about dead. He was bigger than life, invincible." She put her head in her hands, and her body shook. Mostly she felt relieved, but she didn't want them to think she had killed him. There were times when she could have, but she didn't.

"Why would you do that to her?" Sam demanded.

"Two reasons. First, she knew him well and could provide a formal identification. Second, she's been staying at the ranch because she was afraid of him. I thought seeing for herself that he's dead would provide closure and prove she's safe. I'm sorry it was such a shock, Melissa. I didn't realize your feelings for him ran so deep."

"I understand. Thank you for thinking of me." Melissa snuffled. She felt like a complete fraud.

They continued their picnic in silence.

"I've called in another examiner and should be able to get back to my vacation this evening," Jack said as they were packing up. "I'll let you know if I'll be longer."

"Okay." Sam hugged him. "Let me know if you need more food."

"I will." He smiled.

Sam and Melissa watched him go back inside. "He never told us how Peter died. Did he tell you?"

"I didn't think to ask either. It was such a shock."

Jack strode into the morgue, deep in thought. Melissa's reaction had surprised him. *If her reaction was genuine, why didn't she ask how he died? Peter had a lot of enemies. If Sam hadn't offered to pay off Alley's loan, I might have wondered about her, too.* He noted three missed calls and ran a hand through his hair. *I need to stop by the saloon on the way home.*

70

Several hours later, Jack had taken blood samples from the heart and femur, made the Y incision, and was removing internal organs, when Dr. Byron Vanzandt practically bounced through the doors to the lab. "I can't believe you dragged me all the way out here, you dastardly crow!" Byron's sharp eyes danced merrily; his pointed goatee gave him the look of an evil genius.

"Thank you so much for coming!"

"Was it an invitation then?"

"Well, not really, but I do appreciate it."

"You said you needed my expertise. What kind of pretty puzzle do you have for me?"

"It's a doozie. Apparent poisoning by an unknown agent and vehicle. I've recorded my observations at the scene and have been working on collecting blood and tissue samples. I'll let you come to your own conclusions."

Byron studied Jack's notes and nodded. "Very well. I'll work my magic." He smiled.

"Thanks, wizard. I'm going to do some sleuthing and eating while you're weaving spells."

Jack took his leave and headed for Alley's saloon. He stopped on the way to buy a single daisy. The saloon was closed, so he walked around to the side door and rang the bell.

Alley's voice came through the intercom. "Not right now, please."

He pushed the intercom button. "It's Jack. I need to talk to you. Can I come up?"

She didn't answer, but there was a buzz as she unlocked the door.

Jack took the stairs two at a time and bounded into her living room. He found Alley disheveled, sitting next to a bottle of whiskey, and surrounded by photos; mascara running down her cheeks. Jack sat on the floor across from her and reached across with the daisy.

71

She took it slowly and looked up at him. "Where've you been all day, Jack? I've been trying to call you for hours."

"We can talk about that in a minute. What's this all about?"

Alley glanced around and shrugged.

"Did you still love him?"

"No. I was mad at him. After my parents died, Peter and my family home were all I had. He took my home and left me for Melissa; then I had nothing."

"What about the saloon?"

"The saloon never made any money. What he did was trick me into signing papers that said we were exchanging property rights. He became the sole owner of my family property, and I became owner of his debt-ridden saloon. He was so mean."

"So why are you sitting here crying over his photos?"

"I'm not really. I've been crying because I thought you changed your mind. Because you weren't concerned enough to answer my calls. And I was looking at old photos of Peter and me looking happy in my old home."

"Oh, sunshine, I am so sorry." He walked around behind her and sat, wrapping his arms around her. "Let me tell you what happened."

She leaned back against him and closed her eyes. "Tell me."

"Let me start by telling you what I do..."

They talked until everything was put right, and Alley fell asleep. Jack put her to bed, straightened up the living room, and called Sam. "Hi, Sam. What's up?"

"Melissa went back home. Chiquito and I are watching a movie."

"I stopped at Alley's, and she's not doing too well. I'm going to stay if that's alright."

"I'm a big girl. I'll be fine."

Jack hung up then climbed into bed with Alley, fully dressed, and snuggled up with her. She didn't wake but snuggled close and said his name in her sleep. He fell asleep smiling.

Chapter 11

The following morning, Jack woke to the smell of coffee and bacon and the sound of cheerful singing. He splashed some water on his face and went to find the source of all that goodness. She turned as he entered and smiled.

"You're just cute as a button." He pulled her close for a kiss. "The sunlight makes your curls glow, and this robe feels so soft and cozy, like you." He nibbled her ear.

"Oh, stop!" She blushed and swatted at him.

"I might have to if I don't get some of that coffee right away."

She giggled all the way to the cupboard and poured him a cup. "There's cream and sugar on the table. I'm glad to see you don't wake up looking perfect. I was starting to wonder."

"What do you mean? Of course, I look perfect."

She giggled and sat with him to eat.

"I'm afraid it will be another long day today. Will you be okay?"

"I'll be fine now. Thank you for staying last night."

"My pleasure. That was the best night's sleep I've ever had. And thank you for breakfast. I should probably get back to the ranch and get my perfect on."

"Ohh you!" She swatted at him again but found herself being properly kissed instead.

Jack drove home and saw Steven's truck in the driveway. I wonder why he's here? He peeked into the kitchen and saw him sitting across from Sam at the breakfast table eating cereal.

"How's it going?" he asked, making them jump.

Sam shrugged, and Steven looked at him with pleading eyes.

"I've got to get back to the morgue. Did you get some coffee, Sam?"

"No. But I can make it."

"Why didn't you tell me, babe? I could have made you some."

"Don't call me babe. I think you should probably go now."

Steven looked crestfallen, but he stood and headed for the door. "Thanks for breakfast."

Jack made the coffee and sat with Sam. "Are you alright?"

"I guess so. When we got back yesterday, Melissa was already packed. She went upstairs, got her suitcase, and left without saying anything. Then, Steven showed up. It was really weird." Sam blinked and shook her head. "Did you even sleep last night?"

"Yes, why?"

"Your clothes are a little rumpled, and your hair..."

"I know. I need to get cleaned up and go see what Dr. Vanzandt has discovered."

"Who's Dr. Vanzandt?"

"Byron Vanzandt is a genius when it comes to toxicology. He's come up to help with this case."

Sam nodded. "Well, go do what you've got to do. I have a lot of work to get caught up on." She looked around at the mess despondently.

Jack checked in with Dr. Vanzandt shortly after ten.

"Banker's hours?" Byron asked, raising one eyebrow.

"Hey, I'm supposed to be on vacation."

"I know. The only way you can be sure to stay out of things is to leave the country."

"Have you been here all night?"

"Yes. This is quite fascinating."

"Why is that?"

"Well, I can't find anything specific in his blood, but it's obvious something traumatic happened. I'll keep running tests.

74

Did you collect any physical evidence that might have contained what we're looking for?"

"We collected food, cups, soap, and a couple of prescription bottles."

"Where are those? Perhaps I can work backward."

Jack retrieved a box of bagged items from a locker and brought it to the table. Byron opened the box and began examining each item. When he opened the bottle of pomegranate-scented body wash, he looked surprised. Holding it out to Jack, he said, "What does this smell like to you?"

"I don't know. Turnips?"

"Can you ask someone for a list of known poisonous plants that grow in this region?"

"Sure. I'll just call the Sheriff's station. I'm sure they have something available." Jack arranged for Mick to send over a list, and he left Dr. Vanzandt working contentedly.

After Jack left the ranch, Sam decided to ignore the mess for a while and go for a ride. Being outdoors with Ghost always lifted her spirits. She called out to Roger, who always seemed to appear when she needed him.

"Good morning, Ms. Sam. It's a nice day for a ride."

"Yes," she said distractedly. "Where's Red?"

"Oh, he's around." Roger smiled and took off Ghost's bridle.

"Thanks." Sam hopped on Ghost's back and walked her through the open gate. They walked for a while, and Sam watched Roger call Red and head back into the barn. *Maybe I've been wrong to keep him at a distance. He has a lot of responsibility, and I hardly know him. Dad would be appalled.*

She eased Ghost into a canter and jumped the far fence that separated her ranch from Peter's, then stopped and stared across the range at his house. *He was rotten, but who would have killed him? It had to be someone I know, but who hated him that much?* Sam considered her friends and neighbors and couldn't picture any of them as a murderer. She shivered under the hot sun.

Sam and Ghost were sweaty and covered with dust when they returned. Roger appeared and reached for Ghost, but Sam stopped him. "I think I'll wash her before I head in."

"I can do that, Ms. Sam."

"I know. I just feel like spending a little more time with her."

"Okay."

"Roger? Would you like to have dinner with Jack and me this evening?"

He paused for a moment, surprised. "I would love to. Thank you."

"I'm not sure when Jack will be home, but I'll make spaghetti, and we can shoot for seven. He's been pretty busy."

Sam finished washing Ghost, then went inside for a shower. After showering and changing, Sam knelt by her bed and said a short prayer. "Lord," she said, "please help me be a good friend and a good employer. Help me learn to trust, even if it hurts sometimes. And please help me make the spaghetti!" She chuckled a little and crossed herself, assuming God had a sense of humor too.

She made her way down to the kitchen and started on dinner. Although she often berated her own cooking, she knew how to cook. She could even make bread and pies. She just wasn't very creative and preferred to follow a recipe. Everything was ready by seven, and she and Roger were waiting when Jack pulled into the driveway at 7:15. Sam and Roger yelled, "Surprise!" when he walked through the door.

Hand on his heart, he asked, "Do I smell food? And is that Roger?"

"Yes to both. Are you hungry?"

"Famished!"

Jack left before dawn the next morning. He saw Alley's lights on above the saloon when he drove through town and wanted to stop and see her but fought the pull. He had a murderer to catch. *Maybe I should put my personal life on hold. I never realized how distracting personal relationships can be.*

Maybe I didn't know what I was missing. When I go home, everything will be different. I wonder if Alley would come to Albuquerque.

He met Mick at the morgue, and when they entered the lab, Dr. Vanzandt was waving a paper around, visibly excited. "I've found the type of poison!"

Jack didn't need to say anything. He knew Byron would answer all of his questions and some he hadn't even thought of yet.

"It was in the body wash! Remember I asked you to smell it? Something about the smell jogged my memory, and when I looked at the list of local plants, I saw it. Water hemlock grows along the river bank here. It contains cicutoxin and is considered one of the most deadly plants in the world. Cicutoxin is unstable and can't be found in an autopsy, but the postmortem symptoms match."

"Did you test the leftover food that was brought in?"

"Yes. Nothing in the food."

"So we need to find out who would know about this plant and know that it could be absorbed through the skin. Any ideas, Mick?"

"Well, the first that come to mind are Melissa, Alley, and Tia.

"Why Alley?

"Because Peter's land was originally hers and she knows it well. And all ranchers are concerned about invasive, poisonous plants like the water hemlock. The government publishes maps and detailed information about them online."

"I think Sam said that Melissa and Tia are plant experts, right?"

"Yes. Sam would also know about them, of course, since she's also a rancher and goes out collecting plants with Melissa."

"Have you narrowed the estimated time of death, Byron?"

"No, your estimate is sound."

"That makes alibis difficult, but we can ask when we interview our suspects."

"Then there's possible motive," Mick said. "He was allegedly abusing Melissa. He scammed Alley out of her family home, and Tia might be angry about Mark."

"We could set a little trap to see if anyone tries to retrieve the body soap," Jack said.

"What would that look like?" Mick asked.

"Replace the bottle and see if anyone tries to retrieve it. If no one does, then we could give them incentive by mentioning it in our interviews. Perhaps you could have Deputy Flores stake out the property."

✷✷✷✷

Father Garcia beamed and waved to Sam and Jack as they approached the church. "I haven't seen you here during the week, Samantha. Has everything been going well?"

"Yes, Father. I have been taking your advice and praying at home." Sam smiled.

"You seem happier of late. Would this have anything to do with your friend?"

"I prayed for love in my life, and God sent me a cousin. That's why I was here that day. It was the day Jack arrived, and I wanted to say thank you."

"Family is indeed a gift."

After the service, Sam suggested they buy lunch to take home with them, so they went to the Ugly Orange Cafe. Jack looked around and said, "I like how bright and open this is. All the windows, and plants, and the bright orange booths; it's like a cross between a picnic and a retro diner."

Sam looked around and had to agree. "The big, orange and white tiles and the long, white counter add to the effect."

"Hola, Sam. How are you today?"

"Hola." Sam smiled. "Jack, this is Concha Flores. This is her restaurant. Concha, this is my cousin Jack."

"Ohh, I hear about your cousin. Nice to meet you, Jack! Can I get you a booth?"

"No, we'll just get ours to go," Sam said.

78

"And what would you like?"

"Two club sandwiches and a giant serving of french fries."

Concha laughed. "Coming up!"

Concha returned a few minutes later with a large bag. "Here you go, Sam. I hope you love it."

Sam paid for the lunch and smiled. "Thank you! See you later."

They walked outside, and Sam said, "I wonder what she put in there. She had that look in her eye."

"Want me to take a peek?"

"No, we'll find out soon enough. Want to hang out by the pool this afternoon? You've been working pretty hard lately. Sometimes doing something else for a while jogs your brain."

"Sounds like good advice. I want to eat that food before it's cold, though. It smells great."

They pulled up at the ranch, went inside, and Sam opened the bag. Inside, there were the sandwiches and fries Sam had ordered, plus salad, tater tots, and cherry pie. "That Concha! She is so sweet. We'll have to go back soon so I can thank her."

"Is she related to Anita?"

"Yes. Her sister. Their whole family is great. Wait until you meet their mom!"

"When might that happen?"

"They have a lot of parties. I'm sure we'll get invited to one soon. Why aren't you eating?"

"I didn't want to be rude."

"No, eat. Then we can go play in the pool." Sam grabbed a tot.

After lunch, while they were floating around in the water, Sam said, "I never realized how great this pool was until you came. I love hanging out here with you when it's so hot outside."

"Didn't you use it before?"

"Sometimes. But it's not as fun getting in by myself."

"Barbecuing by the pool is a great way to spend the afternoon, but I can see what you mean. If I was by myself, I probably wouldn't bother either."

They floated around until late, just enjoying each other's company, and Sam realized she took a lot of things for granted. *Maybe I should be more grateful for the people in my life and reach out to them more often.* "You should go change the CD." She laughed when he splashed water in her direction.

Chapter 12

A young man tiptoed up to Peter's house and peered in the window the following day. He snuck around the perimeter, making sure no one was watching, then ducked under the tape and tried the door. He took a key out of his pocket and unlocked it before going inside. A couple of minutes later, he emerged holding a paper bag and sporting extra bulges in his pockets.

Mick stepped out of the shadows, and the young man began to run. Unlike televised chases, there was nowhere for the young man to hide. Running flat out across high desert land was just asking for an injury. Mick shook his head, then broke into a sprint. As the pursuer, he had the advantage and was able to take the giant leap to bring down the suspect, using the young man as a nice cushion for his fall. The suspect didn't fare quite so well. He hadn't made it past the driveway, and the sharp cinders poked and scraped him as he slid. Mick cuffed him and stood. "What's your name?"

"Ararat Sahagian."

"Why were you stealing from a deceased person's home?"

"I wasn't stealing."

Mick put on a pair of gloves and picked up the bag Ararat was carrying. "Is this yours?"

"No-o, but the owner asked me to get it."

"Empty your pockets."

"I c-can't." Ararat indicated his handcuffs.

"Your pockets weren't bulging like that when you entered."

"She told me they were engaged, and everything would be hers. She said I could take whatever I wanted. She gave me a key."

"Does she have a name?"

"Yes, but I'd rather not say."

"You will say unless you want to go to jail."

Ararat slumped and hung his head. "It was Melissa Dierkson."

"And what is the nature of your relationship with Ms. Dierkson?"

"We are lovers."

"So she asked you to get something for her?"

"Yes. She was engaged to the man who died, and she left her favorite body soap in his house. There was no harm in getting it for her."

"Why didn't she go get it herself?"

"Melissa is very spiritual. She was afraid his ghost might be there and follow her home. He loved her very much."

"Get in the car, please."

"Don't you need to read me my rights?"

"I haven't decided if I'm going to charge you with anything. I'll need to verify your story with Melissa. Thank you for cooperating."

"She's going to be so mad," Ararat mumbled.

Mick drove his patrol car to Melissa's little green house and got out. He walked up the steps to her porch and knocked. It took a few tries, but she finally came to the door in a bathrobe. She looked sleepy, and her hair was disheveled. "What do you want, Mick?"

"I'm taking you to the station. Would you like to get dressed first?"

She rolled her eyes. "This really isn't a good time."

"Just get dressed, please."

"I'm going back to bed." She turned to walk back to her bedroom.

Mick ran out of patience. He snapped on the cuffs and began to read her her rights. "Melissa Dierkson, I'm arresting you for the murder of Peter Sloan..."

Melissa shook her head, looked at him as if he was crazy, then started to argue with him. When he escorted her to the car and she saw Ararat, she became violent. Mick opened the front passenger door, then the back passenger door "Move to the front, please.". The cage between the front and back seats would keep Ararat safe.

Melissa planted her feet and legs against the car frame, preventing Mick from getting her inside. She was a lot stronger than she looked. She threw her head back, giving him a bloody nose. Finally, he grabbed her legs and slid her headfirst across the seat, slamming the door behind her. Melissa yelled all the way into town. "You know me, Mick! I can't believe you're doing this. Why are you targeting me? What's that guy got to do with me? He's trying to frame me!"

Mick remained silent, carefully noting her words. Melissa demanded a lawyer when they arrived at the station, then stopped talking.

Sam glared as Jack walked into the kitchen. "What have you done?"

"What do you mean?"

"You've arrested Melissa? Why would you do that? She might be confused and a little flaky, but she's no killer!"

Jack took a deep breath. "I didn't arrest her, Mick did, but it was my idea to lay the trap for the murderer. The evidence against her is pretty strong."

"I can't believe I welcomed you into my home and my life, and you're tearing it apart. What kind of family does that? Do you know that Melissa told me the other day that Steven swore he would kill Peter after he saw her bruise? And she told me Alley threatened her when she heard they were getting married." She crossed her arms in triumph.

Jack frowned. "No matter what I think personally, I'm bound to look at the evidence."

"I'm going to talk to her and help her get to the bottom of this. You've obviously decided she's guilty and aren't looking any farther. What kind of policeman are you anyway?" She heard him mumble something as she stomped out of the kitchen and locked herself in her office. Her heart pounded and her hands trembled.

After a few minutes, she heard the kitchen door open and close. When she looked out the window, she saw Jack putting a small bag in his car. He looked back at the house, got in the driver's seat, and drove off.

Sam slumped in her chair, feeling confused and unhappy. *Why did I say all those terrible things? I didn't want him to leave. I just wanted him to listen to me. Now I'm alone, and he's probably mad at me. I couldn't blame him.*

Mick sat in the interview room with Melissa and her lawyer, Ms. Price. Melissa had stopped yelling, but not before Ms. Price got an earful from the hallway. Now, apparently subdued and rational, Melissa sat quietly next to Ms. Price. Mick had worked with her before and knew she was competent.

"Could you explain the grounds for Ms. Dierkson's arrest, please?"

"The body wash she asked Mr. Sahagian to retrieve contained the poison suspected of killing Mr. Sloan. Additionally, Ms. Dierkson is an expert in poisonous plants and has access to them. She created an alibi for the time the poison was used. She refuses to answer any questions, so the evidence speaks for itself."

"Thank you, Sergeant. May we have fifteen minutes to discuss this privately?"

"Of course. Just holler if you need anything."

Mick left the interview room and went looking for a cup of coffee.

Jack felt angry at himself and frustrated that Sam wasn't more understanding about his job. *I can't just change who I am because someone I care about is friends with a suspect. What if Alley becomes a suspect?*

Or Sam? How could I deal with that? I should never have come here.

When Jack entered the lab, Byron looked up with a sparkle in his eyes. You are not going to believe this." Jack raised an eyebrow but didn't need to say anything because Byron was on a roll. "There was cicutoxin in everything. Absolutely everything. And there was an empty ziplock bag with traces of it and a label that said 'water hemlock' on it. Someone really wanted our victim dead."

Jack sat. "Have you sent the label in for analysis?"

"Yes, but I don't have any results yet."

"They're going to have to release her."

"It seems so."

Jack sighed and headed for the phone. He called, but Mick wasn't at his desk. "I'll try again in a few minutes. Where are you staying?"

"Here mostly, but there's a hotel two blocks down that has good rates. I have a room even though I'm not there much."

"I'll see if I can get one too. Would you like to have dinner with me this evening? Maybe if we put our heads together, we can figure this out."

"Sounds excellent. There's a pretty good diner near here called Mary's. Just ask at the hotel, and I'll meet you there at seven."

Mick reentered the interview room after fifteen minutes and sat.

"My client would like to make an uninterrupted statement about the allegations. She may or may not wish to answer further questions because she does not have all the information."

"Ok. Go ahead, Melissa."

"First, I wanted my body wash back. It's my favorite and a little expensive. I didn't poison it. It was mine. Why would I poison my own body wash? Second, I do know about poisonous plants, but so do a lot of other people. You didn't tell me what poison, but I use small quantities of certain plants in salves and always educate my customers about the dangers of using too much. Third, I went to stay with Sam because I was afraid of Peter and because Steven told me to."

"Can you tell me the names of any customers you have talked to about specific plants?"

"Mostly older women who suffer from inflammation."

"Anyone recently?"

"Emily Dade and Victoria Hale are the most recent."

"Have you noticed any stock missing?"

"I've been a little out of it recently, but I can check."

"Deputy Flores stuck her head in the door. "Excuse me, Sergeant. You have a phone call. It's important."

Mick left to take the call, then returned to the interview room and said, "You are free to leave, Ms. Dierkson. If you think of any more names or find anything missing, please let me know."

"Why are you letting me go?"

"We have uncovered some additional information that backs up your statement, but please don't leave town."

Melissa looked at Ms. Price.

"That's a standard request."

"Thank you for helping me today."

"Here's my card. Please call me if anything arises."

Melissa took the card and thanked her again before leaving the room.

Jack found the Adobe Inn down the street.Being a somewhat larger town than Santo Milagro, Las Rodillas had a lot more selection regarding lodging and dining. The Adobe Inn reminded Jack of a Motel 6. It wasn't of historical interest, but it had a bed, a small pool, and a breakfast buffet. Jack had brought his suit and a small bag of clothes from the magic closet. He felt sad when he thought of the magic closet; it reminded him that Sam was angry with him. Perhaps she would feel better now that Melissa had been released.

He checked in and went up to his room, then called to check on Alley before meeting Byron at Mary's. They sat at a booth in the back and indulged in loads of spicy carbohydrates and several drinks each, as they went over everything they knew. The result was two tipsy doctors who knew they needed more information.

Chapter 13

S am answered a knock at the kitchen door and found Melissa standing there. Melissa fell into her arms, and Sam hugged her for a long time. "Are you okay?" she asked, tucking an errant lock behind Melissa's ear.

"Yes, I'm okay but really tired. I don't understand what's happening to me or why my life is so messed up right now."

"It will get better. Come sit in the kitchen, and I'll make some tea."

"Do you have any chamomile left?"

"I keep it especially for your visits. Are you hungry?"

"Yes! I haven't eaten today."

"So, tell me what happened."

"Where's Jack?" Melissa looked around.

"He left earlier because I got mad at him for arresting you."

"Um, he didn't arrest me, Sam. He's not a policeman. Mick arrested me."

Sam sat down in shock. "So I yelled at him for something that wasn't his fault?"

"Maybe."

Sam's stomach churned with guilt. She got back up to finish the tea and get Melissa some chili she had made for dinner. "So why did Mick arrest you?"

Melissa told her everything while she ate. "It feels better talking about it. I didn't understand it at all until I talked to the lawyer, and I'm still not sure why they let me go."

"Your answers made sense. The evidence was circumstantial at best."

"What if they arrest me again?"

"We need to figure out who really killed him, then we won't have to worry. He had a lot of enemies." Sam pulled some note paper and pens from a kitchen drawer and returned to the table. "I don't know anything about sleuthing, but we are both reasonably smart, so we can figure it out."

Melissa took a deep breath. "Peter was a blackmailer."

"Yes, I know. He was blackmailing Mark Carruthers. He tried to blackmail me too."

"Well, he had something on me that I don't want to tell you. He made me do his bidding whenever he wanted. He was cruel and disgusting. I had to break up with Steven because it looked like I was dating Peter, and I couldn't explain."

"So you hated him?"

Melissa's face paled, and her eyes widened. She started to stand, but Sam grabbed her hand.

"Hate is not a crime, Melissa. Lots of people hated Peter. Let's make a list and see if we can narrow it down." Sam started writing:

Sam — *blamed Peter for her father's death.*
Melissa — *was blackmailed and treated abusively.*
Mark — *was blackmailed and coerced into making bad banking decisions.*
Steven — *blamed Peter for losing Melissa.*
Alley — *Peter left her and stole her family home.*

"Who else?"

Melissa gaped at the list. "All those people? I thought it was just me."

"I don't know for sure, but there were several shop owners in town who would stiffen up when he entered their shops, and they wouldn't charge him for things he took. Maybe he had accounts with them?"

"No, Peter didn't like to owe anyone anything. He never used credit."

"Then let's add the shopkeepers I noticed to the list. We can interview them later."

Emily Dade – unknown
Nacho Sanchez – unknown
Tia Connors – unknown

Sam sat back and studied her list. "What about your friend, Ara?"

"I don't know if he even knew Peter. He always followed me around, and he kind of took advantage when I was pretty drunk. I wanted to get my bottle of body wash back because it's my favorite, and it's kind of expensive, so I thought he could sneak in and get it for me. I didn't know there was poison in it. Maybe Mick saved my life."

"If you look at it that way, you were really lucky."

"Ara told them that I said Peter and I were going to be married, so he left everything to me. I did tell him that, but I was lying so he'd do what I wanted."

"Do you think he could have killed Peter?"

"I don't think so, but there's no way for me to know for sure."

"Let's add him just in case. He is involved, and he took some other things from Peter's house."

"How do you know that?"

"Julio told me. He's one of Mick's deputized civilians, and he has a little crush on me. He tells me everything. Oh, what about the customers you mentioned? We already have Emily on our list. Victoria, you said?"

"Victoria Hale."

"Anyone else?"

"No, I don't think so."

"That's a pretty good list. Now we need to talk to each of them and see how strong their feelings were. We will assume that you and I aren't killers, and Ara is unlikely, so that leaves seven. Any thoughts on them?"

"The only two I know anything about are Alley and Steven. I know you like Alley, but she has a different side that you haven't seen. Whenever I run into her, she gets a hateful look in her eye. She kind of scares me, and she says things to people that keep them away from my shop."

"Like what?"

"She says things all innocently like I dabble in witchcraft or I have dangerous herbs in my shop."

"Hmm. Okay. How about Steven?"

"I'm not sure. Steven seems like such an easy-going surfer type, but his personality changed after I broke up with him. He stopped being the fun-loving guy I knew and became sullen and withdrawn. I could feel his eyes on me whenever Peter talked to me in town. He asked me about Peter at the dance, and I told him Peter hit me sometimes. He was furious and started the fight. Peter was angry too. He blamed me for starting it, and he hit me again."

Sam sat very still.

"The thing is, I can imagine Steven getting really angry and shooting Peter or hitting him over the head. But patiently and deliberately planning to poison someone doesn't seem his style. We should remember what kind of murder it was and how it was made to look like I did it."

"There is that. So perhaps we are looking for someone who hated Peter and you too. Or maybe you were just a convenient suspect?"

Melissa put her head in her hands. I no sooner get out of one nightmare and I'm dropped into another."

"Alley hated you both. Mark's her brother, so he may have felt the same. Then there are Emily, Nacho, and Tia. I was going to suggest we split up, but it's probably best if we stick together.

"Okay. We've got a starting place. What could we ask to find out if someone was being blackmailed, if they hated him, and if they knew anyone else who might have been in the same situation?"

Melissa shook her head. "I don't know."

Sam tapped her pencil on the table. "I think we could ask straight out about the blackmail. We could say he tried blackmailing both of us, and we were trying to find out if he had done it to anyone else."

"Then we could watch their facial expressions and body language to see if they're lying," Melissa added.

"And to see if they get emotional. If they say no, we could follow up by asking them if they liked him."

"Yes! That could get an emotional response as well."

"If they answer yes, we could ask if they know anyone else who had problems with him."

Melissa stood. "Sounds good. I'm beat. I think I'll head home if that's okay."

"Sure. Come over tomorrow morning, and we'll get started."

"Thank you, Sam. I don't know what I would do without you."

"We've always been here for each other, and we always will." Sam gave her another hug at the door and waved as she got into her little red Nissan Sentra and drove away.

After Melissa left, Chiquito jumped down from his perch atop the refrigerator and wound around Sam's legs. *At least he's predictable. Poor Jack. I blamed him for everything and wouldn't listen to a word he said.* She turned on the news and sat on the sofa with Chiquito. Sometimes petting him and listening to his purr calmed her, but she couldn't seem to sit still. She went and got the vacuum, working feverishly to stave off her feelings of remorse while Chiquito hid from the noisy machine. She turned off the vacuum to pay attention when she saw the picture zoom in through a restaurant window. There, in a corner booth, sat Jack and another man. The newscaster was talking about Peter's death.

"Dr. Jack Olivares, New Mexico's Chief Medical Examiner, and Dr. Byron Vanzandt, celebrated Pathologist and Forensic Toxicologist, are right here in Las Rodillas at Mary's Diner. Dr. Olivares said they currently have no comment, but they are working closely with law enforcement in Santo Milagro and will keep us updated. Tune in tomorrow for more groundbreaking news!"

Wait. What?" Doctor? Chief? What the heck? She shook her head. She had thought he was some kind of policeman, and here he was, the head of forensics for the entire state. No wonder Mick had come looking for him.

Sam wanted to call him and apologize, but she didn't. She was ashamed and afraid he might not want to talk to her. She went up to bed and stopped to pray before she laid down. On her knees, beside her bed, she said, "Dear Heavenly Father, thank you for Jack and all of the blessings you have given me. Please help me to make things right with him. Help me to be more understanding and less judgemental towards my friends and family. Amen." She crossed herself and went to bed, feeling more at peace with herself and the world in general.

Chapter 14

Sam woke at eight the next morning. She made herself coffee and breakfast, then did some work while she waited. When Melissa still hadn't shown up by eleven, Sam got in her truck and drove to her house. As she pulled into the driveway, Ararat was quietly closing the door with a big smile on his face. "Good morning!" Sam called as she exited her truck.

He turned around, startled. "Uh, hello. Is Melissa expecting you?"

"I think so. We have plans this morning."

"I don't think she's ready." He blushed, and Sam wondered how old he was.

"You're Ara, right?"

"Yes. Who are you?" He spoke with an odd formality that hinted of a second language; not incorrect, but also not entirely idiomatic.

"I'm Sam, a friend of Melissa's. Nice to meet you."

He paused for a moment, then shook her hand. "Nice to meet you too."

"Did you know Peter?"

"Not really. He did business with my uncle when I was a child."

"What kind of business?"

"Something to do with cattle sales. They had an argument years ago, and my uncle went out of business."

His eyes flashed briefly, and his mouth tightened, but he kept his voice light. "I really must leave. Good luck getting Melissa up." He waved and smiled.

Sam spent a couple of minutes knocking, then used her key. "Melissa?" she called, looking around and wrinkling her nose.

The house was so dirty she was sure she saw bugs. Rather than soft scents of lavender or sage, Sam smelled dirty clothes and rotting food. She was shocked by the state of Melissa's house; it was usually so clean that it didn't look lived in. And she was confused by Ararat's presence. *She just told me she was in love with Steven.* The bedroom door was standing open, and she knocked as she peeked in. "Melissa?" She was there, sleeping peacefully with a smile on her face. A half-empty carafe and a note from Ara were on the bedside table. The note read, *I had to go¡ sexy mama. See you tonight.* Sam was disappointed that Melissa had a change of heart, but she let herself back out of the house. *I guess I'll just have to investigate on my own.*

Sam drove to town and looked at her list. She decided to begin by interviewing the shop owners she had added to see if she was on to anything. *I'll just work my way up the street.* She parked in front of the pharmacy and went inside. Sam didn't know if it had a name; the sign just said 'Pharmacy.' She supposed the town was lucky to even have one since it was so small.

Emily Dade had moved to Santo Milagro a few years earlier and set up shop. She was a prim, quiet woman who kept to herself, and although Sam had been to the pharmacy many times, she felt like she didn't know Emily at all.

The little bell tinkled as Sam entered, but otherwise, there was silence. She looked around at the shelves and displays. The shop always looked very clinical, from the white shelves to the laminate floor. It reminded Sam of a hospital. "Hello?"

"Just a moment!" An elderly lady with a cloud of white hair and the heavy scent of lavender appeared from the back. "Welcome! Sorry to make you wait. How can I help you?"

"Hello. I was looking for Emily."

"I'm so sorry. Emily left on vacation two days ago. The pharmaceutical agency sent me to cover for her."

Sam stood processing that for a second. "It was unplanned?"

"I guess so. She told me she had to visit her sister and didn't know how long she'd be gone."

"Thank you. I'll just wait until she gets back to talk to her." Sam smiled and left the shop. *Strike one,* she thought, making a note.

Nacho Sanchez was next on the list. He owned the hardware store two doors down and was outside hanging some sale fliers. Unlike the sterile environment inside the pharmacy, Essentials pulled people inside with splashes of color and engaging displays.

"Hello, Mr. Sanchez." Sam waved.

"Mija! It has been so long since I saw your lovely face." His face creased into a thousand wrinkles, and his eyes twinkled as he smiled. "Your papa, I miss him every day." He hugged Sam.

"I miss him too."

"I know. I am so sorry."

"Can I ask you something?"

"Of course, Mija."

"You knew Peter, right?"

Nacho's eyes narrowed. "Yes, I knew him."

"He tried to blackmail me and a friend of mine, and I wondered if he had tried it with anyone else in town."

"I don't know about the blackmail, but he did some tricky stuff. He would get that man from the bank to call in loans, then offer to pay them off. His interest was so high that people couldn't pay it, then he would threaten to take their business."

"Did he do that to you?"

"No, I don't like the loans. But he did it to Emily."

"I noticed he left without paying for things here. Did he have an account with you?"

"No, Mija. He told me I could help Emily with her big payments by subtracting his purchases from what she owed him. But when she showed him the receipts, he just laughed and said he never told me that. He said my English is so bad I didn't understand him." He frowned.

95

"He was a terrible person."

"Un diablo." Nacho nodded, then turned as another customer stopped in front of his store. "Excuse me, Mija." He smiled. "Buenos días, Señora Flores."

Sam watched Mr. Sanchez helping Anita's mother. Seeing him always brought back happy childhood memories. He and his wife were central to Santo Milagro and a part of any festivity.

Tia Connors was the owner of Magical Forest, an aptly named plant store. Tia reminded Sam of a plant. Her light green accessories reflected against her very pale skin. Golden hair wound atop her head, and her green eyes glowed. The shop felt like a tropical jungle, and Tia was practically camouflaged when she stood still. "Hello!" Tia called as she wound her way through the foliage.

"Hi, Tia! You have such talent! It's beautiful in here!"

"Thank you!" Tia's calm demeanor was soothing.

"It's extraordinary how the space you create is so peaceful. I feel happy in here."

"Me too! That's my inspiration." Tia seemed to almost glow.

Sam felt guilty bringing up Peter. "Tia? Could I ask you something personal?"

"Of course!"

"You knew Peter Sloan?"

The shutters went down, and Tia turned away.

"I'm sorry, Tia. He was trying to blackmail some of us and acting like a loan shark with others. I just wondered if you were one of us."

"I'm sorry too, Sam. I hate the way I feel when I think of him. He was such a bad person."

"What happened?"

Tia sat on a stool and looked at her left hand. "I was engaged to Mark Carruthers. Did you know that?"

"No, but then I don't know him as well as I thought I did."

"I heard you dated him for a while after we called off our engagement." Tia smiled sadly. "But I believe you. That was after he changed."

Sam ran a finger along the purple veins in a giant leaf while she waited for Tia to decide what to tell her.

"He did something at the bank; I'm not sure what. Peter somehow got proof and started blackmailing him. Mark denied it when I asked him, but there were large amounts of money going from our bank account to Peter's. Then it stopped, and people started complaining to me about Mark calling in their loans when they were a little late with payments. We had a huge fight, and I broke off our engagement."

"I'm so sorry, Tia. I had no idea."

"It's better I found out what he was like before we got married."

"Did you hate Peter for that?"

"No, I'm not very good at hate." She gave a little sigh and spritzed water on a couple of the plants. "If I was going to hate someone, it would have been Mark. Whatever he did, it wasn't good. Otherwise, Peter wouldn't have been able to blackmail him."

Sam nodded. She had to agree; Mark had done something that could get him into a lot of trouble. "Thank you for talking to me, Tia. I appreciate it."

"Oh, Sam, you're very welcome. Please visit anytime you want. The plants like you."

Sam waved at Tia, standing in the window, as she left.

After Sam left Tia's, she walked across the street to the saloon. She still needed to talk to Alley, and she was getting hungry. When she walked in, Alley came bustling over with a menu and a smile. "Hi, Sam!"

"Hi, Alley. Have you had lunch yet?"

"No, Rhonda called in, so I've been busy. I think it's settled down now."

"Can you have lunch with me?"

"Now that's an invitation I can't refuse," Alley said, giggling. "What will you have?"

Sam didn't need to look at the menu; it hadn't changed in three decades. "I'll have a Reuben with a side salad and a Modelo Black."

"I knew it! Be right back!"

Someone said something loud at the bar, and everyone laughed. A middle-aged woman with tight jeans and long, stringy, blonde hair sneered at Sam, popping a giant bubble.

When Alley returned with a couple of beers, Sam asked, "Have you heard from Jack?"

Alley got a goofy grin on her face. "Yes. He's been in Las Rodillas, but he calls two or three times a day. We're supposed to go out tomorrow."

"I think he's upset with me, but I need to talk to him."

"He's not upset. I'll give you his number before you leave." Alley smiled. "Hold on. The food's ready!"

She jumped up to get it and returned, juggling plates and bowls.

They ate in silence for a few minutes before Sam said, "I didn't realize how hungry I was. This really hits the spot."

"I'm happy to hear it. I'm a big fan of our Reubens, too."

Sam looked at her carefully and said, "Something's different. I can't quite put my finger on it, but you seem... happier?"

Alley blushed. "Maybe. Since I started seeing Jack, I stopped feeling like a victim. I haven't been drinking as much or feeling hungry all the time. I've started feeling like I can do things."

"That's great!" Sam smiled. "Can I ask you something?"

"Of course."

"It's about Peter."

Alley scrunched up her nose but nodded.

"Was he always mean? Trying to blackmail people, cheating, abusive?"

Alley tilted her head to the side and paused. "No... it started little by little after he accused me of cheating on him."

"Cheating?"

"Yes. Peter was twenty-three years older than me, and I didn't always look like this." She grimaced and spread her arms. "I was slim with long golden ringlets, makeup, fashionable clothes. Peter thought I was a great prize."

"So, what changed?"

"For some reason, he got it into his head that I cheated on him with his business partner, Levon Sahagian. We both told him he was wrong. Levon was happily married, with two children, and we had never even been alone together."

"You have no idea what put that into his head?"

"No. It doesn't matter now, but that's when he began to change. He moved out of our bedroom and started doing everything he could to ruin his partner. Then, he had me sign the papers that said he owned my house and land. He didn't explain what they were, and I was trying to be cooperative. I wanted my husband back. He set things up carefully and divorced me three years later. I was told by the judge that since I had done the title exchange, the saloon and its debt were mine, and we were to split the contents of our bank accounts and our credit card debt. Peter left me in a bad spot, and he tried to make it worse every step of the way. He really hated me."

"So Peter's personality changed after the two of you divorced?"

"I don't know if he changed. He was always kind of controlling, but he was nice to me. I didn't start hearing complaints about him until after we split up."

"Have you heard anything about his will?"

"No. I am kind of hoping he left me the house, but it wouldn't surprise me if he left everything to a complete stranger just to spite me."

"You never know. If he didn't make a will at all it might go to you. I don't know all the rules."

"Me neither. We'll just have to wait and see."

Sam nodded and pulled out her list. "One more thing. Melissa said that you hate her. Is that true?"

99

Alley's shoulders slumped, and her eyes turned sad. "I don't hate her, but I don't trust her. I never quite understood why you're so loyal to her. She scares me a little."

"She told me you glare at her when you see her in town, and you tell people lies about her shop to keep them away."

Alley sighed. "That's what I mean. She acts nice to my face, but she's not a friend."

Sam leaned forward and studied Alley's face, trying to decide if she was speaking the truth. "You used to be friends, right?"

"Yes. She was one of my first friends after I got divorced. I think you were off at college. Melissa introduced me around and invited me to dinner with her and your dad."

"My dad? Why would she have dinner with my father?"

Alley's eyes widened a bit, and she turned away for a second. Then she reached out her hand. "Can I see your list?"

Sam handed it to her and waited while she looked it over.

"You have possible motives for the people at the top of the list. Why are the others on here?"

"They are people who might have motive, means, or opportunity. I included everyone I could think of."

"What about Ara and Victoria?"

"They have been hanging around Melissa and might know about the poison or have access to it."

"What kind of poison was it?"

Sam blushed. "I don't know. Some kind of plant."

Alley nodded but had a faraway look on her face. "I don't want you to get your hopes up, but I might be able to help. I need to talk to someone first." Alley brightened suddenly. "Why don't you see if you can get a hold of Jack, now. I wrote down his number for you, and you can use the phone on the counter there." She pointed to the phone by the cash register, then got up and began clearing their table.

I guess that's the end of that conversation. I must have hit a nerve. "Thank you, Alley. I appreciate all of your help." Sam called Jack and made plans to meet him for dinner the next day.

Chapter 15

On the way to Las Rodillas, Sam thought about what she had uncovered. She had added notes to her list so she could explain everything without making it confusing. "Even though I learned a lot, I just ended up with more questions. Maybe it's not helpful at all." Sam saw him standing outside the diner before she pulled up, and he gave her a big hug when she jumped out of the truck. "I'm so sorry, Jack."

Jack smiled and put his hands on her shoulders. "Family doesn't hold grudges. I know you were just upset."

"I saw you on TV night before last." Sam grinned. "You were here with some other doctor, *Doctor* Olivares."

"It's my new hangout," he said, ignoring her jab. "Let's go in and get a drink."

They sat in a back booth.

"You sure have a lot of friends here for an out-of-towner, Jack." The waitress raised an eyebrow and smiled at Sam.

"It must be my charming smile, Greta." Jack grinned.

"What can I get you two?"

"Modelo Negra," Jack and Sam said in unison.

Greta smiled and walked off with a little swing of her hips.

Sam looked at him with awe. "Look at you making friends and influencing people."

"Jack laughed. "So what have you discovered, super sleuth?"

"Everything and nothing. Let's wait until your fan club gets back with the drinks and order something to eat. I'm hungry. Do you have paper and a pen?"

"Sounds like this is going to be good."

Greta delivered the drinks and a bowl of tortilla chips. "Are you ready to order?"

"What's the special today, Greta?"

"Enchiladas."

Jack looked at Sam. "I don't really feel like enchiladas today," she said. "How about the beef stew? It smells really good."

"With all the smells in here, you can smell the stew? I think I'll have some too."

After Greta left, Sam showed Jack her list and relayed what each person had told her.

"Nice work, Sam, but you should stop now. This could get dangerous. We can turn all of your information over to the Sheriff's office; the Captain is back now, and they'll be able to take it from here."

Greta came back with their orders and some warm rolls. "Thank you, Greta. This looks great!"

"Enjoy," she said with a smile.

Jack took a bite of the stew and chewed it slowly. "It's really good. Thanks for the suggestion, Sam."

They ate quietly for a few minutes before Sam said, "Jack, Alley said a couple of things that I didn't understand. When I asked what happened between her and Melissa, she changed the subject. But she mentioned Melissa inviting her to have dinner with my father. Was Melissa trying to set them up? And then, she asked to see my list and said something about maybe being able to help, but she needed to talk to someone first. I don't know if she was still talking about Melissa? It was a strange conversation toward the end."

"Thank you for letting me know. I'll see if she'll talk to me about it. By the way, Steven asked if we wanted to go see him race tomorrow. Do you want to go?"

"That would be really fun! Can Melissa come too?"

"I can't see why not."

"I'll text her now. I love being able to actually use my phone when I'm in Las Rodillas," Sam said as she tapped out her message.

"She said she'll come. Do you want to meet us there, or will you be coming home tonight?"

"Since we'll be out tomorrow, I might stay over and check in with Dr. Vanzandt in the morning. Do you know where it is?"

"Yes, I can find it. This has been fun, Jack. I've missed you, even if it's only been a couple of days."

Jack left some money on the table and walked Sam out to her truck. "See you tomorrow." They hugged, and Sam headed home.

Chapter 16

Sam invited Melissa to spend the night and had some scrambled eggs and toast ready when she got downstairs. Sam eyed her disheveled appearance and said, "I already got my shower, so I'll do the dishes afterward so you can have yours."

"It's okay." Melissa waved her off and tripped on her way to the table.

"You don't want to get gussied up for Steven?"

"Not really. He's seen me at my best and my worst. I don't think he really even looks at me anymore."

"Do you still love him?"

"Sure." She ate half her eggs and a bite of toast. "Do we have coffee?"

"Yeah. It's not as good as Jack's, though."

"Jack, Jack, Jack. He's all you ever talk about."

Sam brought coffee for both of them and sat down. "Are you feeling okay, Melissa?

"I'm fine," she snapped. "Let's just get going."

Sam put their coffee in travel mugs, and they left the house.

As they drove to the race track two towns away, Melissa drank her coffee, and her mood improved. She started smiling and singing to the songs on the radio. "I've never seen Steven race. This is kind of exciting."

Sam was a little afraid to say anything that would set Melissa off again, so she smiled and nodded.

When they arrived at the track, they met up with Jack. Then they made their way to the stands and climbed the bleachers to the top.

Melissa seemed a little off-balance, so Sam linked arms with her, and other than a couple stumbles, they made it unscathed. Sam could spot Steven a mile away. His shoulder-length blonde hair and tall, sinewy frame were easy to identify. "Look! There he is!" Sam said, pointing.

"Steeeven!" Melissa shouted.

Everyone at the track turned to look at her waving, and Steven waved back.

The cars pulled into their spots behind the starting line. Steven's bright blue car with a big white wave on the side stood out against the evil-looking, black car that idled next to him. A beautiful girl in a bikini top and short shorts came out with a flag. Sam looked over at Jack when the girl held the flag high, and her top rose dangerously, then she bent over, so her shorts rode up her backside.

"What?" he asked.

"Nothing. He's really good isn't he."

"Yes." Jack nodded without looking away.

Steven drove full speed into the corners, then braked hard and drifted halfway through before speeding up again. His car was fast and nimble. Melissa was on her feet, shouting and jumping up and down as he approached the finish line. The other spectators, who were regulars, just smiled and nudged each other at her enthusiasm.

Steven accepted his trophy with one eye on Melissa, and when he raised it in the air, she bolted down the bleachers. Sam tried to grab her, but she was too slow. She watched in horror as Melissa ran down the steps, but somehow she made it out onto the track and gave Steven a giant hug. The two prize party girls stared daggers at her but had to stay back while the photographers had a field day.

"Ohh, you were so amazing!" Melissa said breathlessly.

"I was inspired." Steven grinned. He kissed her soundly, and the photographers clicked wildly. "Ready to go celebrate my win, babe?"

Melissa backed away from him, then turned and ran toward the parking lot.

"I need to get her home, I think," Sam said.

"That's fine. I'll probably stay over at Alley's, and we'll come by tomorrow."

"Ok. Sounds good. Let's have a pool party. Invite Steven, and maybe we can find out what happened today." She turned and ran after Melissa, catching up to her by the truck. "What happened?"

"That wasn't Steven."

"What?"

"You might think I'm crazy, but I have been with Steven for a long time… off and on, you know. But I know his aura and his kiss, his smell. That was not him."

"Come on. Let's get you home. We'll figure it out later."

They drove back in silence. Sam was very worried. Melissa was completely unlike herself. Sam asked her if she'd like to stay over again, but she wanted to go home. Sam dropped her off and headed back to the ranch with a heavy heart.

The next morning, Sam made some coffee and pulled out an old, dog-eared novel that she'd read several times. The Cat Who series by Lilian Jackson Braun was an old favorite, and Sam was currently reading The Cat Who Said Cheese. Chiquito seemed to know when Sam was reading books from the series and sat on the coffee table staring at her. "What?" Sam asked him.

Mrow

"Come sit with me if you want." She patted the cushion next to her, but he stayed where he was. "You're a weird cat."

Sam read for about an hour, then made some snacks and got into her swimsuit. Finally, tired of waiting around, she went outside to find Roger.

"Hello, Ms. Sam."

"Hi, Roger. Could you help me take the cover off the pool?"

"Sure thing!"

They walked in that direction, and Sam suddenly stopped. "We're having an impromptu pool party and barbecue.

You're invited too if you'd like to come."

"Thank you. I'll at least come by for lunch."

Sam was floating in the pool when Jack and Alley arrived.

"You started without us!" Alley said. "I'll go in and get my suit on."

"I got bored. There are some beers in the cooler. Help yourself."

"I brought some meat for the barbecue, just in case."

"You think of everything, Jack. I got some, too, so we aren't in danger of running out. Is Steven coming?"

"He grows on you, doesn't he?"

"That's not why I wanted him to come."

"Why then? He said he'll try to make it."

Sam paddled over to where he was standing so she wouldn't be overheard, then explained about Melissa's reaction at the race track.

"She might be…"

"I know, but something about him freaked her out. We might as well get his take on whatever's going on."

"True. I'll go get changed. Want another beer while I'm here?"

"I haven't had any yet. I was waiting for you. So, yes, a beer sounds good.

Steven and Roger arrived at the same time, already wearing their trunks and having an animated conversation about the race. Roger waved, and Jack told them to each grab a beer. Jack was returning to the hot tub with two beers when Steven took a running jump into the pool, right where Sam was floating. He surfaced with a grin. "Hey, Sam."

"Good thing it's hot today, or I might be upset."

"Just trying to help keep you cool, babe." He winked, then swam easily to the other side of the pool, where the hot tub sat. He pulled himself out of the pool right as Jack handed Alley a beer. Jack joined her, and Steven sat on the edge of the hot tub with his legs dangling over the side.

"He's out harassing the cows."

"Maybe we should put some field fence around the yard so he can hang out with us."

"He's ok. He just follows me around most of the time, but that's nice of you."

They had walked into the kitchen, and Sam started pulling things out of the refrigerator.

"How well do you know Melissa?"

"I don't really know her at all. I was surprised to see her with Steven at the race."

"Really? They've dated off and on for years."

Roger shrugged. "I've only known him for about a year."

Sam let it drop and piled up his arms with food. "Race you!" she said, taking a couple of quick steps, then laughing. "Just kidding. I wouldn't do that to you." Both were smiling when they returned to the barbecue area.

Jack took the meat from Roger and arranged it on the grill, and Sam passed out plates and buns. When they had all loaded up their plates and found a seat, Jack sat back in a wicker chair, watching the others talking and eating and taking pictures with his phone. They all seem to be enjoying themselves. Alley and Sam had their heads together, and when they were finished eating, Sam put on a Scorpions album. Steven and Roger were talking about cars.

Jack watched quietly until Alley approached him and said, "I should probably be getting home."

"Ok. Let's help Sam get things cleaned up, then we can go." He stood and started gathering condiments to take inside.

Sam followed him with a stack of leftovers. "Jack? Can you make sure Steven and Roger leave when you do? I'm not sure what it is, but something is making me feel uncomfortable."

Jack nodded. "Alley feels it too."

Once the food was cleared away, Jack said, "I guess we'll wrap this party up since most of us have early starts tomorrow.

Can you help me with the pool cover Steven?"

They got on either side and started to unfold the cover.

"Roger, you and Steven can take some of the extra beer home if you like," Sam said.

"Nah, let's leave it for next time," he said grinning.

"Speak for yourself. I'll be happy to take some off your hands, babe. Want me to carry the cooler into the house?"

"No. We can leave it out for tomorrow." Sam turned to Alley. "We didn't eat your dessert!"

"That's okay. It'll keep for a few days."

"Do you want any of the leftovers?"

"No, thank you, but Jack might need lunch tomorrow."

Somehow Jack helped herd everyone from the patio. He gave Sam a hug and escorted Alley to the pickup Sam let him use. Sam gave them a wave and locked herself in the house. Maybe I'm just imagining things. She shook her head. Chiquito looked at her expectantly, so she gave him some food and grabbed his tail, gently gliding her hand to the tip. Sam smiled. His tail was like its own entity, and Chiquito didn't seem to mind her messing with it. He flicked it back and forth and took a bite of kibble before following her upstairs.

Alice Kanaka

Chapter 17

S am wandered downstairs the next morning and saw a manila envelope lying on the floor, inside her kitchen door. She picked it up and set it on the table, then set about making coffee. Once it was brewing, Sam opened the envelope. She was still gaping at the contents when Jack arrived. Peter was a serious pervert.

"What's wrong?" he asked.

'Looks like we've got a new blackmailer in town."

"May I?" He pulled a pair of gloves from his pocket, put them on, and held out his hand.

"Do you want the whole packet or just the letter?"

"There are photos in the packet?"

"Nudes. I was skinny-dipping in the pool. Peter was such a perv."

"So you never gave in to his threats?"

"No way. That would have given him power over me. I laughed in his face, and he never did anything with them as far as I know."

Jack took the packet and nodded but inside, he was roiling. "I wonder where this blackmailer got the photos."

"I don't know. We should visit everyone on the list and see if they got a letter too."

"No. We should let the Sheriff know."

Sam frowned. "I wonder if Melissa got one."

"Stop! I'll take your letter and our list and pay Mick a visit, but first, I'll make us some pancakes. Did you actually make your own coffee?"

"Yes. I wasn't sure what time you'd get here. It's not as good as yours."

Once they'd finished breakfast, Sam said, "So what's the plan?"

"I was thinking I'd drop in at the morgue and the Sheriff's office, then go have dinner with Alley. She's an amazing cook. How about you?"

"I have things to do around here. Let's meet up for breakfast tomorrow."

"You just want me to cook for you."

"No fooling you!" Sam laughed. "And call me if you find out anything about the letter!"

Jack went to the station first. He met with Mick and Captain Blatt. The Captain took himself very seriously, but was duly impressed to have the Chief Medical Examiner in his small district. He shook Jack's hand and thanked him for his assistance.

"Here's the letter. I gave you the list Sam made and a report of her results."

"Yes, thank you, Doctor. You might have saved us some legwork. Encourage her to stay out of it now, if you can."

"You both know her, so you know the odds, but I'll try."

It was nearing lunchtime when he left so he decided to drop in on Alley at the saloon. Ben and Rhonda seemed surprised to see him. "We haven't seen her this morning. We figured she was with you."

"I'll go see what she's up to. Could you make us a couple of club sandwiches with side salads? I'll come back down and pick them up."

"Sure! No problem," Ben said.

Jack went around the side of the building, prepared to ring the buzzer, but the door was unlatched. He took the stairs two at a time and then froze. Alley lay face down in a pool of blood. He stood there a moment while his brain seemed to short circuit. "Alley?

Alley!" he cried out. He dropped to his knees next to her and felt for a pulse, but he could see she was dead. He knew he needed to call it in, but he couldn't move.

His chest heaved, and his stomach cramped. Jack had seen a lot of death; it was his profession. But finding a loved one at a murder scene was incapacitating. Rhonda came up to tell him their lunch was ready and found him there on his knees.

"No! Not Alley!"

"Call the sheriff's station, please," Jack whispered.

Rhonda backed up to the phone with her hand over her mouth and tears falling as she watched Jack grieve. "Hello, I want to report a murder." Her voice was shrill in the receiver"

"Did you see it take place?" asked the voice on the phone.

"No. Please come now. It's Alley Carruthers, and we're in her apartment over the saloon."

"Who's we?"

"Me and Jack."

"Someone will be right there."

The connection ended with a click. Mick and Captain Blatt ran from the station, shouting instructions to Deputy Flores to call Dr. Vanzandt, Sam, and an ambulance. Mick started taking pictures before he spoke to Jack because Jack had entered the crime scene. Then he handed the camera to the Captain and approached. "Jack?"

"No."

Mick could see Jack's pain, and he wanted to hurt someone. He had never seen anything so heartbreaking. He put his hand on Jack's shoulder. "I'm sorry, Jack. Can you let us process the scene so we can find whoever did this?"

"Who would want to harm a hair on her sweet head?" He reached out to touch her, but Mick stopped him. "Jack! Stop! You'll compromise the evidence, and they'll get away with it!" He took Jack's arm and helped him up. "Come sit over here. Dr. Vanzandt and Sam will be here soon."

Jack was sitting in a daze when he heard a pitiful little cry and looked around for its source. Alley's tiny kitten was curled up between her head and right shoulder, nudging at her and mewling.

That was it for Jack. He carefully picked up the kitten and held her close, walking into Alley's bedroom and shutting the door.

Dr. Vanzandt and Sam arrived at about the same time. He proceeded her up the stairs and stopped on the landing. "You must be Sam," he whispered. "Glad to meet you." They shook hands. "I'll leave him to you."

"Thank you,'" she said. Her own eyes welled with tears, and she hoped she could keep it together for Jack. She found him sitting on Alley's bed, gently holding the kitten, rocking back and forth with red eyes and a drawn face. She sat down next to him and hugged him. There was nothing she could say to make it better, but she sat with him as he grieved.

After they were given the all-clear, she grabbed the kitten supplies and helped Jack to the truck.

Chapter 18

Jack was a zombie for the next three days. He stayed in his room, or he walked. He walked for miles. Alone. He didn't talk or even look at anyone. If anyone had asked where he'd been, he wouldn't have been able to tell them. His mind was snarled with emotions he didn't know how to handle. *I should have been able to protect her. I shouldn't have left that morning. How can I go on? Is this how my father felt when my mom died? Is this why he couldn't love me?*

He had no appetite, and he couldn't sleep. He laid down for a while, then got up and paced. Finally, feeling claustrophobic, he'd leave the house and walk some more. He couldn't escape his thoughts.

On the third day, Jack again walked for miles and ended up in town. Father Garcia rushed forward as he stumbled into the church and fell to his knees.

"Water."

The priest helped him up and half-carried him through to the office, sitting him on a chair before rushing through to the kitchen for a pitcher of water and a glass.

"Do you need an ambulance?" he asked as Jack gulped. "Be careful not to drink too much too fast. You'll be worse off if you vomit."

"Thank you for the reminder."

Father Garcia watched him carefully.

"I'm okay now," he said as he continued to sip.

"What brings you here?"

"God, I think. I've been walking aimlessly for two days, and today, my feet brought me here. I need to talk."

"It's about Alley?"

"Yes."

"Tell me about her."

"She seemed like goodness and light, but I sensed her darkness, and it drew me to her."

"Her darkness?"

"She was full of anger and sadness. She hated herself and thought she was unworthy."

"Unworthy of what?"

"I don't know. Love, affection, happiness, maybe. I set out to woo her and make her feel special and loved but what happened is she taught me how it feels to be loved. She gave me something I haven't felt since my mother died."

"And you loved her for that."

"Yes. More than anything, I wanted her to be happy and to love herself again."

"And was she? Did she?"

"I think so. But just as she was finding joy, someone cut her life short. I keep thinking I should have saved her. I failed to keep her safe."

"Do you believe in God's will, Jack? That he has a plan for you?"

"I don't know. I guess so."

"Sam prayed for someone she could love and trust, and you were brought here. Perhaps you were also brought here to learn about love. And Alley, once her soul was cleansed of sorrow and bitterness, was able to join Jesus at the foot of God where she belongs.".Jack thought about that for a minute. "That's a nice way to think about it."

"She came to see me before she died."

"She did?"

"She hadn't been to church in years, but she asked me to pray with her. She asked God to forgive her for shutting him out when her marriage fell apart. Then she thanked him for bringing happiness and love back into her life.

She thanked him for you and asked him to bless you and look after you."

"Did she know she was going to die?"

"That I couldn't say, but she seemed happy and at peace, so whatever she thought, it didn't seem to be anything bad."

"Could you pray with me too, Father? I'm a little out of practice."

"Sure. I will start, and you can add the specifics."

They prayed together for quite some time, and then Father Garcia gave Jack a bottle of water. "Would you like a ride home?"

"No, thank you. I think some time alone with my thoughts and prayers might do me some good. You've helped me a lot, Father. I think maybe I can heal now."

"Don't forget to thank God too. I am only his vessel."

Jack smiled and shook his hand before he left.

He walked home, arriving after dark and showering before having the first full night's sleep in days.

On the fourth day, Jack came out of his room, stomped out of the house, and got in his car. Sam ran after him. "Where are you going, Jack?"

"Get in if you want. I'm going to the morgue."

Sam swallowed. "The morgue?"

"Yes. It's what I do. It's who I am. I will be there for Alley in death and find whoever did this to her."

"Will they let me in?"

Jack shrugged. "I don't even know if they'll let me in."

"I'll come."

They drove in silence. Sam texted Mick and asked him to meet them there.

When they pulled up, Dr. Vanzandt was waiting for them. "I'm glad you're here. I need your help."

Jack nodded, and they walked inside. "Are you coming?"

Sam ran to catch up.

Mick arrived minutes later. He hustled in and stared at Sam. "What did I miss?"

"Nothing," Jack said. He was like a soldier going into battle. "Describe the scene for me, Mick."

"But you were..." He stopped when all three of them stared at him. "Sorry. The entryway had not been broken into. We found a single fingerprint on the doorknob. The victim was hit on the head by a solid, heavy object. I will let Dr. Vanzandt speak to that. There was a metal cross, taken from the wall, lying on the floor, on the left side of the victim. Compromising photographs and Peter Sloan's last will and testament were lying as if dropped on the victim, along with one large white button and one medium-length brown hair. There were newspapers with letters cut out, scissors, and a glue stick on the coffee table."

"Anything else?"

"There didn't appear to be a struggle. There were no other injuries and no prints other than the one on the door. Sam found a piece of bubblegum near the door and asked me to have it tested."

"Byron?"

Dr. Vanzandt paused, but he knew what Jack was doing. "The blood and matter on the cross were consistent with the head injuries. It appears that the perpetrator surprised the victim with two left-handed blows from the back. Approximate height is five feet six inches, which is the height of most of our suspects."

"May I see the photographs, please?"

Mick handed them to him. "They were mixed up, but I sorted them." He looked at Sam and blushed.

Jack sorted through and handed Sam's to her. The rest were of Melissa, Mark, Alley, Steven, and Anita.

"Who is this?" He handed the photos of Melissa to Sam.

She gasped and studied them closely, looking at the dates. "No wonder she let Peter control her." Jack looked at her curiously.

"These photos are of her and my dad after he returned from heart surgery. He might have died while he was in bed with her." She looked so immensely sad that Jack momentarily forgot his own grief. "They seem so happy together. Then Peter came along and made it into something ugly. I'll have to think about that for a while."

"I'm sorry, Sam. It's a lot to process."

Jack put down another stack with Mark as the star. "What are these, Mick?"

"We looked at those with a magnifying glass. Mark appears to be signing papers in someone else's name and altering dates. Possible proof of fraud."

He showed two photos of Alley and a man. "These?"

"They may be what Peter thought was proof of Alley's affair with his business partner. They're much older and inconclusive," Sam said. "Alley denied there was an affair, and although the photos look like they might be about to embrace, they don't really show anything. He didn't blackmail Alley; he just hated her because he felt betrayed."

Jack set down the photos of Steven. "Steven didn't mention being blackmailed."

"Maybe he wasn't. Alley wasn't. Maybe Peter was keeping them as insurance."

"What do they show?" Jack asked.

"It looks like he's tampering with someone else's car. He wouldn't do that, would he?" Sam asked.

"We'll have to ask him. I know these are Deputy Flores and Dr. Moe. I met him at the card game Roger took me to. Were they being blackmailed?"

"Anita told me Peter tried to blackmail her a week before his death. She and Dr. Moe weren't doing anything wrong, but since he is technically married, she didn't want to give him a bad reputation," Mick said.

"Technically married? What does that mean?"

"His wife has been in a sanatorium for years and refuses to see him."

"Now show me the will." Jack held his hand out.

Mick passed it to him. "Peter didn't change it after they divorced. Alley was the sole recipient."

Jack thought for a few moments. "What it looks like to me is a left-handed person... wait. Where were the scissors and glue stick in relation to the newspapers?"

"They were on the left," Mick said..

Jack nodded. "A left-handed person tried to make it look like Alley was the blackmailer. They also tried to make it look like the killer was angry about the blackmail and the will. The button and the hair could be clues, or the evidence could have been planted. The victim obviously knew the killer since she buzzed them in and was not afraid to turn her back on them."

"The button belongs to Melissa, but she's right-handed, and there's no way she'd leave those pictures," Sam said.

Jack nodded again. "None of the people being blackmailed would want to leave those photos. Do we know anyone who's left-handed?"

"Steven is left-handed," Sam said, "but he's too tall."

"Why would anyone care about the will?" Jack asked.

"Melissa told Ara she and Peter were going to be married, although that's kind of a stretch."

"I want to go over the forensic evidence again. Mick, you find out more about Ara and Steven's backgrounds. And ask Peter's attorney if he was in touch lately. Sam, you talk to Melissa and see if you can find anything out, but please be careful."

"I'll come back and get you this evening."

"Yes, that's fine," Jack said distractedly.

Sam left, but Mick stayed.

Jack pulled the body from the refrigerated storage chamber. He sucked in some air and steeled himself to see her again. Mick and Byron stood still, afraid to intrude.

Jack was imbued with superhuman strength. "You said she was struck more than once?"

"Yes," Byron said. "Do you see where there are two depressions right next to each other?"

"Yes. I am going to find this person, and they will pay."

Byron nodded. "We will find them."

"I want to go back over everything we've learned from both crimes. The link seems to be that they were married, and the first victim's possessions went to the second victim, although I don't think she was aware of that."

"Is it possible that she sent out those letters?" Mick asked carefully.

Jack almost snarled, but he quickly regained his professional composure. "First, she is right-handed. Are her prints on any of those items?"

"No," Mick said.

"Second, Sam had already received her letter by the time I got home from…" Jack stopped. "By the time I got home. So no, it's not possible."

Byron and Mick nodded. It was painful watching Jack fighting to overcome his loss.

"I'll go start digging if you don't need me anymore."

"Thank you, Mick. Let me know what you find."

Jack and Byron went over all of the medical evidence again but didn't find anything else.

"Do you think it might have been two different murderers?" Byron asked. "The crimes are very different."

Jack thought about that. "I don't know. The first crime seemed to point at Melissa because of the water hemlock, the blackmail, the body wash, and her possibly staged alibi. There was so much evidence. It was almost overkill."

"And the second?"

"The second is also pointing at Melissa. We have the button and the hair.

121

But then there are the incriminating photos and the fact that she's right-handed."

"Actually, Mick forgot to mention Melissa's photos were found stuffed under a sofa cushion. They weren't with the others."

Jack didn't say anything for a few seconds. Finally, he looked at Byron. "We have three possibilities. Either Melissa is a very clever murderer, someone is trying to frame her, or she is working with a second person."

"I hadn't thought of that last one. Are you worried about Sam asking her questions?"

"Ordinarily, I would be, but Melissa has been very intent on saving their friendship. I don't think she would harm her."

After seeing the photos of her father and Melissa, Sam was a lot more shook up than she let on. She needed to take some time to process what those pictures meant, so she rode Ghost to her favorite place along the river. She dismounted and let her graze while she sat on a boulder and watched the water flow by.

Her first thought was that they had both been keeping a huge secret from her. She felt angry and betrayed that the two people she was closest to didn't feel like they could confide in her. Sam stood and paced as she mulled that over. *Would I have been understanding? Angry? I don't know the whole story since they never told me.* She sat down and took her boots off, gasping as she plunged her feet into the freezing water.

She let her mind drift to her second thought regarding the blackmail. Melissa was so afraid that Sam wouldn't understand that she let Peter control and abuse her. On the one hand, it showed Sam how important their friendship was to Melissa. But on the other hand, the lack of trust and faith in their relationship was heartbreaking. Melissa had been hiding what happened for a year and hiding the relationship for much longer. She had hidden her grief and pain during the funeral and afterward when Peter got his claws into her.

If Sam was honest with herself, she had returned home brokenhearted from college and wasn't paying attention to what was going on around her. *I didn't confide in her either. Have I been a terrible friend?* Should I have noticed what was going on? It would never have occurred to me. She put her head in her hands. Her eyes were dry, but her brain felt snarled with guilt and confusion. I need to talk to her. She's the only one who can help me understand.

Sam put her boots back on and called to Ghost. She snuggled her face. "I'm so lucky to have you." Then she mounted and rode her home at a leisurely pace, letting go of her thoughts and focusing on her surroundings.

Later that day, Sam pulled into Melissa's driveway and looked around. The ordinarily pristine garden was withered and unkempt. She wondered, not for the first time, what was going on with her friend. *Is she still grieving?* Melissa didn't answer her knock, so she let herself in again. "Melissa? Melissa!" She ran to the phone and called for an ambulance. "Please send someone right away!" She knelt by her friend and checked her pulse. "Yes, she's breathing, but her pulse is very weak. Please hurry!" She called Mick next. "Hurry, Mick! I don't know how long the ambulance will be!" Sam sat with Melissa and held her hand. "Stay with me, Melissa. Help is coming. Don't give up."

Mick and the ambulance arrived at the same time. He and Sam watched as the paramedics whisked Melissa off to the hospital.

"Tell me what happened."

"There was no answer, so I let myself in."

"You have a key?"

"Yes."

"Does her house always look like this?" He glanced around at the drawn shades and the mess.

"It didn't used to, but last time I came by, it did. About a week ago."

Mick took some pictures, then opened the blinds. He put on some gloves before bagging a glass and a half-empty carafe.

"What are you doing?"

"Just checking everything. Do you think her odd behavior might be because she's been taking drugs?"

"I never thought of that. She has been acting differently."

"Look around and see if you notice anything out of place, but don't touch anything."

Both of them wandered around looking for anything out of place, then met back in the bedroom.

"I found this stuffed under the bed," Mick said, holding up a dress with a missing white button." And a baggy full of something in a dresser drawer.

"I didn't find much other than garbage," Sam said, "but I also don't see any of Ara's things. He seemed to be practically living here last time I came by."

"I'll post a deputy here to watch for Ara and head over to the hospital when she gets here. You go ahead if you want."

"Thanks, Mick. Someone should let Jack know too."

When Sam arrived at the hospital, she wasn't allowed to see Melissa.

"Come on, Celia, you know we've been like family our whole lives. She doesn't have anyone else."

"I'm sorry. I could get fired over that. Patient privacy is one of those rules you don't break."

"How long before she can have visitors?"

"I don't know. I can have her call you."

"Thank you, Celia," Sam said despondently. *Now what?* She decided to pick Jack up in Las Rodillas and give him an update on the way home.

124

Chapter 19

During breakfast the next morning, Sam said, "Jack? I've been thinking. Would you be willing to go on an overnight horse camping trip with me while the sheriff wraps up the interviews?"

Jack looked at her like she had just spoken to him in some unknown language.

"We've been under a lot of stress, and it might help us clear our heads. Plus, there's nothing we can do right now except wait," she added.

Jack thought about it while he sipped his coffee. "Yes, that might be a good idea. We're too close to everything right now. Maybe a day or two away will give us a better perspective."

"I don't know about you, but when I'm outdoors, surrounded by nature, I feel better. My stress goes away, and my mind seems to clear."

"Let's pick up some supplies in town, then leave in the morning."

Sam prepared to pull into the last parking spot at the market when a rusted, sputtering pickup truck cut in front of her and took the spot. The driver sat in the truck until Sam found a spot on the street, and when she approached the entrance, the driver got out slowly and gave her a sneer before popping a bubble and entering first.

"Who is that lady? She suddenly seems to be everywhere."

"What lady?"

"The one who took our parking spot."

Jack shrugged, so Sam let it go. "I have most of the supplies at the ranch," she said as they entered the market.

"You can't have a proper camping trip without beer."

"True. We should probably get some food too." Sam laughed.

"You know, I'm starting to feel better already. I wish we could leave tonight."

"I suppose we could. We just won't get very far before dark."

"It's ok. We can get our packs together, and I'll let Mick and Byron know where we'll be. If we get to bed early, we can head out at sunup."

"I am so glad you're here, Jack, and I love how much we have in common."

"It's funny, isn't it, since our upbringings were so different."

As they walked through the produce aisle, the lady from the pickup elbowed Sam when she walked by, causing her to fall into a large bin of oranges. Sam looked up, and there she was, lazily chewing her gum and waiting to sneer at her before rounding the corner. The stock clerk came running, and Sam apologized, mentioning she had been pushed.

"It could happen to anyone. Don't worry about it. I'll get them all picked up."

She looked at Jack with consternation, but he just laughed, assuming she had been clumsy.

When they got home with their groceries, Sam said, "I'll start pulling out supplies, and you put the food in the fridge."

"Yes, ma'am!"

It was five o'clock by the time they were finished, so Sam pulled out some leftovers and challenged Jack to a game of ping pong.

Sam and Jack had the horses packed up and ready to go at daybreak. "Go ahead and mount. I'll be right back." Sam ran into the house and came back with a handful of small tubes.

"What are those?"

126

"Essentials. Coffee and creamer!" She jammed them in her backpack and mounted Ghost. "Feels weird to use a saddle, but it's easier on both of us with all this gear."

Jack nodded. "You ready?"

"Yep. Let's head out!"

"I haven't been this way before," Jack said.

"There's a bridge down here. The other side of the river is forested and better for camping."

They rode in companionable silence for most of the way, each lost in their own thoughts. Over the wooden bridge, past the guest cottages, and into the forest beyond. After about two hours, Jack asked, "Is this still your land?"

"No, this is government land, but we can camp here. I have an annual pass if any rangers happen to be around."

"Good to know I have such a law-abiding cousin." Jack chuckled.

"How about that clearing up ahead?"

"Looks like someone has camped here before."

"Guilty," she said, raising her hand and smiling at him.

"Do you come out here alone?"

"Yes. No one has ever bothered me, but I have pepper spray... and a shotgun."

"Good."

"Let's get the tent set up, then we can gather some wood and set up the other stuff."

The tent was a six-person tent and six feet high at the center. It was the same tent she and her father used when they went camping, and she hadn't bothered to replace it since there was nothing wrong with it.

They hiked around for a long time collecting wood. "How long are we staying here?" Jack asked. "This seems like a lot of wood."

"It's better to have too much than too little. We have three meals a day to cook plus campfire time."

"True," he said, watching her as he finished stacking wood.

Sam went over to the packs and started pulling out gear. "This is a portable toilet." She unfolded the metal legs attached to a small, plastic toilet seat and produced a bag and some toilet paper. "And this is a little tent for privacy."

"Whaaat?"

"We could make do without, but I don't really like to have to dig a hole behind a tree." She then pulled out some flat metal pieces and somehow formed them into a small box. "This is our stove and these are our chairs." Out came two small, folding camp stools.

"Is there anything else in there?"

"I have a block of dry ice and a soft, thermal bag to put the food in. You brought the food, right?"

Jack rushed over to his pack and unloaded the perishables. "Do we have room for the beer in there too?"

"Just enough room," Sam said with her impish grin. "I have a small cook set and some water, lanterns for each of us, and fire starters."

"You are a pro. I'm impressed. I thought I knew how to camp, but I'm realizing there's a difference between car camping in a designated campsite and horse camping in the middle of nowhere."

"My dad started taking me camping when I was little."

"Did your mom go too?"

"No, she hated camping. She made us cookies to take with us." Sam smiled at the memory. "She died in a car accident when I was five, so Dad had to be Mom and Dad."

"I'm sorry, Sam. My mother died when I was young too. How old are you?"

"I'm 25. How old are you?"

"I'm 28, and my mom died when I was eight. She was visiting someone, and there was an accident. Were they together?"

"Maybe. That's pretty weird. I wonder why our dads never told us we had family. We could have grown up playing Legos together."

"Maybe we should look into it when we have a free moment. Is it time to eat yet?"

Sam laughed. "It's past lunchtime. Why don't we have something simple and go for a swim?"

"Do we have something simple?"

"Ham, cheese, onion buns, and tortilla chips."

"To put inside," they said in unison.

"Sounds perfect." They threw together a couple of sandwiches and put everything away.

"See that platform?" Sam asked, pointing up into a nearby tree. "That's where we'll keep our food bag and garbage to keep the critters away."

"And the toilet waste?"

"If we tie off our waste in a grocery bag, we can leave it in the larger bag with the lid closed, and it won't smell too much. I have some little deodorizers too."

"So smart."

"Says the doctor. Bring something to swim in."

"Uh…"

"I knew you'd forget, so I brought you some trunks." Sam laughed. "The horses will enjoy the water too. One thing we don't have is a shower, and it's pretty hot. Ready?"

"I hear water. I'm ready. We could grab a couple of beers."

Jack felt peaceful as they sat on the rocks around the pond and drank their beers in the hot sun. The horses had gotten in the water and were happily grazing nearby.

"Thank you for bringing me here, Sam. You were right about this place."

"I come here when my world gets overwhelming. We haven't really had a chance to talk about everything that's happened. I'm really sorry, Jack."

"I've never been in love before, and even though I didn't know Alley for very long, I loved her because she loved me. I loved the feeling I had when I was with her. My heart felt safe.

Then all of a sudden, she was gone. Her laughter and love and trust. I felt sick. I still feel sick. It seems like I should have known she was in danger, been able to protect her. She said some odd things at the pool party, but I didn't get a chance to ask her about them."

"What did she say?"

"She asked Steven about his mother and said she frequented the saloon. And I think she said Steven was the nice one, but I didn't understand what she meant. Then, later something seemed off, but I couldn't figure out what it was. Maybe it was Steven. I need to figure out what happened to her. It's the only way I can feel whole again."

"I'll do whatever I can to help. We'll figure it out together."

Jack got a lump in his throat and felt a crushing sadness. "Alley didn't deserve to die. She never caused anyone harm." His voice cracked, and he took a deep breath. He sat in silence for a few minutes. "I'm sorry, Sam, I didn't mean to ruin our retreat."

"You're not ruining anything. I brought it up. Sometimes sharing our pain can help us through it. You've been through a lot lately."

"It does help being here with you. Knowing I'm not alone in the world helps."

Sam's eyes teared up, and she gave him a hug.

"I shouldn't be so selfish. I know you are worrying about Melissa too."

"I'm glad I have you, too. Let's try to focus on fun while we're here and let our burdens wait for our return."

"You got it. Waaahooo!" he shouted as he jumped off his rock. Sam jumped too, and they splashed around until they were tired.

When they returned to camp, Sam secured the horses, built a campfire, and put some smaller branches in the little stove. Jack volunteered to cook their first meal. He was fascinated by the little metal stove.

"This is amazing!" Sam mumbled. "What is it?"

"It's just steak and veggies with some salt and pepper." Jack shrugged.

"It must be the onion. Steak and onion always taste good cooked over the fire."

"Or maybe it's the can of beans you heated up." Jack laughed.

"You laugh, but beans always add a little something extra. Why don't you grab a couple beers, and we can play some cards."

As the sun began to set, Jack became aware of the sounds around him, and he started feeling a little nervous. "Sam, is there anything we need to keep an eye out for? Any poisonous insects, bears, snakes?"

"Sometimes. But I've camped here many times and never had a problem."

"Not putting me completely at ease."

"We could come across a black bear. If we do, just don't run. We have to keep food put away and should change clothes before bedtime, especially if we've barbecued."

"Is that why you have the campfire so far from the tent?"

Sam nodded. "Since people around here don't usually make a habit of leaving food and garbage out, we haven't had a lot of problems."

They stayed up late playing cards and talking about music and pets and their pasts. Once they got in their tent, Jack laid awake for a long time, thinking about Alley and Sam and how much he owed them before finally drifting into a fitful sleep.

Sam was just getting ready to put their breakfast on plates when Jack emerged from the tent. "Hey, sleepyhead," she said. "I've made you a special treat for breakfast."

"You cooked something?"

"It's the one thing my dad could make."

"I am very impressed! What is it?"

"Ta-da!" She set a plate in front of him. "Chilaquiles!"

"Oh my god. I haven't had this for years. It looks great. How do you make it?"

"I'm not sure I should give you my secret." Sam grinned.

"You saute some tortilla chips in green salsa, then put refried beans, eggs, cheese, and sour cream on top. Actually, there are a million ways to make it, and you can add whatever you want. We can use the leftovers for burritos tonight."

Jack dug in with gusto. "This is so good! Stop staring at me and eat."

"Sorry." She smiled. "I am ridiculously happy you like them so much. You always make such amazing meals." Her eyes sparkled.

"I like to cook, but sometimes I get bored with my own repertoire. It's nice to try something different."

Sam nodded and looked down at her plate. "I shouldn't take advantage of you the way I do. I can cook. Yours just tastes better."

"I knew you could cook. I've seen your pantry." Jack grinned. "But like I said, I enjoy cooking, especially for an appreciative audience."

"What's on the agenda today?"

"I thought we could ride out to the waterfall if you want. We can swim there and explore the cave behind it."

"That sounds great! Should we take some lunch?"

"Yeah, and some beer?"

"That's a given." He laughed.

"It's an hour ride," Sam said. "We'd probably better get a move on."

The ride was beautiful and went by quickly. Sam always enjoyed heading up the mountain. Sunlight pierced the thick pine canopy, and colorful wildflowers peaked between smaller plants and shrubs on the forest floor. She could hear the water as they approached. When they turned the last corner, Jack gasped.

"Do you like it?" Sam asked.

"It's amazing!"

Sam looked at him.

"When you said waterfall and swimming, I was expecting something much smaller. This is... epic!"

"It is pretty amazing." Sam smiled. "It's one of my favorite places. Not too many people know about it. We should be able to let the horses play too. Ghost knows this place well."

"Why do you call her Ghost?"

"My dad gave her to me when I was little. She was a pony and just the right color, so you couldn't see her in the fog. I would go looking for her in the field, and she would appear like magic. I told my dad how she could vanish and reappear like a ghost, and he said I'd found the perfect name for her."

"So you've had her most of your life."

"Yes." Sam hugged her.

Jack smiled when Ghost seemed to hug her back. "She loves you, too."

Sam smiled. "She does. Let's go play. Race you in!"

She sat down to tug off her boots, so Jack did the same.

"Hey! I can't get my boot off." Jack had his leg bent at a strange angle and was doing his best to find some leverage. "Can you give it a tug?"

Sam pulled and fell on her backside when it came off. "What's the matter with your foot?"

"I don't know. It was fine this morning."

"It's huge!" Sam crawled forward and looked at it. "Did you twist it?"

"Not that I remember. It's been really itchy though. I thought it was just the heat."

Sam lifted and examined his foot. "I found a stinger. Where's that boot?" Jack handed it to her, and she shook it upside down. "There's our culprit. You had a bee in your boot. Let me try to pull the stinger out."

"What's taking so long?"

"Done! I didn't want it to break off. The cold water might help with the swelling, and I have some Benadryl in my pack."

"Should I ask why?"

"Stuff happens. I have a basic first aid kit with me all the time.

Let's see if we can get that swelling down so you can get back in your boots."

"I am a doctor, you know."

"Do you have some better advice for yourself?"

Jack beamed. "No. You'd make a great doctor. I'm impressed by your quick diagnosis and treatment. Wow! The water is freezing!"

"It's always cold. And the reason I could diagnose your bee sting so quickly is there are only a few things that could cause that kind of swelling while riding a horse with boots on." She sat next to him and put her feet in the water too. "Yikes! That is really cold! Probably a good thing we didn't jump in! Want some lunch while we're sitting here?"

"Sure."

"Can you drink beer when you've taken Benadryl, doc?"

"I probably shouldn't, but I will. Just one. You won't leave me here if I fall asleep, will you?"

Sam laughed. "You never know. I don't think I could lift you onto Parsnip."

"I'll make sure to stay awake then. What's for lunch today?"

"Same as yesterday."

"Yum."

"We'll explore the cave another time, huh?" she said as she sat back down and handed him a sandwich.

"Yes. This is such an amazing place. Can people camp here?"

"I guess so. The ground is pretty uneven, though, and I don't usually camp right near water."

"Why not?"

"Animals come to drink from it, and we might accidentally scare them away or pollute the water. Plus it's more of a treat if we have to make a special trip to get here."

"True."

"How's your foot?"

"I'm not sure. I think it's frozen."

"Let me see. The swelling's down.

Maybe we can get your boot back on." Sam brought Jack's socks and boots over, along with a small towel. "I'll dry it off and get a sock on it, then we can try the boot."

"Owww! Take it easy, will you?"

"I guess it's thawing. Why don't you put the sock on?"

Once the sock was on, Jack gingerly put his foot in his boot but stopped when it reached the hard bend. "I think you're going to have to help. It really hurts."

"Does it hurt like it's too swollen to fit, or is it just tender?"

"Just tender, I think."

"Would you rather ride back without the boot?"

"No, I think that would hurt too, and it's a long ride."

"Okay." Sam got on her knees behind him and grabbed both sides of the boot. "The quicker we do this, the sooner it'll be over. I'm going to pull the boot, and I need you to push with your foot, even if it hurts. Push hard. Are you ready?"

Jack gritted his teeth. "Ready."

Sam yanked hard when he pushed, and his foot settled into the boot.

"I'm glad that's over."

"Let's get the rest of our boots on and see if you can stand." She packed up their things and called the horses, then helped Jack up. "How's it feeling?"

"I'll live. Thanks, Sam."

They rode most of the way back in silence.

"We're here, Jack. Wake up! You're lucky you have good balance, or you would have fallen off 30 minutes ago."

"I guess I'm not immune to Benadryl."

"The activity, the pain, the icy water; they'll wear you out, too. Let's get your boot off, and you can lay down for a while."

Once Jack was resting, Sam pulled out a book she had brought along.

"What are you doing?" Jack's voice startled her.

"Are you up already? I'm just reading. I've been so busy, and it's taking me a lot longer than usual to finish it."

"Do you read a lot?"

"When I have time. The ranch usually keeps me pretty busy. How's your foot?"

"Much better. Are you ready for dinner?"

"Yes, sir! Up for burritos?"

"Sounds good. Am I making them?"

"It's just a matter of heating things up, so I think I can manage. Have a seat, and make-shift campfire burritos will magically appear on your plate."

"Why is it," Jack asked, "that food tastes so much better when you're camping?"

"Are you saying my burritos are delicious?"

"Yes, they are delicious, but you know what I mean, right? Take the steak and veggies from last night. If we were at home and I'd made that, no one would be very impressed, including me. But out here, it tasted amazing!"

"I think it's partly cooking it over a fire and partly because all of this fresh air and exercise makes us hungry!" She made her fingers curve like claws.

"You're so funny!"

"What'll it be, doc; Benadryl or beer?"

"Beer, definitely. I'll have to start behaving myself once we get back." He patted his stomach.

"I have one more guilty pleasure. S'mores!" She pulled out graham crackers, marshmallows, and chocolate bars.

"Honestly, your pack is like Mary Poppins' bag. I don't know how you fit so much stuff in there. Do s'mores go with beer?"

"They do not. So let's have our s'mores first, then we can pull out the tortilla chips."

After a few hours of cheer around the campfire, Sam said, "I don't know about you, but I'm beat."

"Me too. It's been a pretty eventful day."

"Let's get some sleep, and we can pack up in the morning when there's light."

Sometime during the night, Sam sat up in her sleeping bag and grabbed her shotgun. It was very dark in the forest and suddenly very quiet except for the horses.

Jack rolled over and said, "What is it?"

"Shh. Take this flashlight," she whispered. "Something's spooking the horses. Crouch on the side of the tent flap, and when I say 'when,' turn it on and shine it on the horses." She quietly unzipped the tent and shouted, "When!" She cocked her gun at the same time he turned on the powerful flashlight.

A hooded figure froze in front of the log where the horses were tied. Then the person turned and ran blindly into the forest, crashing through bushes and trees while swearing under their breath.

"There, he's got his light on." Sam could see a spot of light bobbing through the trees, heading back toward the river. "He must have been completely blinded by the flashlight. He's still getting farther away, so we probably won't see him again."

"This flashlight is really bright! How do you know it was a man?"

"I don't. It might have been a woman, I suppose."

"What do you think they wanted?"

"The horses, I guess, but I don't know why. It's okay now. They know there are two of us, the horses are tied up well, and we're armed."

"Well, I don't like it. What if they'd had a gun? What if they wanted to let the horses loose so they could attack us, and we wouldn't have transportation? There's a murderer out there, you know."

"Jack! Talk about thinking the worst. You want to try to travel in the dark?"

"Has anything like this happened to you before?"

"No. But my dad always said to be prepared. Once, we had a bear come into camp." She saw from his face he wasn't amused. "It'll be sun-up in a couple of hours. Let's try to get a little more sleep, then we can leave once it's light."

Jack agreed, but Sam knew he wasn't sleeping. She knew how he felt because she was nervous too.

The next morning, as he boiled water for coffee and made pancakes from a mix, he tried to imagine the intruder. "Sam, did you get a good look at that person last night? I mean, how tall was he compared to the horses, for example. How was his gait? Was there anything noticeable about him... or her?"

"He was kind of hunched over the reins when you turned the light on, but when he turned to run, he seemed tall. He was slender and had a long gait, even running blind. I guess that's why I said he. The height and figure didn't look like a woman. Of course, I might look like that too."

"Could it have been Steven?"

"Maybe, but why would he try to steal our horses? And he didn't know where we were."

"No idea. I was just wondering if the body type fit." They finished eating in silence and packed up again. "I'm sorry we didn't have a little more time out here," Jack said. "I felt like I was having a real vacation for the first time in years."

"We'll do it again."

Chapter 20

Sergeant Mickelson walked forward and shook hands with Jack and Sam. "Thank you for coming in. Dr. Vanzandt and Captain Blatt are already here." They walked into the conference room at the back of the station. "Good afternoon, Captain. Byron. You've both met Sam, I believe."

"Yes," Captain Blatt said. "Thank you both for coming. Sit wherever you'd like."

They sat together at the end of the table then Jack said, "You have updates?"

"Yes. I've been to the hospital a couple of times," Mick said. "Melissa is not allowed visitors. The doctor reported that she has been taking Ambien mixed with alcohol for quite some time and has developed a double addiction. Melissa claims she never takes Ambien and usually just has a small glass of whiskey before bed to help her sleep. Perhaps you can help here, Dr. Vanzandt."

"The liquid in Melissa's glass and the decanter contained high amounts of Ambien. It is possible someone else has been adding the Ambien, and the last of the alcohol in the decanter had a higher dosage as it settled. It's also possible Ms. Dierkson had a second glass the last time she drank."

"So, basically, she overdosed on the combination."

"Yes. This has been going on long enough to cause liver and kidney damage and addiction."

"Does that explain her messy house and why she was sleeping so much?" Sam asked.

"Probably."

"There's one other thing," Mick added. "She's pregnant. When the doctor asked her who the father was, she said she had no idea. She said she hadn't had relations for months."

"That is obviously untrue since she is pregnant; however, Ambien alone, especially when mixed with alcohol, can cause parasomnia," Dr. Vanzandt explained.

"What's parasomnia?" Sam asked.

"It's when the mind is asleep, but the body is awake. People can eat, have sex, or even drive while they are asleep and not remember any of it."

"Could they kill someone if they were given the suggestion?" Mick asked.

"I'm not sure. It seems possible, but with their mind asleep, it might not go too well."

"Poor Melissa," Sam whispered. "I hope that's not what happened."

"At this point, Ms. Dierkson is under constant medical supervision as she is experiencing severe withdrawal symptoms."

"Thank you, Dr. Vanzandt. Could you tell us about the other major update?" Mick asked.

"Ah. This is very interesting. As you know, we have been looking into the death of Peter Sloan. Dr. Olivares took several blood samples, one of which was tested for his DNA."

Jack nodded.

"Recently, while conducting the final tests on the household goods brought in, I found a long, blonde hair. When I ran it, there was a match with the victim on ten of the twenty critical markers."

"What?!" Jack exclaimed.

Sam looked at him, surprised. "What does that mean?"

"It means," Jack said, "the hair belonged to someone closely related to Peter."

"A parent, child, or sibling," Byron clarified.

"Peter was an only child, as far as I know, and his parents are deceased. I was at their funerals.

So what we need to find out is whether or not he has any living children," Mick said.

"And this will tell us the identity of the murderer?" the Captain asked.

Byron nodded. "Quite possibly."

"Wonderful work, Dr. Vanzandt!" Jack beamed. "So, what's next?"

"I'm going to look for another DNA match for the hair. See if I can find the owner or the owner's mother."

"Emily just returned from vacation, so Sergeant Mickelson can pay her a visit," Captain Blatt said. "We'd like to know her history with Mr. Sloan, where she went, and about any prescriptions for Ambien she's filled lately."

"Yes, sir."

"We still need to look into Ararat and Steven's backgrounds," Jack added.

"I'll put Deputy Flores on it. They've both disappeared, so we're looking for them."

"What about Mark Carruthers," Sam asked? "No one has mentioned him since…"

Everyone looked at Jack.

"Stop walking on eggshells, please. I am perfectly aware of what we're investigating."

"Are we assuming Mark is in the clear now?"

"I'd almost forgotten about him, to tell you the truth," Mick said. "Why don't you and Jack pay him a visit?"

Jack nodded, and they stood to take their leave.

Once Sam and Jack were back in her truck, she asked, "Why are they letting me sit in on meetings with such confidential information?"

"Because I asked them to. You've been unofficially deputized as a consultant. I told them I needed you there for support and pointed out you're a local expert."

"Thank you, Jack. I won't let you down."

141

"I know you won't. Want to go grab some lunch before we tackle Mr. Carruthers?"

"Yes! I think I hear my stomach rumbling."

As they entered the Ugly Orange Cafe, Jack saw the woman he had seen in Melissa's shop and at the grocery store. "Who is that?"

"That's the lady that pushed me into the oranges at the grocery store." Sam frowned and stared at the menu. "Have you decided what you want?"

"Yeah, I'm going to have the club sandwich. You'll have the Reuben, right?"

"I can't. It was one of the things Alley and I shared."

"Tell you what," Jack said. "I can't get a club because it was one of the things we shared. So, I'll order the Reuben, and you order the club, and we'll get an order of tots to share."

"Okay."

When their orders came, Sam stared longingly at Jack's Reuben until he snatched her club sandwich. "I can't stand it! Give me that club!" He pushed his plate at her before taking a giant bite. "Mmmm," he said, chewing and relaxing in his seat.

Sam picked at the Reuben as she watched Jack eat. Finally, she gave in and picked it up. "You did that on purpose."

"Maybe. But it was the right thing to do. Alley doesn't care if you're enjoying her favorite sandwich. You knew her well. She wanted everyone to be happy, and it would crush her to know that we feel sad every time we think of her. Maybe we need to remember the happy times and celebrate them, and we can start by enjoying her favorite food."

Sam got a little teary. "When did you get so smart? Here's to Alley," she said and took a big bite of her sandwich. "Mmm. This might be the best one yet. So good."

"You can thank me later. How do you think we should proceed with our interview?"

"I don't know. Offer condolences. Ask Mark if he got a letter like mine?"

They finished their lunch and were about to take their bill to the register when Sam put her hand on Jack's arm. "Wait. Look over there."

"Is that Mark? Who's he sitting with?"

"That is Emily. They look pretty cozy."

"I saw him arguing with Peter on the day he died. Should we join them?"

"Why don't you text Mick, and we can just sit here and observe."

Mick strolled in a minute later and looked around. He saw Sam and Jack sitting by the window on one side of the restaurant. Sam gave him a little wave. On the other side of the restaurant, tall booths nearly concealed Mark and Emily from view.

"Party of one?" the waitress asked.

"No, I think I'll join my friends. Maybe you could bring me a cup of coffee?" He veered to the right and plopped himself in the booth across from Mark and Emily. Mark dropped Emily's hand like it scorched him, and they scooted apart. "Hope I'm not interrupting."

"Of course not," Emily said primly. "I was just offering my condolences."

"I wanted to talk to you both, so it seems lucky to find you here together."

They looked at him expectantly.

"I understand that you were both treated badly by Mr. Sloan." Mick paused for dramatic effect. "The day he died, you went on vacation, Emily. Why is that?"

She visibly paled, and her hands shook as she set down her coffee cup. "It wasn't really a vacation. My sister was going in for surgery and wanted me to watch her kids."

"Could I have her name and contact information, please?"

"Of course."

"And your travel information."

She nodded.

"Mark, I wanted to ask if you have received any threatening letters recently. Some of the others have."

"Yes, two. The first was just mildly threatening. The second told me to leave some money in a manila envelope next to the bank in some bushes. I put it there and tried to see who picked it up. I even gave a kid some money to watch, but whoever it was didn't pick it up until I left."

Emily's mouth formed a small oh, and she put her hand on Mark's. "When did that happen?"

"The day you came back."

"I caught Ara climbing out of the dumpster behind that little park on the same day. I asked him what he was doing, and he told me he'd accidentally thrown out something he needed with the garbage. When he tried to retrieve it, he fell in, he said, and he had a manila envelope in his hand. He wouldn't do that to you, would he?"

"He and I don't know each other very well. Perhaps he doesn't approve of me."

"I'll have a word with him," Mick said.

"I appreciate it. I need to get back. My lunch is about over."

"I guess I should go too," Emily said. "If it turns out Ara had something to do with the blackmail letter, please go easy on him and find out why. He's not a bad person."

"I'll do what I can. When can I get your travel information?"

"Could you come by the pharmacy in about half an hour?"

"Of course. I'd also like a list of any recently filled prescriptions for Ambien."

"May I ask why?"

"I'm not at liberty to say."

"I'd like you to get a warrant for that, so I'm not liable for divulging confidential information."

"Thank you for your cooperation. I'll bring one with me."

Mick watched the two of them stand and head toward the exit. He hadn't really given the two of them much thought, but if Peter was blackmailing Mark and gouging Emily on interest, they both had a motive. *I need to find out what Mark was being blackmailed about and why Emily took that trip.*

After Mark and Emily left, Mick took his coffee to Sam and Jack's table.

"Learn anything new?" Jack asked.

"Maybe. I've got a few more things to look into. Thank you for getting me over here."

When they got home, Sam suggested they go back over her list and see if they had made any headway. They were about halfway through when Steven knocked on the door. He tried to hug Sam, but she pushed him away.

Jack came to the door, and Steven said, "I'm sorry about Alley, dude. Is it okay that I'm here?"

"Of course. Come in. We were wondering what happened to you."

"I had to go see my mom; she's sick. And I didn't wanna bring you a bunch of memories when you're grieving, you know? But it's been too long since I've seen you both, so I come bearing beer."

"Beer is always welcome. Maybe we can have a little soak in the pool. What do you think, Sam?"

Sam was looking at the two of them, trying to figure out if Steven was the right height for the camp intruder when she noticed them both staring at her. "What? Sorry."

"The pool?"

"Oh. You know, I want to see Melissa, so I think I'll go see if they'll let me visit. You guys have a good time."

Sam got in her truck and spent the short drive to the hospital thinking about how she would get in to see Melissa. Calling it a hospital was being pretty generous for the small building and minimal staff.

It was more like a clinic with a small emergency department and a handful of rooms for in-patient use, like childbirth. Sam knew some of the doctors and nurses and even the security guards, so it was hard to pull a fast one. *I might have to just hide around the corner and make a break for it when they aren't looking.*

She entered the building and took the elevator to the second floor, then she got lucky. She didn't know the nurse at the desk, and no one else was around. She approached the desk "May I see Melissa Dierkson, please."

"Are you a relative?"

"Yes. I'm her sister."

To her surprise, the nurse let her in. The easy success was a relief but a little bit of a letdown after all of her contingency planning. *I'm such an idiot.*

Melissa struggled to sit up and gave Sam a weak smile when she entered. "Sam! You're here!"

"I've been trying to see you since they brought you in, but they wouldn't let me because I'm not a relative."

"Is that why no one came?"

Sam nodded. "Today, I told them I'm your sister."

"You are." Melissa held her arms out for a hug as tears rolled down her face. "I thought no one cared about me anymore."

"Who else do you want to see?"

"Steven. Ara. Alley. Jack. You. Mostly you."

"Steven and Ara both disappeared when you were brought in. Steven just came back. He said his mom wasn't well, and he didn't seem to know you were in the hospital."

"He knows. He always knows everything."

Sam raised her eyebrows a little at that. "Alley is dead."

Melissa tipped her head to the side and scrunched up her face. "What? Not Alley! How could that happen? She was so young."

Sam sat in the little chair next to Melissa's bed. "She was murdered in her apartment. I thought you didn't like her."

146

"Oh, Sam! I was jealous of her." Melissa pounded the bed with her fist. "I wanted to make things right, and now I can't. Once they started my detox, I realized how messed up I've been." She pulled at her hair. "I don't know how long I was taking that stuff, but there are periods of time I don't even remember."

"Who do you think was putting it in your decanter?"

"Ara and Steven were the only ones who came over, so it must have been Ara. Steven wouldn't do that to me. And the doctor said I'm pregnant! I always use protection. I don't know what happened, but Steven wouldn't hurt his own baby!"

"How do you know it's Steven's?"

Melissa looked at her in shock. "Because he's the only one I've been sleeping with."

"Ara claimed you were lovers."

"Oh, no. He's just making things up."

"You should probably have a paternity test. I've heard people on Ambien can seem like they're awake and do things in their sleep: eat, have sex, even drive."

"That sounds really dangerous."

"It is! And it's much stronger when mixed with alcohol."

"I'll ask the doctor about it. Thanks for telling me. How's Jack?"

"He's grieving Alley, but he'll be okay."

"He was with Alley?"

Sam thought back. "You really haven't been around much. The changes in you were so gradual, I didn't even realize them at first. Yes, they were getting pretty serious."

"I wonder what else I missed."

"Your house and yard are a mess. When was the last time you visited your shop?"

"I don't know... I can't remember going in since we went into town with Jack."

"Why didn't you like Jack?"

"I don't know. I want to ask the doctor about that too.

I had thoughts in my head that didn't seem to be my thoughts; like someone was planting them there. Jack was one of those. I thought he didn't like me; he was spying on me, wanted to cause me harm. Maybe it was the drug." She shook her head.

The nurse stuck her head in. "I think that's long enough for your first visit."

"Can I put Sam down for release of information? I don't have any other family."

"Yes, I'll go grab a form."

When the nurse left, Sam said, "Why don't you give me the key to your shop, and I'll check it out? And I'll get your house cleaned up before you're discharged."

"The key is at my house, on a hook by the door. The doctor told me I can probably go home in a week." The nurse came back, and Melissa filled out the ROI for Sam. "Thank you for coming!" Melissa hugged her. "I feel so much better now."

"I'll be back tomorrow," Sam promised.

She was deep in thought as she walked through the lobby. She had wanted to talk to Melissa about her father and the photos, but it hadn't seemed like a good time. She started when Emily walked up next to her and touched her arm.

"Sam, do you have a minute? Could we sit down in the coffee shop?"

"Of course." She followed Emily down the hall, where they each ordered coffee and sat down at one of the little round tables.

"I'm not sure where to begin. I think you have met my brother, Ara."

"I didn't know he was your brother, but yes, I've met him."

"I didn't know either until a couple of years ago."

"What happened?"

"Apparently, Peter and our father were business partners. For some reason, Peter decided our father was having an affair with his wife and set out to destroy him."

It was his father, not his uncle.

148

"My mother left with me, and my father committed suicide. The authorities couldn't find us, so Ara was placed in foster care."

"Then what happened?"

"Mother must have heard about his death at some point because she remarried. My step-father adopted me and gave me his last name. I don't know if she looked for Ara, but she died five years later, and I was raised by my step-father."

"How did you find Ara?"

"I didn't. He found me. I was only three when all of that happened. He was nine. I didn't remember our family life before my mother left. When Ara found me and showed me photos, I was very surprised. I asked my step-father a lot of questions, but he said my mother didn't like to talk about her past, so he didn't know much."

"That was a horrible thing to happen, and all of it a mistake. I'm glad Ara was able to find you after all that time."

"Yes, me too. I care about him very much, and he loves Melissa. At first, he was trying to woo her because he thought she was with Peter and he wanted revenge, but he fell in love with her. He's been with her almost every night for weeks. The nurses won't tell him anything and won't let him see her, so we've been taking turns sitting in the lobby, trying to find out if she's okay."

"Poor Ara. Does he know what's wrong with her?"

"No. They won't tell him anything."

"Let's go talk to him. I'll have Sergeant Mickelson meet us there, and he can explain."

"Thank you, Sam."

"You're welcome. I'll keep you updated if you like, until Melissa can have visitors."

Sam texted Jack on her way out of the hospital to let him know where she was, then she and Emily walked down the street to the station.

Chapter 21

Ara's apartment was not far down the street from the station. The twelve-unit complex was the only one in town and was located behind the small park, next to the bank. Sam had filled Mick in on her conversation with Emily and asked him to accompany them.

"I know it's kind of run-down, but it's all he can afford," Emily said as they walked up the stairs.

Mick knocked, and Sam could hear someone moving quickly, opening and shutting drawers or cupboards, and other muffled sounds before Ara opened the door.

Sam gasped. Gone was the dashing young man. Ara's face was drawn, and his eyes had lost their twinkle. He was wearing baggy boxers, a housecoat, and... duckie slippers.

He tried to slam the door shut, but Mick stopped him.

"I'm sorry, Ara," Emily said. "I saw Sam at the hospital, and I think she has some news for you."

"Why's he here?"

"He's been trying to get a hold of you."

Ara slumped and stepped back to let them in. "Sit wherever you can find a spot." He moved his arm like a lazy waiter. "Tell me about Melissa."

Sam looked around, trying to figure out where to sit. There were books and papers stacked up everywhere. She finally put a pile from the sofa on the floor and sat. Mick did the same, and Emily brought a chair in from the kitchen.

"We'll get to her," Mick said. "I'd like to ask you some questions first."

Ara's eyes squinted at that, but he nodded. "What do you want to know?"

Mick took out his notebook. "First, what do you do for a living?"

"I make computer games."

"Doesn't that pay pretty well? Why do you live here?"

"Peter was charging my sister so much interest on her loan she wasn't able to pay it."

"We've been living on Ara's income for over a year," Emily said.

"So both of you benefit from his death."

Emily sat up straight in her chair and shook her head.

Ara frowned.

"When did you take up blackmail?"

"I am no blackmailer!" Ara said.

"You took an envelope of money from Mark Carruthers."

"It was just an experiment, and, honestly, he should be helping with Emily's difficulties if he wants to marry her."

Emily turned and gaped at him.

"How did you find out about the photos?" Mick asked.

"Several photos were laying in a small pile somewhere, I don't want to say."

"You need to tell me."

"I'd rather not."

"They are part of a larger murder investigation, so if you don't want to go to jail, you'll have to."

Ara thought about that. If I tell him, he'll get the wrong idea. If I don't tell him, he'll find out anyway, and both of us will get into trouble. Ara sighed. "I found them on Melissa's dining table, but that doesn't mean she's a blackmailer or a murderer. I tried sending out letters the night I found them but forgot to put some kind of instructions on them, so I made just one more to try it out."

"Why would you do that?"

"Curiosity, I guess. I haven't been quite myself since Melissa went to the hospital. I haven't been sleeping. I don't really have any explanation why."

"Return the money to him, and he might not press charges."

"Yes, sir."

"And I will need the photos."

Ara got up and pulled them out of his desk drawer. There was one of Alley embracing Peter's business partner, one of Sam in the pool, and one of Mark looking behind him as he stuffed cash in a briefcase.

"Are these the only ones you found?"

"Yes, that's all."

"Tell me about your relationship with Melissa."

Ara's eyes softened, and a small, dreamy smile crossed his face. "Melissa is the most amazing woman I've ever met."

"How long have you been seeing her?"

"About two months. At first, it was just one time, but then it became once or twice a week. Recently, I have been seeing her every night except Thursday."

"What happens on Thursdays?

"I teach an online programming course."

"Have you noticed any change in Melissa's behavior?" Sam asked.

"Yes... but it has been gradual. I think maybe I've been wearing her out. I should be more considerate."

"Tell us about the changes."

Ara thought for a minute, pulling his robe closer and running his long fingers along the soft, fuzzy fabric. "When I first met her, Melissa was very busy. She was running her shop, gathering plants, making soap. Her house looked like no one lived there; it was so clean. Then she... I don't know what happened, but she was always in bed when I went over. I didn't mind because she always wanted wild sex, but the house became extremely dirty. Sometimes I had to pull her into the shower with me and change the sheets because she was... not very clean." He wrinkled up his nose at the memory.

"Did you ever see her drinking?"

"She usually had a glass of whiskey from a bottle on her nightstand before bedtime."

"Did you drink with her?"

"No. I'm a recovering alcoholic. I never touch the stuff."

"Did you use protection when you were intimate?"

"At first, we did. She made sure. But, after a while, she didn't care. She didn't want to wait. Why are you asking me these things? And why is she still in the hospital? Will she recover?"

Sam looked over at Mick, and he nodded. "Someone has been drugging Melissa's whiskey for quite some time. She almost died from an overdose, and she's going through medically supervised detox right now."

Ara sat very still. Emily put her hand on his shoulder, and he looked at her with a haggard face. "I should have known something was wrong," he said hoarsely. "I was so selfish. She could have died."

"There's more," Sam said.

Ara looked at her with trembling lips and fear in his eyes.

"She's pregnant and thinks it's someone else's. She doesn't remember sleeping with you after the first few times."

"How can that be!"

"Have you heard of parasomnia?"

He shook his head.

"It's like sleepwalking. The person's mind is asleep while their body seems awake. The drug that's been in her drinks causes that."

Ara seemed to crumple. His shoulders slumped, and his face sagged. Sam wished she hadn't had to tell him. "Maybe she'll remember once she gets it out of her system. But since she's asking for a paternity test, you might offer to have your blood tested as well."

Mick looked at him sternly. "I'll need an account of your movements the night of Peter's death, the day of Alley's death, and the day Melissa went to the hospital; the sixth, the thirteenth, and the sixteenth. Can you bring that information to the station tomorrow and sign an official statement?"

Ara nodded.

"Thank you," Mick said as he stood.

Sam stood too, and Emily showed them to the door. "Please let me know if you have any updates on her condition," Emily said. "And perhaps you could let her know that Ara is thinking of her."

"I'll do that." Sam smiled and hugged Emily.

Mick gave Sam a ride to Melissa's house, where Jack was sitting on the porch waiting. "I got your text," he said to Sam. "Why don't we go inside, and you can tell me what's going on. It's getting chilly out here."

"Good idea. I'll make some tea." Sam cleared off the table and gave them their mugs. She and Mick got Jack caught up on Sam's visit with Melissa, Emily's approach at the hospital, and their conversation with Ara.

"Before we left, I asked him to bring information about his whereabouts during both crimes to the station tomorrow and sign a statement." Mick finished his tea and put his mug in the sink.

"So, how does our case look?"

"That's tricky," Sam said, turning her mug around in a circle. "Technically, any of our suspects could have killed Peter. Did anyone check his house after the photos and the will surfaced?"

"Yes. I forgot you two were out of town." Mick leaned against the kitchen counter. "There was an open safe under a floorboard in his bedroom. No prints and no idea how anyone knew it was there."

"Given the probability of parasomnia, it's quite possible Melissa gave out that information," Jack said.

"Right," Mick said. "So someone went to Peter's house to find the photos and possibly the will, and got very angry over what they found."

"What makes you think that?" Sam stopped playing with her mug and looked up at him.

"Because the next day, they killed someone else."

The kitchen was silent, with palpable tension.

154

Mick had even shocked himself with his matter-of-fact statement. Jack stared at him with a raised eyebrow, and Sam gaped.

"Sooo, the murderers don't have to be the same person, but you think whoever broke into Peter's house killed Alley?" Sam asked.

"I think so, yes."

"Let's talk about what that person found and why it would make them angry," Jack suggested.

"They found the pictures," Sam said.

"Yes, why would they make someone angry? Everyone knew he was a blackmailer."

"Emily might not have known Mark was embezzling," Mick suggested.

"If Steven and Melissa have been together this whole time like Melissa claims, the photos could make him very angry," Jack said. "Although according to the evidence, he seems to be too tall."

"Ara might be angry about the will since Melissa told him she would inherit," Sam said.

"He could have been angry about the pictures of Alley and his dad, and decided she was in on it since she inherited everything. Also, Steven and Ara are both left-handed. There are a couple of things we're not considering, though," Jack said. "One is the relative whose DNA we found from the hair in Peter's effects. That person would be very angry about the will. And the other, whoever was at our campsite, if it was related."

"There's also the batch of blackmail letters that went out before Alley was killed," Sam added. "I thought whoever killed Alley sent them out and tried to make it look like she did it, but since Ara is the one who sent them out, and he only had three photos, it looks like that might be a red herring."

"I don't know," Jack said slowly. "Something is off. I think we need more information. Maybe you can get search warrants for the homes of Ara, Mark, and Steven. If anything's here, I imagine it will be found by our clean machine." He gave Sam a nudge.

"I'll keep an eye out for long blonde hair, too," she said.

Jack got up and thanked Sam for the tea. "I have to get back to the morgue. Just a few more missing pieces, and we'll crack this wide open."

Mick stayed and helped Sam clean. They split up and made quick progress. After about an hour, Sam said, "Hey, Mick? Come here a minute."

He entered the bedroom to find Sam on her hands and knees, looking at a pile of lint, Kleenex, and wadded-up papers. "What are you doing?"

"I shook out the bedding, and all of this stuff came out. Can you help me look through it?"

They put on gloves and sifted through everything until Mick sat back on his heels and said, "Well, lookee here. I almost missed it."

"What is it?"

"A long blonde hair."

They both stared at it in silence.

"I'll go get a baggie," Sam said. "I found a couple of things too."

Mick bagged the hair and went to see what Sam found. "It might be nothing, but I found this picture of Melissa and my dad. Just the one, and I found a used condom. I know it's gross, but it can provide DNA, can't it?"

"Yes. We'll want two more bags and some more gloves. Maybe we'll find all kinds of evidence. It looks like she hasn't cleaned in months."

"I know. I didn't want her coming home to this."

After another hour, she heard the vacuum cleaner and went to see how Mick was doing. He stopped vacuuming. "The kitchen is respectable, and the living room is getting there. Can we adjourn for the night?"

"The bedroom floor is picked up, and the bathroom is clean, but I'd kind of like to clean up the furniture in the bedroom before we leave. There might be something important laying around."

"Yes, you're right." He sighed. "I'll be in as soon as I'm done here."

"I'll just take some baggies with me." Sam started with the night table on Melissa's side and worked her way to the one on the other side before Mick came in.

"Find anything?"

"Melissa's side doesn't look like it's been opened in a long time; just a lot of garbage on the top. The other side had a box of condoms and a bottle of prescription Ambien, both bagged. They might have fingerprints."

"What else do we have?"

"You take the bookshelves, and then you can vacuum. I'll take the dresser top and drawers; I can straighten them at the same time. Then I'll put away the clothes in the dryer, and we can go."

Mick nodded and got to work. They were both surprised when Jack showed up with a pizza. "I thought you might have worked up an appetite." He grinned.

Sam did an odd little happy dance. "Did you get the pepperoni, pineapple, and jalapeno?"

"Of course I did." Jack's eyes widened in mock surprise. "How could I forget?"

They sat down at the kitchen table and made that pizza disappear. "I didn't realize how hungry I was," Mick said, patting his stomach.

"I guess none of us did." Sam laughed.

"Thank you, Jack. I should be getting back to the station now."

"Thanks for helping me out," Sam said.

After Mick left, Jack pulled out a couple of beers and handed one to Sam. When she raised an eyebrow he said, "I only had two."

"Gotta have priorities." She looked around. "Maybe I can work in the garden next. It looks so much better in here."

"If you're coming over here again, then I am too."

"Thanks, Jack! That is so nice of you, but you don't have to."

"There's a lot happening and a lot of evidence pointing at Steven. I think we should stick together right now."

Sam nodded. "In that spirit, I vote we take the evidence to the sheriff's station, since Mick forgot to take it. And before I forget, I should take the key to Melissa's shop so I can check on it for her."

"Good idea. If anyone's been watching us, we don't want them breaking in to steal it. We should probably change the locks on Melissa's doors, too. There seem to be multiple keys around."

After Sergeant Mickelson returned to his desk, he sat making a mind map to show all of the relevant connections between the suspects and the two murders. He was wondering if Melissa's poisoning should be added as well. He looked up at the sound of footsteps and conversation, recognizing Sam's melodic voice before he saw her.

"Hi, Mick," she said. "You're still here?"

"I've been working on a timeline and a mindmap. Sometimes everything starts running together."

"May I see?"

Jack and Sam put their heads together to study the sheet of paper Mick had been working on. "That looks great," Jack said.

"Thanks. It helps me get my thoughts in order. By the way, I was going to go over and help Sam in Melissa's yard tomorrow, but I have a meeting with the Captain. Could you take my place? I don't really want her going over there alone right now."

"Of course!"

"Why isn't anybody asking me?" Sam said. "Alley's funeral is tomorrow. Anything else will have to be postponed."

Jack's face fell. "You're right. I must have been blocking that out."

"If it's the day after tomorrow, then I can go and help, Sam."

"After mass, of course."

Jack pulled Mick aside as they left and said, "If you have to leave, take her with you. Don't leave her there alone."

"Don't worry. I won't."

Chapter 22

On the day of Alley's funeral, the church bells pealed every hour until the service began. She was a beloved member of the church and the community. The women had gathered to bake desserts and decorate the church with flowers, and the pipe organist was playing dramatically beautiful music. Jack had felt the sense of community in Santo Milagro, but seeing this outpouring of love for one of their own touched him deeply. Everyone stood as the organist began Mozart's Requiem Mass, a piece that always gave Jack goosebumps. The pallbearers brought the coffin down the aisle, and Sam squeezed his hand.

They sat, and Father Garcia led them in prayer after a beautiful eulogy. Many in the congregation had something they wanted to say, and Jack felt he should say something too, but he was afraid he might not get through it. When Father Garcia invited him to come forward, he looked out and saw a sea of kind, compassionate faces, and his tears came. He wasn't aware of them trickling down his face as he spoke.

Alley was the first person I met in Santo Milagro. I didn't have the privilege of knowing her for years like most of you did, but she taught me about love. She changed my life with her trust and her sunshine. I am grateful to her for loving me and grateful to all of you for your outpouring of love for her today. You've all shown me the true meaning of community." He turned and looked at her picture above the coffin. *"I hope you know how special you are and how much we love you. And I hope you are there with Jesus smiling down on us today as we celebrate your life.*

159

With that he returned to his seat, completely unaware there wasn't a dry eye in the congregation. Father Garcia led them in another prayer and a final hymn before inviting them into the hall for refreshments, but Jack stayed in the sanctuary for a long time. Sam sat quietly beside him while he was lost in thought and started when he said, "Let's go join the others, shall we?"

The next morning, Sam followed the scent of coffee downstairs and found a plate of pancakes waiting for her. Jack had already left for the morgue, but there was a note.

To my favorite cousin,
Here are your coffee and pancakes. Wait for Mick to pick you
up, and don't take rides from strangers or suspects. I'll be back
to make dinner. Love, Jack.

There was a rap on the door, and she went to let Mick in, but it wasn't him. Steven entered and tried to hug her. She pushed him away. "What are you doing here?"

"I just got back. Aren't you glad to see me?"

"What? You were just here the night before last."

"No, I wasn't."

"You came over and went swimming with Jack. Are you just messing with me?"

"No… Where's Jack?"

Sam didn't want to be alone with him, so she was relieved when Mick knocked on the door and stuck his head around the corner.

"Hi, Mick. Want some pancakes?"

"Sure! That sounds great." He nodded to Steven and sat down.

"I have to go." Steven frowned.

Sam stared at Mick for a moment after he left. "What on earth is going on?"

"I'm not sure, but let's stick together."

They ate their breakfast, filled up on coffee, then headed for mass. Afterward, she and Mick walked down the street to Melissa's shop. Sam looked around.

The layout was always a mystery to her, but nothing appeared out of the ordinary, other than the dust. She was about to suggest they leave when a gap on the shelves behind the counter made her pause.

"What is it?" Mick asked.

"I think there's something missing from that shelf." She walked toward the shelf and grabbed a step stool. Once she was closer, she could see that the shelves were neatly labeled and contained similarly labeled jars. The jar that read 'water hemlock' was missing and had been for a while, based on the layer of dust. She pointed it out to Mick. "I was planning to buy new door knobs for Melissa's house. We should probably get one for the shop too."

Mick agreed, so they walked another block to Mr. Sanchez's hardware store, but it was closed. "Darn, I forgot he's closed on Sunday. I'll stop by tomorrow and get them. Let's just head over to Melissa's and take care of the yard."

They walked back to Sam's truck and drove the short distance to Melissa's house. Although Main Street was only three blocks long, the sparsely populated town of Santo Milagro stretched across miles of high desert. Melissa lived on three acres, one mile down the unnamed dirt road that led to Sam's ranch. Once they got to Melissa's, Sam began unloading gardening supplies, a broom, and some white paint.

"What needs to be done?"

"Melissa has always had a pristine garden. We need to make it look like it hasn't been neglected for months. We can start in the front."

They pulled weeds and watered the drought-resistant plants, which were surprisingly parched. Sam swept the porch while Mick cleaned the windows.

"Do you think we should add a coat of paint to the porch? Or am I being overkill?"

"You're probably being overkill." Mick laughed. "What about the back?"

They headed around the side of the house, freezing at the sight. "This is too much for one afternoon," Sam said.

161

"Maybe it's not as bad as it looks. Let's at least get the patio cleared." Mick took a broom and swept the flagstone, switching to the rake after a few minutes. Sam put on some gardening gloves and started pulling the weeds growing up between the cracks. She found a hose and washed off the plastic lawn furniture and the cleared patio.

After several hours, Sam said, "It looks pretty good. Let's make one more pass through the house."

"Sure." Mick followed her through the house then stopped and said, "Sam?"

"Yeah?"

"I know you've been through a lot recently but—"

A rap on the door interrupted him. Sam went to investigate and was surprised to find Steven waiting on the porch. He was wearing the same clothes he had on that morning and looked like he had been running his hands through his hair.

"I need to talk to you"—he glanced around her shoulder and narrowed his eyes at Mick—"in private."

Sam folded her arms.

"I don't know what's going on," he said quickly, "but I want you to know I really like you, and I think you're in danger. It might have something to do with my mom. I went to see her yesterday, and she was acting like she was drunk and talking gibberish about Peter and Alley and the will. I don't know how she even knew about that."

"And day before yesterday?"

"I told you, I was at my mom's. I stopped in on my way back."

"On your way back from where?"

"I was racing in Cali. You guys weren't home, so I left a note. Maybe I'm going crazy, but I swear it wasn't me the other day. I have to go now. Just please be careful." He jogged back to his truck.

Sam stood on the porch and watched him speed down the road.

Mick stepped beside her. "You okay?"

"Yes, but very confused."

"What happened?"

"We should go find Jack, and I'll tell you both. It's very strange."

They drove to the morgue in silence. Mick had a million questions, but he was a patient man. When they arrived, the officer at the front desk rang the lab and let them through. Sam wondered how many people worked there because there was always someone different working the desk.

"Hello, you two. This is a surprise."

"We had a little incident," Mick said. "Sam wanted to talk it through with you."

Jack's eyebrows rose, and he looked at Sam, who started pacing back and forth.

"When Steven came over on Friday, did he seem odd to you?"

"A little, yes, but I can't quite pinpoint it. He wasn't slurring his words together as much and seemed... a little harder? More serious? He also didn't get some of our usual jokes, and he'd forgotten some things we'd talked about before. What happened?"

"First, he stopped by the ranch just before Mick got there and denied being there Friday. He was acting very strangely."

"Then," Mick said, "he came to Melissa's."

"What?!"

"He said he didn't know what was going on, but he thought I might be in danger. And he thought it might have something to do with his mom. He told me to be careful."

Jack thought for a minute. "Let me show you what Byron and I found, then we'll circle back."

"Okay," Sam said.

"When we requested a DNA match, the response was a request for additional information. We added the fingerprint from the condom and got a match."

Sam's heart raced as she waited for Jack to continue.

"It was a one hundred percent match and also contained ten of the markers linking it to Peter." Jack paused. "The person who came up is named Andrew James. He was accused of arson—the burning of his family home—and the subsequent deaths of his adoptive parents in Texas, but he fled the state before he could be arrested."

"Does that mean Steven is really Andrew?" Sam asked.

"It could mean that. The request for additional information is odd. My best guess would be that there are two individuals in the database with the same DNA, so we need fingerprints to specify which person we are looking for."

"Two people with the same DNA?"

"We might be dealing with identical twins. We've got some digging to do," Jack said. "Would you two like to join me for dinner?"

"Back to Mary's?"

"I'm in," Mick said.

"I need to visit Melissa afterward. Will you come with me, Jack? She was asking about you yesterday."

"Yes, okay. Maybe we can ask her if she's noticed anything different about Steven."

The three had a nice dinner at Mary's, although the diner was unusually loud. A large group had pulled up on motorcycles just as they were ordering. Sam thought it interesting to watch them, but it did make conversation challenging. She caught bits of Jack and Mick's conversation, but she mostly watched the bikers. They appeared middle-aged, perhaps in their forties and fifties. And as she watched, one of the women strutted over and said, "Why are you staring? Do you have a problem with us?"

Sam smiled. "No! I was just admiring you and your friends. You seem so vibrant and confident. I imagine you have some amazing stories to tell."

The woman laughed. "Now that is a first. I'm Cathy. Let me buy you a beer." She took Sam's hand and pulled her from the booth, slinging an arm around her shoulders and leading her to the bar. After she had introduced her around and pushed a beer in her direction, she and her friends took turns telling Sam of their escapades.

Sam excused herself half an hour later when she saw Jack and Mick slide out of the booth. "It was great meeting you, Cathy. I hope the rest of your trip is as fabulous as the first part."

"Always remember to make your own adventures, young lady. No one else is gonna do it for you." Cathy winked and slipped her a card, then waved as Sam followed Mick and Jack out the door.

"What was that all about?" Jack asked.

"Nothing. Just making friends." She looked at the card Cathy had given her and smiled. It read, "Have a great day!" with Cathy's name and phone number below.

"Are you joining us at the hospital, Mick?""

"No, I want to look into a few things."

They watched him walk off, then got in the truck.

Sam said, "I'm having trouble wrapping my head around all of this." She clicked her seatbelt into place.

"Me too. We'll figure it out. Maybe Melissa can help."

When they got to the hospital in Santo Milagro, it was quiet. The nurse on duty was the same one who let Sam in to see Melissa the day before. She smiled at Sam but then caught sight of Jack and frowned.

"Only relatives are cleared to visit," she said.

"By order of whom?" he asked.

"Sergeant Mickelson."

Jack flashed his badge. "I just had dinner with him, and he knows I'm here."

She looked at his badge carefully. "Let me just make sure she wants visitors."

"Tell her Sam and Jack, please."

The nurse nodded and went to check before leading them to her room.

"You came!" Melissa said with a smile. "Both of you! I thought you forgot."

"Of course not. Actually, I have something to talk to you about in private." Sam turned to Jack. "Could we have a few minutes alone?"

"Sure. I'll be just outside. Let me know when you're done."

After he left the room, Sam sat down in the chair next to Melissa's bed and took her hand. She looked into her eyes and said, "I saw the pictures."

Melissa's eyes widened, and she tried to sit up.

"It's okay. I've thought about everything quite a bit, and even though I don't know the whole story, I know you, and I knew my father. If you were together, it was because you loved each other. And if you chose not to tell me, it was because you were somehow trying to protect me. It's not my business, so you don't have to tell me anything, but I'll listen if you need to talk sometime."

Melissa had fat tears rolling down her face. "I'm so sorry, Sam. I wanted to tell you, but your dad wanted to wait. Then he passed away, and I didn't have the courage to do it by myself. Then Peter... he made everything seem so ugly."

"I know. He was a horrible man. I didn't want to upset you with all this. I just wanted you to know that it's not a secret anymore and that we're okay."

Melissa reached out her arms for a hug. "Thanks, Sam. It's such a relief not having that big secret looming over me."

"I'll tell Jack he can come back in, and I have before and after pictures of your house." Sam pulled out her cell phone and handed it to Melissa, then she went over to the door and called Jack. Heading back to the bed, Sam said, "That's what it looked like when I found you."

Melissa scrolled through the pictures and wrinkled her nose. "Oh my god, how could it have gotten like that? Ewww."

"And here it is now." Sam smiled, scrolling through more photos.

"You are the best friend ever! I don't know how to thank you."

"Mick helped a lot. And we'll change your locks because it seems quite a few people have keys."

"I don't even know who because apparently I've been pretty loosey-goosey." She looked down, ashamed. "The doctor told me the baby is Ara's. I don't even know how that's possible."

"He said you've been having unprotected sex almost every night."

"I will never touch another Ambien for as long as I live! And Jack?"

"Yes?" He walked forward from the doorway.

"I am so sorry for how I treated you. I don't remember everything, but I know I said some rotten things to you, and I'm sorry."

"You seem like a different person now." He smiled. "So, let's start over. Hi. I'm Jack." He extended his hand.

"Nice to meet you, Jack. I'm Melissa." She laughed and shook his hand.

"Speaking of seeming like a different person," Sam interjected. "Can I ask you some stuff about Steven?"

"Like what?" Melissa tensed.

"Do you know anything about his past?"

"A little."

"His parents? Brothers or sisters?"

"No, he said that he grew up in California... sometimes he talks about his mom."

"Have you noticed any changes in him?"

Her eyes softened, and she gave a weak smile. "He seemed really sweet and gentle when I met him, but after I broke up with him because of Peter, we got back together, and he was different. He got kind of bossy and didn't laugh as much."

"When did you get back together?"

"About a week before Peter died. He's the one who told me I should go stay with you."

"When did you start feeling out of it?"

"I'm not sure. It was gradual." Melissa picked at a piece of fuzz on her blanket. "It might have been around the same time."

"Did you bring your carafe with you when you came to stay at the ranch?"

"Of course." Melissa laughed and then stopped. "Oh. He helped me pack and told me not to forget it."

Sam's forehead wrinkled. "What about when he stopped by the house, and you told him to go away?"

"He told me to say that if he came over."

"Didn't you think that was strange?"

"He said so many weird things, especially at night when I was groggy." Melissa shrugged.

"Do you remember going to the car race with us?"

"Yes... sort of. There was someone there who looked like Steven. But he wasn't Steven. I think I might have been hallucinating." She shrunk in on herself, and her eyes flicked back and forth.

"We'll get to that in a minute. How does Ara fit in?"

"I don't know. I don't remember Ara being there, except that once. I can't believe I was sleep-cheating. No wonder Steven got mad at me."

"He got mad at you?"

"Yes, he called me a hopped-up whore and said he didn't have any more use for me.

That's why I had an extra glass of whiskey." Melissa began to cry. "I had forgotten about that."

"Think back, Melissa. Would the Steven you were dating before you met my dad have ever said anything like that? To anyone?"

Melissa looked at Sam with a red, tear-stained face. "I would never have guessed he could be so cruel."

"I'm going to show you a picture of him," Jack said, "and I want you to tell me if you notice any difference, anything at all."

168

It was a picture of Steven in his swim trunks, grilling hamburgers. Melissa had a hard time looking at it at first but then enlarged it on the screen and sat up. "His nose is a little different. It has a bump on the bridge where it was broken. He has a tattoo of a skull on his upper arm." She looked closer, "It could be the sun, but I think his eyebrows might be a little darker... he doesn't have that scar on his leg. When was this taken?"

Jack and Sam looked at each other. "It was taken just before you were brought to the hospital," Jack said.

"But that's not Steven."

"Did Steven ever say his name? After you got back together?"

"No, but I called him that. You're frightening me."

"We think Steven has a twin, and that twin might be responsible for a lot of things that have been going on."

"Does he know?" Melissa whispered.

"I don't think so," Sam said. "You just relax and get better. Mick and Jack will solve this." She gave Melissa another hug and promised to visit again the next day.

Sam waited while Jack called Mick from the nurses' station and gave him an update. He showed the nurse a photo of Steven and said, "If this person asks for Ms. Dierkson, please don't leave him alone with her and call the police immediately."

"May I know what this is about?"

"It's an active police investigation. We think she could be in danger."

"Okay. I'll keep my eye out. Thank you."

Chapter 23

When they returned to the ranch, Roger wandered over to the truck, followed closely by Red, who always had a bounce in his step. He leaned in the window and said, "I was wondering where you two were. Steven stopped by looking for Jack and I wanted to talk to you about our feed vendor."

"I'll go on inside," Jack said as he got out of the truck.

Sam got out of her side and followed Roger to the barn. He pointed out the remaining inventory. "The vendor has been late on shipments the last few months and his prices are going up again. Carlos told me that Peter was using Forever Feed. He said that they are very timely and cost about ten percent less."

"I trust you to make the right decision, Roger. Just remember that relationships are important and keep me in the loop."

"Thank you, Ms. Sam." Roger grinned and headed back toward the barn.

Sam watched him go. He's been here a long time. I need to let him take on more responsibility. The feed is a good first step.

When Sam went inside, Jack asked her about her security system. She showed him how it worked and said, "Do you know I've never even used the alarm before?"

"It could come in handy right now. Better safe than sorry."

"Yeah. You know what? It's really sad that with all of her memory loss, the one thing Melissa remembers is the man she loves calling her names. Isn't that horrible?"

"The things we are most likely to remember are those linked to a powerful emotion. His words must have been traumatic."

"Poor Melissa. She's been through a lot."

The next morning, Sam trudged down the stairs later than usual to find Jack wielding coffee and comfort food. It was a quiet, peaceful morning, welcome after all of the recent emotional turmoil. Sam watched Jack as he kept busy clearing the table and washing the dishes. "I feel exhausted. How do you manage to have so much energy?"

"I don't, really. I just feel like I should be doing something. Why don't you pick out a movie, and I'll make some brownies."

"Or we could play a game of ping pong. I am still the champion, you know."

"Pure luck! Your reign is about to—" He was interrupted by a loud banging at the door. Seeing Steven standing outside, Jack called Mick.

Steven saw Sam and yelled, "Sam! Open up!"

"Take off your shirt," she said through the door, her heart pounding.

"Are you getting a little frisky, babe?" He took off his shirt.

Sam saw his clean shoulders before a bullet whizzed through the air, nicking one shoulder and hitting the glass window. The alarm went off, mixing with police sirens a few minutes later, as two squad cars pulled up. Sam crouched down, cracked the door, and yelled, "There's a shooter, Mick!" She and Jack pulled Steven inside.

Mick's partner drove closer, providing him coverage to slip into the house. She crawled across the seat and out the passenger door as Mick covered her.

Once everyone was inside, Deputy Flores said, "We seem to have scared him off. Any idea who it was?"

"Yes," Mick said. "Steven, I'm going to arrest you for your own safety. We'll need some information about your family."

"Can I come too?" Sam asked.

"We'll all go. It's not safe here," Mick said.

They drove in a caravan to the station and got comfortable in the back conference room. "Who wants coffee?" Anita asked.

"It's not terrible; I made it myself."

Everyone's hand went up. "Guess I'll be making another pot." She chuckled as she left the room.

Jack got busy patching up Steven.

"Oww. Who would've shot me?"

"Someone who didn't want you to take your shirt off," Sam joked.

"Let's get down to business here," Mick said. "Would you like to start with a statement, Steven?"

"I guess it's time," Steven sighed. "My brother and I came to town to help our mom."

"What is your mother's name?"

"Victoria Hale."

"Alley knew your mother," Jack said.

"I think everyone knows her, even if they don't know her name. Anyway, we didn't have enough income for a caregiver, so we decided to share an identity."

"Because you are twins?" Mick asked.

"Right. My brother was here first, and everything was working out fine until I met Sam." His eyes slid sideways to glance at her.

Mick asked, "What does Sam have to do with this?"

"I like her, and I wanted to get to know her, but my brother was dating Melissa and kept messing things up. I finally told him I was going to come clean, and now he and my mom are mad at me."

"Who is Andrew James?"

"I have no idea."

Mick squinted at him. "We need to have you in custody for your own safety. We'll drive you to Las Rodillas. That will allow you a little more anonymity."

"You're arresting me? For what?" He scooted his chair back and stood.

"We think you're in danger, and you might need an alibi. This is to keep you safe, not to punish you."

"Will it go on my record?"

"No."

"Jack and I can stay in Las Rodillas, too, so we'll be nearby," Sam said.

"What could happen if we're all here?"

"We don't know, but someone is planning something," Jack said. "May I take a blood sample?"

"I don't like this. If you won't tell me what this is about, then no."

Jack took a deep breath. "I'd like to verify your identity."

Steven stared at him and then laughed. "Right."

"Deputy Flores, transport Mr. Chapman over to Las Rodillas. Jack, could you come with me? The Captain would like a brief."

"What do I do?" asked Sam.

"Why don't you come with us?" Steven grinned.

"Yeah, ok. You can tell me about your mom."

"That's not so bad then. Show us the way, copper."

Mick and Jack arrived at the jail in Las Rodillas to discover Sam had gone shopping and made Steven's cell very homey. The other prisoners were complaining. She bought him a soft blanket, noise-canceling headphones, and a sleep mask so he could ignore the uproar, then went to find a hotel room.

"Steven looks very comfortable," Jack said.

"I guess it's only fair," Mick said.

"Are you staying here tonight too?"

"Might as well. Want to meet for breakfast?"

"The hotel has a free breakfast buffet at eight."

"Okay, let's meet up then."

Jack found Sam in the hotel bar.

"Hey, Sam."

"Hey," she said, swaying a bit.

"You look blue."

"I really want to believe Steven. But something's not right."

"Tell me what you're feeling. It doesn't have to be right."

"I just… I don't know. When he came over that day and I left to see Melissa, did he have a tattoo on his shoulder?"

Jack paused. "No, I don't think so."

"Something's wrong. Tell me again why we think the twin is a killer?"

"Because his fingerprint was on the condom."

"Did that fingerprint match the one found at Alley's apartment?"

"No… "

"And why do we think Steven is innocent?"

"Because…"

"What if Steven is Andrew? No one has tested his DNA or taken his fingerprints, right?"

"Do you think he's Andrew?"

"No. I don't know. I just feel like something is wrong."

"Steven is in custody, so we have a little time."

"Did you get a room?"

"Not yet."

"They're full, but I have two beds. You can stay with me."

"Have you eaten anything?"

"No. I'm not hungry."

"Tell you what, I'll buy you another drink if you share some appetizers with me."

"Nachos."

The waitress came over, and Jack said, "Could we get some nachos and the sampler plate?" Sam looked at him. "And two more of whatever she's having?" Sam nodded.

After the waitress left, he said, "I'm just trying to make sure you don't end up vomiting all over our hotel room."

"How kind." Sam rolled her eyes.

"Come on, Sam. This isn't like you."

"Maybe it is. You haven't known me very long."

"I have seen the loss and grief in your eyes. I have seen you bombarded by betrayal. I see the stress mounting.

But I have never seen you give up. You're always looking out for your friends and coming up with plans."

Sam looked up from her glass.

"I remember what you did for me when I lost Alley."

"What I do for others is not necessarily the same as how I cope on my own."

"I'm aware of that, but think about the stakes here. Whoever killed Peter and Alley and drugged Melissa... that person is evil. If it's Steven or his twin, he needs to be stopped. He could go after Melissa or his mom, or his twin, even us."

"I know, Jack." She sighed. "I am just so confused. All of this stuff is happening, and none of it makes any sense. If the twins... if there are actually two of them... if they were adopted by two different families, how did they find each other? How did they both end up here?"

"It would be helpful to talk to their mom."

"I asked Steven about her on the ride here. His mom is Victoria Hale. She was on my list of people to question."

"Do you know what she looks like?"

"Steven said she is tall and thin with long blonde hair and a kind of weathered face. I've seen her around. She's the one who pushed me into the oranges."

"I've seen her too, actually. If it's the person I'm thinking of, I saw her in Melissa's shop. Alley asked Steven about her at the pool party."

The food arrived, and Sam started to eat. "I guess maybe I was hungry," she said between bites.

"We can always order more."

"This is a lot, but maybe they can bring us another quesadilla. That was so good... and another drink?"

Jack flagged down the waitress and placed their order. "Have you looked through all of your dad's things?" he asked.

"Most of them. I haven't been through his bedroom or the attic. Why?"

"I was thinking. Since we have some time on our hands, we could see if he had any old family pictures or journals that might explain why we didn't grow up together."

"Yes. Good idea. But didn't Mick say it wasn't safe at the house?"

"Maybe he'd let us be bait."

Sam looked skeptical. "I guess we could ask."

Chapter 24

The next morning, Mick was sitting in the hotel restaurant with a big plate of food when Jack entered. "Good morning. Have you been up all night?"

"How'd you guess?" Mick asked sarcastically.

"The bags under your eyes? The two days' stubble, the giant mound of food? Three coffee cups?" Jack laughed.

"Don't kick a man when he's down. Where's Sam?"

"She was drowning her sorrows last night and didn't want to get up."

"Too bad I missed it."

"No, it wasn't party drinking. This case is getting to her. She feels like something about Steven's story isn't right."

"Like what?"

"She said it's hard to pinpoint, but one concrete example is the day he came over, and she left to visit Melissa. He claimed it wasn't him. Melissa told us the twin had a tattoo, but the Steven, who was over that day, didn't have a tattoo either."

Mick stared at him. "So, what does she think?"

"What if he's the twin? Or what if there is no twin? Or the twin isn't involved? We need to speak with his mother."

"Already on it."

"Now I have a request."

"Yeah?"

"Sam and I have our own little family mystery, and since we are playing a waiting game, we'd like to search her house for old pictures or journals."

"No."

"If we're both there and armed and the alarm is on, it should be fine. You could even post someone outside if you wanted to."

"Absolutely not."

"We could be bait, perhaps."

"Jack, I really like you both, and there's no way I'm going to take a chance like that."

"Think about it. Are we any safer here? No guards, no alarm, Sam sleeping upstairs with only a flimsy lock between her and whoever wants to get in our room."

Mick stood up fast and knocked over his coffee.

"Sit back down, Mick. I'm not trying to freak you out. I'm just pointing out that you would have more control over the circumstances at the ranch."

"Get some breakfast, and I'll think about it."

They ate without much conversation, then Jack went to see about getting breakfast and coffee for Sam.

Mick looked at the heaping plate Jack was carrying and said, "Does she really eat that much? I don't know if I can afford her." He laughed.

"First, don't ever let her hear you say something like that. She'd probably knock you down a peg. Second, she might have a hangover appetite. It's best to be prepared."

"Well then, let's go brave the lioness in her den."

Jack knocked and stuck his head in. Sam just groaned and pulled her covers over her head."Sam? I have coffee… and a Bloody Mary, and Mick's with me."

Sam sat up fast and grabbed her head.

Mick thought, I'd marry her today, even if I'd never met her.

Jack laughed at her. "You look like a little kid!"

"Shut up and give me the Bloody Mary." Then she caught sight of herself in the dresser mirror. "No wonder you're laughing. Not all of us can wake up beautiful." She stuck her tongue out at Jack and took a swig of delicious, tomatoey tonic.

178

"I think you look beautiful!" Mick blurted out. Then both blushed, and Jack laughed again.

"I think he's a keeper," Jack said. "Hair sticking out at all angles, wrinkled sheet impression across your cheek, and... he leaned closer, is that dried drool on the side of your mouth?"

"I am this close to throwing my hangover remedy in your face. Be gone!" she commanded with a wave of her hand.

They laughed.

"So, Mick. Did Jack run our proposal by you?"

"I wasn't sure you'd even remember that conversation."

"I wasn't that drunk."

"Hmm."

"I wasn't!"

"Yes, he did," Mick interjected, thinking they acted more like siblings than cousins.

"And?" Sam looked him in the eye.

"I don't want anything to happen to you."

"Granted. I don't want anything to happen to me either, but if we are together, inside, with the alarm on, we should be fine, right?"

"Remember the twin and the house fire?"

"Think about it this way," Sam said, "Steven is out of the picture right now. If we can trap the twin, we can figure this out once and for all. If he doesn't take the bait, we still get to look for clues to our family mystery. The twin might be the one you have locked up, and Steven might want to talk."

"Augh! You two are going to drive me crazy. How can I say no?"

Sam smiled sweetly.

"You should fix your hair," he said gruffly. Then in answer to Sam's sad look, he said, "It's giving me impure thoughts."

He turned and walked out the door.

Mick was back in the restaurant with coffee and a piece of pie. He felt like a complete idiot.

"Why didn't you stop me?" he moaned to Jack when he came downstairs.

"There was no stopping you. That was brilliant."

Mick glared at him.

"I'm serious. You totally took her by surprise and made her see you in a new light."

"She wasn't mad?"

"She didn't even get it at first." Jack laughed.

"And she didn't look disgusted?"

"I didn't see any evidence of disgust."

"Thanks. I know she's your cousin and all, but she looked sexy as hell. My thoughts came out of my mouth before I could stop them."

"She doesn't see herself that way. She thinks she's a no-nonsense cowgirl; no makeup, no frills, short hair. Her only concession is the bright red hair color. Any idea what color her natural hair is?"

"No idea. I know her skin is naturally very light because she has a farmer's tan, and her eyes are green, so…"

"Our fathers were both Mexican, so chances are her hair is brown."

"Who are we talking about?" Sam asked, sitting down at the table. "Can I have a bite of your pie?"

Mick gave her a bite and watched as she closed her eyes to savor it.

"Mmm," she said. "So who?"

"You, actually," Jack said. "I was wondering what color your hair is under the red."

"We may never know." Sam smiled. "I was thinking of changing it. I dyed it red to prove I was a girl."

"The girl thing is pretty obvious," Mick said.

"What I mean is, other girls started wearing makeup and high heels, but I didn't have a mom to show me that stuff, and my dad thought it was dumb. So, one day when I was at the hairdressers, I saw a photo in a magazine and asked Georgia if she could make my hair look like the photo.

180

I just meant the color, but she thought I meant the style. I cried when I first saw it, but once I got used to it, I loved it."

"It suits you," Jack said.

Sam smiled. "I'm just getting a little tired of the red. I kind of like the color of your fancy little car."

"It is a nice color," Jack said.

"I like the red," Mick interjected. "But the blue-green might bring out the color of your eyes."

Sam smiled at that too. "I need more coffee. Did you guys come up with a plan?"

"Nope," Jack said.

"I'll check in with Steven and call the hospital, then we can drive out to the ranch. Please stay together, and I'll be back shortly."

When Mick got back, Sam and Jack had moved from the restaurant to the bar.

"Do you two ever do anything besides eat and drink?"

"Nope!" Sam said with her impish grin.

"We've packed up and checked out. Does that count?" Jack asked.

"I suppose so." Mick rolled his eyes. "Are you ready to go?"

"Not quite. Don't you have some updates to share?" Sam looked at him expectantly.

"Well…" He paused when he saw Sam waving at the waitress with two fingers.

"What? Carry on."

"I checked in with Steven. He's a little grumpy because you didn't stop by, and he's still refusing a blood test."

"That is interesting," she said.

"I'll drop you off at the ranch. I have a deputy stationed, out of sight, hopefully."

"Can you drop us at the station instead, since both my trucks are there?"

"Sure. Can we go now?"

"What are you waiting for?"

As he turned to leave, she asked Jack, "Did he just roll his eyes at me? Hey, Sergeant, are you rolling your eyes at me?"

He turned and put his hands on her shoulders, put his stubbly face very close to hers, and whispered, "If you don't stop it, I'm going to kiss you right here in front of God and everyone." Then he turned and walked out of the bar, leaving her wide-eyed and a little breathless.

"You asked for it." Jack chuckled as he passed her.

Everyone rode in the front, with Sam in the middle, right next to Mick, who was pretty muscular, she found. *Do I like Mick? He's nice, smart, patient, honest, kind of hot, looks at me like I'm chocolate cake, and I just got excited when he got in my face. He has really nice lips. What is wrong with me!?*

"Are you okay?"

"Yeah, did I miss something?"

"I was telling Mick about our treasure hunt, and he offered to help with some research."

"That's nice of you. Thank you."

Mick squinted at her. *Why is she being so polite? Have I scared her?* "Be careful," he said when he dropped them off.

Jack gave him a nod, then told Sam he'd follow her home with the second truck.

Chapter 25

When they arrived home, Sam whispered, "I don't see a deputy.".

"I think that's the point," Jack whispered back. "Let's get in the house and reset the alarm."

"Should we look around and make sure no one's in here?"

"The alarm was set, so I don't know how there could be, but we can if it makes you feel safer."

"I'm feeling pretty creeped out. I think I'll keep my gun with me."

"Not a bad idea. We can check each room and end with the one we're going to start in."

Sam nodded and followed him around. "This is the first time I've ever been nervous entering my own house."

Once they searched the entire house, including the closets, showers, and under the beds, Sam pointed to the attic door. "I haven't been up there since I was little."

"Well, let's check it out." Jack pulled on the string, and stairs gently slid down.

"You go first."

"You're the one with the gun."

"You want it?"

"No, thank you." Jack laughed. He climbed up quickly to get past his nerves. "All clear. Is there a light switch?"

"I think so. Do we need a flashlight?"

"No, there's natural light and a lot of dust." He sneezed.

Sam joined him at the top of the stairs. "I think I remember a hanging light with a string. Here." She pulled the string and turned a bright bulb on.

"Much better." Jack looked around. "What is all this stuff?" He saw piles of boxes, toys, decorations, and a rack of dresses. "It looks like a rummage sale."

"I don't know what all's here. A lot of it seems irrelevant to our treasure hunt, though. We're looking for photos, documents, or journals, right?"

"Yeah."

They searched for an hour before Jack said, "Sam! Over here! Look at these!"

"Photo albums?"

"Yes! Look inside."

"Is that us? We were just babies."

"There are our fathers riding together, drinking beer, and barbecuing. Our moms hugging and laughing. It looks like we were one big happy family."

"So what happened? How many years do these pictures continue?"

They flipped through several books until they got to the last one; it was only half full.

"Oh, look. The funeral. Two caskets. There's me and my dad and gran."

"My father. Angry and stoic. He stayed that way for the rest of his life."

"Is that you?"

Jack looked at the picture of himself as an eight-year-old boy. He looked so lonely and sad. "There was no more love or joy in my house after that day. I wasn't allowed to grieve her or even speak of her. I blocked it all out so the pain would stop. I can remember you now, seeing these pictures. You were such a spunky little kid."

"Why don't I remember? I was five. I should remember something."

"I don't know. Maybe it will come back gradually. I still don't know why my father was so angry like it was your dad's fault. He never spoke of him again either. When I lost Alley, it felt like I lost my mom all over again, and I was finally allowed to grieve. That unconditional love and happiness I felt from her was what I lost when my mom died." He stared at a photo of himself and his mother. I can almost feel her hug.

"I don't know the right words to say, but I'll always be here for you."

He smiled sadly at Sam. "My father was not the most loving parent, but I'll always be grateful to him for sending me here to find you."

Suddenly tears were sliding down her face. "Jack-o. That's what I called you. And you used to give me piggyback rides. I remember now. I lost my mom and you on the same day, and I can remember crying at night because I missed you."

They sat together, quietly looking at pictures of their childhood and reliving fond memories until the phone rang downstairs, and they both jumped.

"It might be important," Jack said as he raced for the stairs. The phone had stopped ringing by the time they got to it, but Jack grabbed it when it started again a second later.

"Hi, Jack. I wasn't able to contact the deputy on duty, so I wanted to tell you to be careful, and I'm on my way."

"Thanks, Mick. See you soon."

He hung up the phone. "Let's close up the attic for now and go look around your dad's room. Mick's on his way."

"Why did he call?"

"He couldn't get a hold of the deputy. I'll run up and turn off the light."

"I left my gun up there. Could you grab it for me?"

They wandered into Sam senior's room. "I feel a little safer in here, for some reason. The attic always seems a little scary," Sam confided.

"That's probably my fault," Jack said sheepishly. "You were being a brat one day, and I locked you in there. When our parents found out about it, I was in a lot of trouble, and I felt really bad because you were crying."

"Maybe if I remember that, my irrational fear will go away."

"Maybe," he said doubtfully. "Childhood trauma can cause funny reactions. We can clean it up and make new memories there." He looked around his uncle's room, noting the bookshelves and the large desk. The room itself was light and airy, making the heavy furniture and dark fabrics seem out of place.

"Where should we look first?"

"His desk seems like a logical starting place."

"There's a lot of stuff here. I hope I didn't miss anything important."

"It's been a year, right? I'm sure anything immediate has been taken care of."

Sam turned suddenly. "What was that?"

"What?"

Someone was knocking on the door, so they tiptoed down and looked around the corner through the kitchen. Mick was standing there, holding Anita upright. Jack took one look at her and flung the door open. "Come in! What happened?"

"I'm not sure yet. I knew this wasn't a good idea."

Deputy Flores groaned, and they all focused on her.

"Deputy? Can you hear me?" Jack quickly felt for a pulse.

She opened her eyes and started. "Where am I?"

"You're in Sam's house. Do you remember what happened?"

"Someone was coming, so I moved to stay out of sight, and I tripped on something. I must have hit my head

186

I felt someone lift me and lay me down somewhere. They checked my ankle and my head, then left."

"They didn't hurt you?"

"No, they made sure I was alright."

"Interesting," Jack said. "How do you feel now?"

"My head hurts, but I'm okay, I think."

"Let me just check your pupils. Can you follow my finger?" He turned to Mick. "We'll need to assume she has a concussion since she hit her head. I'll get her an ice pack. Can you make sure she stays awake?"

"I'm sorry to be so much trouble," Anita said. "You can take me over to my mom's house, Sergeant. She'll keep an eye on me."

"Why don't the two of you stay for dinner? Then we can take you to your mother's," Sam suggested. "I can make some chili."

The next day, Sam and Jack drove into town to visit Melissa. She was still under medical supervision at the hospital, but she was showered and dressed, sitting at the window with a sketchpad. Melissa smiled when she saw them and hugged them both. "You came!"

"Yes, of course."

"You didn't yesterday."

"We had a little emergency yesterday. It sounds like you'll be discharged soon."

"Yes, I'm so happy to be returning to the sources of my energy."

"And what would those be?" Jack asked.

"My crystals." She smiled and hugged herself.

Sam looked at Jack surreptitiously. "Did you have any of those at home?" she asked Melissa.

"I have dozens of them!"

"Are they valuable?"

"They are to me. I have spent years letting them find me."

"I meant monetarily."

"Not really. I used to tease poor Ara and tell him they were my treasure. He thought Peter was my sugar daddy."

"Are you staying occupied? Do you need me to bring you anything?" Sam asked.

"Actually, they are letting me lead some classes for long-term patients, drawing and flower arranging, and small tours around the hospital gardens. It's fun for me and helps the other patients focus on life and beauty rather than illness and death."

Melissa talked more about her plans to continue teaching at the hospital and her shop after she was discharged.

"You are one amazing lady," Sam said. She gave Melissa a hug. "I'll see you tomorrow, sis. Sleep well."

"Thanks for coming. I am feeling much more positive."

"By the way," Jack asked, "did you happen to have any water hemlock at home?"

Melissa tilted her head to the side. "I'm not sure. I sometimes ground up the roots at home because I have to be so careful with it, but I always kept it in a clearly labeled, sealed container."

"What did you use it for?"

"It can be used for skin conditions and inflammation in very small amounts. I sometimes make salves with it."

"Thank you," Jack said. "See you soon."

As they walked back out to the truck, Sam said, "We need to talk to Ara. There weren't any crystals at Melissa's house."

Jack thought about that for a minute. "I guess that would be okay. We should notify Mick, though."

"Let's check in with him afterward, then we can hear what he found, too."

"You're just afraid he'll tell us not to."

Sam smiled impishly. "Onward, James."

"You're driving. That would make you James."

"Can't get much by you," Sam said, giving him a light punch in the arm.

Sam knocked on Ara's door, and he answered in his robe and duckie slippers. The apartment looked slightly more organized.

"Oh, hello, Sam and Jack. Come in."

"Did we catch you at a bad time?" Sam asked.

"No, no." He looked down. "I always work in my house coat."

"How are things? Is Emily doing okay now?"

"She has moved in with Mark. The financial burden is lessened."

"Do you miss her?"

"Not really, no."

"Have you spoken to Melissa?"

"I had this fantasy built up in my head. I thought even though I'm a geek, I had met this gorgeous, perfect woman who wanted sex with me all the time. All of it was a lie. Everything."

"What about the baby?" Sam asked gently.

"She doesn't want it. I don't know how to take care of a baby. He will end up like me, in foster care." His head hung in defeat.

"Maybe not. You never know what will happen. The real Melissa is very different from the one you met. Perhaps you should try to get to know her."

Ara nodded. "I will take your advice."

"May I ask you something?"

He looked up.

"Do you happen to have Melissa's crystals?"

"Yes. Another lie. She told me that they were her treasure. But they are worth almost nothing."

"Did you need money that badly?"

"No, I wanted revenge on Peter. I stole his woman and his treasure. But it was all lies."

"Ara, those crystals really are Melissa's treasure. They're very important to her. If you let me have them, I could return them to her."

Chapter 26

Mick was waiting for them when they got back to the ranch. "That took a while. Learn anything new?"

"Yes. Let's grab a beer and compare notes," Jack said.

"I suppose I'm technically off the clock."

"It seems like you're always working, Mick."

"I'm kind of unofficially on-call round the clock when we have an active investigation."

"I'm just going to check in with Roger. I'll be back in a minute."

Jack and Mick walked toward the house.

As Sam walked across the cinder drive, a rusty pickup truck screeched to a halt in front of her. The driver grabbed her arm and propelled her into the truck before taking off in a cloud of dust.

Mick heard Sam shout and raced toward the driveway, Jack right behind him. The plume of dust showed the direction of the speeding vehicle, and Jack ran for Sam's truck while Mick called for backup before following. He didn't know who had kidnapped Sam or if Jack was armed, but he was certain Sam's life was in danger.

Inside the speeding pickup truck, Sam's heart was pounding, but she tried to hide her fear. She looked at Steven and screamed, "Are you out of your mind?"

"My mom wants to talk to you."

She held on for dear life as he flew down the primitive dirt roads, sending dirt and rocks flying behind them. Every pothole he hit bounced her on the seat and jarred her ribs and back. "What is wrong with you? Are you a psychopath or something?"

"Shut up!" Steven hit her in the face with the back of his hand.

She blinked back tears from the pain, needing to stay in control of her emotions, and felt blood on her lip. "You told me you were mad at Peter because no man should ever hit a woman."

His jaw stiffened. "I also told you to shut up! Next time it will be my fist," he growled.

Sam slid closer to the truck door, trying to get some distance between them.

"Don't even think about jumping out. I will run over your skinny ass and throw you back in the truck. A little blood doesn't bother me at all."

Sam was pretty sure this wasn't the Steven she knew; at least, she hoped it wasn't. *This guy is going to kill me.*

Forty minutes later, Steven took a sharp turn onto a narrow dirt driveway and stopped in front of a dilapidated, single-wide mobile home. It had once been white, Sam guessed, but it was so dirty she couldn't be sure. Steven got out and yelled, "We're here, mama." There was no answer except the broken screen door swinging in the breeze. "Get out," he said. "Mama!"

Sam pulled a small pistol out of her boot and cocked it as she walked around the truck. When he could see her, she cocked the gun and said, "Give me the keys." Her voice was steady and her eyes glinted dangerously.

"No." He looked around. "Mamaaa! I need backup."

"I will shoot you, and my aim is good."

"No, you won't." He lunged at her and he was fast, but she shot him in the right leg to slow him down. She knew she was supposed to go for mass if she had to shoot, but she didn't want to kill him. Her aim was true, and he yelled, "Augh! You bitch!".

"Give me the keys, now!" Sam was yelling partly from adrenaline and partly because the gun made her ears ring. Her shoulder ached from the recoil, and she wanted to be safe.

Steven squinted at her, breathing heavily, then lunged again, and she shot him in the left knee. He sat down hard and put the keys under him. "You'll have to kill me to get them."

The screen door banged loudly, startling Sam. She shooed gnats away from her face and looked up to see a middle-aged woman with a shotgun, looking unsteady on her feet.

"You must be Victoria." The woman did not look well. Middle-aged and dirty, Sam could smell her from the driveway. "Are you okay?"

"Never mind that. Why are you messin' with my boy?" She lifted the shotgun, which looked heavy, and wobbled as she took a shot at Sam. Her aim was poor, but shotguns were like horseshoes and hand grenades. Sam ducked behind the truck, but the ringing in her ears intensified. Her whole body trembled. "Put the gun down, Victoria!"

Victoria leaned her weight against the railing and aimed again, so Sam shot her in the shoulder. Victoria let the shotgun drop to her side, put her hand on her shoulder, and then stood there panting. "That's it, son. I can't hold the gun no more. I need another drink. You finish her off." She hobbled across the porch and let the door slam behind her.

Sam was staring after her when she felt a hard tug on her ankle. She fell and hit her head on the gravel, her gun landing out of her reach. She shook her head, trying to clear her vision. Steven had drug himself over while she was occupied with his mother and was trying to use her boot to pull himself closer. If he got close enough, she wouldn't have the strength to fight him off. She couldn't hear what he was saying, but the look on his face scared her more than anything she had ever seen. His pupils were dilated and his lips were pulled back, lending a feral look to his clenched teeth. He was sweating profusely and reminded her of a rabid dog. Sam's adrenaline surged, and she began yelling and kicking hard and fast with the heels of her boots.

Jack raced up the driveway and jumped out of Sam's truck as her right boot connected with Steven's nose.

He howled and let go of her boot to hold his nose with both hands.

Sam was hyperventilating when Jack reached her, and she fought him off as he tried to help her up.

"Sam! Sam, it's me. Let me help you."

She pulled with her arms and pushed with her feet until she had scrabbled a safe distance from Steven. Finally registering Jack's presence and realizing she was safe, she stopped fighting him. "Mom... shotgun... inside." Sam pointed before she passed out.

Mick was right on Jack's heels but didn't interfere with his interaction with Sam. Instead, he cuffed Steven and waved to a medivac helicopter arriving from Las Rodillas. After Sam passed out, Jack looked at him. His eyes were flicking back and forth and he was breathing hard. "Are you alright, Doc?"

"I'm not sure." Jack put his hand to his chest then bent over with his hands on his knees. "Sam pointed at the house and said..." Jack took a couple of breaths. "Victoria's in the house with a shotgun." His breathing was becoming more normal. "We should check it out."

"No, you stay here with Sam. Let me handle it."

Mick called his deputies and cautiously approached the door. "Sheriff!" he called out. "Open up!" He didn't get a response, and the door wasn't locked, so he moved along the entryway with his gun out and his back along the wall. He swung around the corner and saw Victoria lying on the kitchen floor. He wasn't sure what was wrong with her, but she looked much like Melissa had when Sam found her, and she had a glass and a bottle of alcohol nearby. "Bag the glass and the bottle, Flores. I'll be back in a sec."

Mick ran outside and flagged down one of the medics from the helicopter. "You'll have two passengers. The other is in the house. She may need her stomach pumped. And do you have an extra blanket?" He took the blanket to Jack and helped him wrap Sam in it and move her to the backseat of her truck. "

Why don't you go ahead and get her to the hospital? I'll stop by later after I take care of this mess."

"Thanks, Mick," Jack said before peeling out of the driveway toward town.

Mick went back into the house, rubbing his hands over his face. *Looks like an all-nighter.*

Chapter 27

Sam drifted in and out through the night. She vaguely remembered nurses coming in to check on her. They gave her medication for the pain and were there to soothe her when she woke, terrified from her dreams. She could still see the evil in Steven's face and feel the panic welling up inside her when she closed her eyes.

When she awoke the next afternoon, Jack was sitting in a metal folding chair by her bed. "Sounds like we're lucky you're such a fighter."

"Jack! I'm glad you're here."

He smiled softly. "I've been here for a while. I snuck you in some food if you're hungry. I think you missed a couple of meals."

"I might be a little hungry. What happened after you came to Victoria's?"

He leaned forward and handed her a paper bag. "I thought you might want to know about that. Why don't you eat and I'll tell you the whole story. I brought you a selection because I wasn't sure what you could manage."

"What is all this?" she asked, looking in the bag. "Pudding? A banana? A quesadilla? Tater tots?"

"Don't question. Just eat. Eat whatever sounds good to you, and if you need more, I'll go get it."

"You're the best, Jack!" Her hands trembled slightly as she peeled the banana.

"I got to the house last night, just as you broke Steven's nose. You were kicking hard to keep his hands off your boots and one of your heels connected.

Once you realized you were safe, you pointed at the house and indicated I should check it out, then you passed out."

"I was so scared."

"I can't even imagine. I'm sorry it took me so long to get there."

"It's better that you didn't. It would have just put you in danger too." Sam shivered. "What happened after that?"

"Mick arrived shortly after I did, and after he cuffed Steven, he went inside and found his mom passed out on the kitchen floor. Her glass was nearby, so Mick bagged it and sent it to Byron. He told the helicopter team that they would need to transport two people to the hospital and asked if they had a mobile lab. Steven was yelling about his mom and asking what had happened. Mick wrapped you in a blanket and put you in the backseat of your truck, so I could get you checked out at the hospital."

"I don't know who that was, but it wasn't Steven. That guy was a bad dude."

Jack nodded. "Even if he wasn't in custody, I don't think he'll be walking around any time soon."

"Did they find any evidence in the house?"

"Yes. Byron is at the lab working feverishly. We'll see what he finds out soon enough. Get some more rest, and they'll discharge you tomorrow."

"Thanks, Jack. Could you ask Father Garcia to stop by?"

"Of course."

"You get some rest too. And thank you for the tasty breakfast... lunch?" She smiled crookedly before dozing off again.

Jack left her room, placed a call to the priest, and went in search of the on-call doctor.

"Hello, I'm Jack Olivares," he said, shaking his hand.

"Nice to finally meet you, Dr. Olivares. I've heard a lot about you. I'm Daniel Wolf."

"I was wondering if I could speak with the patient who was brought in last night with a gunshot wound and an overdose."

"Ah, yes. Is this part of the official inquiry?"

"Yes, Dr. Wolf. I believe Sergeant Mickelson is working on a court order for her current medical records, but I just wanted to ask her a couple questions if she's well enough."

"Come with me. I'll just look in on her first and see how she's doing."

Dr. Wolf stepped into the room for a moment, then returned. "Ms. Hale said she doesn't mind having company. Try not to excite her and terminate the visit if she starts getting tired."

They walked in, and Jack noted that Victoria looked significantly better than she had the night before. "Hello, Ms. Hale. How are you feeling?" Jack asked.

"Well, I have a bullet wound, and I've just found out my son has been poisoning my booze, so I'm not very happy."

"Do you know which son did that?"

"They are twins, but one is good and one is bad. Cain and Abel. I know which one."

How cryptic. "Did the bad son drug your drink?"

"Of course."

"What did you name your boys?"

"Andrew and John."

"Is John the good son?"

"Oh, no. That would be Andrew. I wish he would come see me."

Jack blinked in surprise. "He will soon. How do you tell them apart?"

"Mostly how they act, but there's differences if you see 'em both at once."

Jack decided to try a different tact. "Did you know Peter Sloan is dead?"

"Why would I care about that?"

"Because he was your sons' father?"

"I wasn't allowed to talk about that. It was a secret," she said, folding her arms.

"Can you tell me why you were trying to shoot Sam Olivares?"

Victoria glared at him. "Who are you again?"

"I'm the Chief Medical Examiner."

"Well, chief medical examiner, I don't think I have to tell you that. I'm tired now. You should leave." She rolled onto her side, facing away from him.

Jack could see they were done, so he shrugged and went to find Dr. Wolf.

The next time Sam opened her eyes, Father Garcia was sitting by the window in her room. He approached the side of the bed. "Hello, Samantha. How are you feeling?"

Sam's smile didn't quite meet her eyes. "Emotionally or physically?"

He put the tips of his fingers together. "Let's start with emotionally."

Sam leaned forward in her bed. "Imagine, if you will, sitting in a truck with someone you thought you knew and seeing evil in his eyes; real evil. Not only does he hit you in the face and threaten to run over you if you jump out, but his eyes are completely void of humanity."

"That must have been horrifying. What did you do?"

"I recited the 23rd Psalm to myself and asked God for strength and guidance."

He nodded. "Did that help?"

"It did. My head was clear until the end. I hit my head and went a little nuts."

"Well done, my dear. It sounds like your faith may have saved your life."

"I fired my gun at two people. I haven't ever done that before. I was trying hard not to kill them, just to defend myself. I don't know if I could have… the whole thing was terrifying."

"It's a very difficult position to be put in. I'm thankful that you don't have to deal with taking a life. Are the people who kidnapped you badly hurt?"

"One of them is. I shot him in the knee. He just kept coming at me, and I didn't know how to make him stop." Sam began to shake again, reliving the fear.

"You're looking a little tired, Samantha. Why don't we say a prayer of thanksgiving together, and you can rest."

Sam nodded sleepily. She listened to Father Garcia pray and felt gratitude in her heart as she sank into a peaceful sleep.

Jack decided to visit Byron at the lab rather than sit around the house by himself. Mick was there as well.

Byron was clearly excited, practically bouncing on his toes. "You will not believe what I found. Where to begin?" he muttered, pacing the room. "You know that we found long blonde hairs at Peter's and Melissa's, right? And the DNA showed ten of the primary markers which show that the owner of the hair was closely related to Peter?"

"Yes?" Jack waited patiently.

Dr. Vanzandt brought up a Powerpoint slide, sat on a tall stool, and continued, "We now have John and Andrew's fingerprints and blood samples. Andrew's are a match for the fingerprint and DNA on the condom from Melissa's house. His fingerprints, along with his mother's and John's, are all over the trailer. The fingerprint on Victoria's vodka is Johns's."

"Can you tell us more about the twins?" Jack asked.

"Yes, Andrew, the man who kidnapped Sam, grew up in Texas. John grew up in California and is wanted for desertion."

"Do either of them have an alibi for the times the murders were committed?"

"That's difficult since no one seems to know which twin they saw when," Mick said.

"And their mother, Victoria?" Jack asked.

Byron swung around and said, "Her medical records show a long history of moderately severe mental illness, and a blood test shows that she is the twins' mother."

"Was she any help?" Mick asked. "You spoke to her at the hospital, right?"

"She claims she can tell them apart and calls them the good son and the bad son." Jack took a deep breath.

"We're getting there," Mick said.

"What did you find in the trailer?"

"What didn't we find? We found a journal, along with a bag of crushed plant matter and a hairbrush. Those were in the master bedroom."

"We need to find out if Melissa can tell them apart. If she can identify *her* Steven then—"

"She was so drugged toward the end, a jury might not believe her," Mick interrupted.

"Has anyone read the journal?" Jack asked.

"I looked at it, but it's not a regular journal. It looks more like the ravings of a lunatic. There are formulas and abbreviations, phrases like 'I hate her! She deserves to die!' crude drawings, scribbles. I've given it to our forensic psychologist to see if she can decipher it," Mick said.

"Arrange to have everyone meet at the hospital at ten the day after tomorrow; that way, everyone can be there. I'll give you a list."

"I don't see what good it will do," Mick said.

"Trust me." Jack smiled.

The next day, Sam was sitting up watching TV when Jack knocked softly on the door. "Jack!" She smiled. "What do you have there?"

"I have illicit snacks. How are you feeling?"

"I'm fine now. Can't I go home?"

"I'll ask the doctor."

"Do you have any more information about the brothers?" she asked quietly.

"Yes, I wasn't sure if you'd want to hear about them."

"I need to." She looked away from him, out the window. "I can't get his face out of my head. It wasn't Steven, was it?"

"His name is Andrew. The man you know as Steven is actually named John."

Sam shuddered.

"We'll be having a meeting tomorrow morning to go over all of the information. I have some paperwork to look at, then I'll come back and hopefully take you home." He smiled and squeezed her hand.

Jack looked back at Sam as he left her room. Physically she was fine, but he suspected it would take a while for her to get over what had happened. He had pieced together most of the puzzle, but he didn't yet completely understand the why. He put it on the back burner and went to the chart room to confer with Dr. Wolf.

They sat together, looking over Victoria Hale's medical records. She had a long record of psychiatric treatment both before and after the birth of her twin sons. A blood sample and fingerprints had been sent to Byron. The records dated back to childhood and began with general height and weight, milestones, and vaccines.

At age ten, there was an entry that read:

Tentative diagnosis of Bipolar disorder. Patient referred to
Dr. Allen in Las Rodillas.

There was no further mention of her mental health until she became pregnant. At age twenty-three, the entry read:

Pregnancy at 16 weeks. Attempted suicide. Referred to Sacred
Heart for inpatient care.

I'll need to get a court order for the records at Sacred Heart. "Do you think she was taking the Ambien, or was it added to her alcohol by someone else?" He asked Dr. Wolf.

"From what she said, I believe someone else added it, but I don't have any real way of knowing that. She is pretty unstable right now."

"I've asked everyone involved in this case to attend a meeting tomorrow and would be grateful if you could accompany her."

"Of course. We might like to have an orderly with us as well."

Jack nodded. "Thank you. For everything. Also, Sam has asked if she can go home this evening."

Dr. Wolf stroked his small mustache. "I think that should be fine. She seems completely recovered. Just try to encourage her to rest."

"Try being the operative word." Jack smiled.

Chapter 28

The following morning, Sam was at the hospital early with a coffee from the cafe. Mick was there looking haggard. His uniform was wrinkled, and he had a day's beard growth, but he had a determined look in his eyes.

"Good morning, beautiful," he said without much enthusiasm. "How are you feeling?"

"I might feel how you look. When was the last time you slept?"

He shrugged. "I'm not sure. A couple of days ago, maybe."

Sam put her hand on his arm and looked him in the eye. "Thank you for coming to the rescue."

He couldn't hold her gaze but said, "It's my job. But I would have been... really upset if anything had happened to you."

"I've never been so scared in my life."

"But you kept your head and defended yourself. We could use you on the force."

Sam figured he was kidding, but she blushed anyway. "Thanks, but I don't want to be in that situation ever again. What's going on this morning?"

"I don't know. Jack's got something cooking."

"Are you talking about me?" Jack said from behind them.

They both turned. He was practically crackling with energy. Sam had never seen him so sure and focused.

"Is everyone here?" he asked.

"Except our three patients."

"Let's go into the meeting room then. You've placed the name cards?"

"Yes," Mick said wearily.

Jack stood on one side of the room, in front of a whiteboard. John was brought in by one of the deputies, who sat with him next to Emily. The others moved uncomfortably, wondering why he was in handcuffs. Andrew was brought into the room in a wheelchair by another deputy and placed between John and Ara.

When John saw him, he lunged, placing his cuffed hands around Andrew's throat. Everyone seated nearby got out of their seats and moved away as fast as they could. "You tried to kill her!"

"I didn't. Mom just wanted to talk to her. Look what she did to me!"

The deputies separated them quickly as they glared at each other.

Once everyone had regained their seats, Melissa walked in of her own accord and sat next to Sam. She took her hand and looked around at the others in the room, doing a double-take when she saw the twins.

Finally, Victoria was wheeled in by an orderly accompanied by Dr. Wolf. Captain Blatt followed them in and stood by the door with his arms folded in front of him.

Every eye was on Jack as he walked across the room. He stood tall in a suit and tie, exuding an air of authority and confidence. "We have had two murders, two attempted murders, and an abduction in Santo Milagro, along with a lot of unnecessary confusion caused by lies and false information. Before we begin, Ms. Hale, are you able to tell us which of your sons is 'the good son?' Andrew?"

Victoria sat up straight with an air of importance. "Of course I am. I know my own sons. That's my good son." She pointed to the twin on the left, with the bandaged knees and a broken nose.

"Mama. I thought we talked about this," he hissed. "She can't tell us apart."

Jack ignored him and focused on Victoria. "Why do you call him the good son?"

"Because he minds his mama."

"Thank you very much." Jack walked to the other side of the room. "Melissa, can you tell us which brother you refer to as *your* Steven?"

She tilted her head slightly. "Yes. Can I touch them to make sure?"

"Yes."

Captain Blatt walked around the table with her as she approached the twins. She outlined Johns's head and shoulders with her hands, feeling his aura, then put her arms around his shoulders and nose in his hair, near his ear, and he stiffened. "You were at the race track." Then she did the same to Andrew, and when he tried to push her away, she said, "This is my Steven. I would know his chemistry and his dark aura anywhere."

"Can't you ever keep your mouth shut?" he growled.

"Thank you, Melissa."

She squeezed past Ara, Mark, and Sam, closely followed by Captain Blatt. When she was once again seated, Jack said, "Let's go back to the beginning, now. A year ago, Melissa was seeing Stephen to hide her relationship with her best friend's father, Mr. Olivares. Is this correct?"

"Yes," Melissa said, glancing sadly at Sam.

"When Mr. Olivares died from a heart attack, you thought it was your fault."

Melissa nodded. "Then Peter showed up with photos and threatened to show them to Sam. I don't have much money, so he took his payment in other ways." Melissa shuddered.

"Meanwhile, Peter was also blackmailing Mark, correct?"

Mark drew himself up. "Don't be ridiculous!"

"We have the photographs. There aren't any more secrets." Jack said sternly.

"Fine." His shoulders slumped. He caught me cutting corners and forced me to call in slightly delinquent loans early so he could buy property inexpensively or offer to take over the loan and charge very high interest."

"That is what he did to Emily. Correct?"

"Yes," Mark and Emily said at the same time.

"Emily moved in with her brother Ararat to decrease expenses, but you also had reason to hate Peter, didn't you?" Jack walked over and looked at him pointedly.

Ara nodded but didn't say anything.

"You blamed him for what happened to your family."

"Yes. I lost everything because of him. I wanted him to feel the pain of losing someone he loved, so I decided to steal his woman."

"That would be Melissa."

Melissa leaned forward to look at him. "You were *using* me?" she asked in a high-pitched voice.

"Yes," he looked at her pleadingly. "But then I fell in love with you."

"You stole her crystals, thinking they were from Peter and valuable," Jack said.

He nodded. "Sam told me they were important to you, though, so I took them back to your house."

"Unbelievable," Melissa muttered.

"I don't know what this has to do with me," John said.

"You will." Jack sipped his coffee. "My point is that all of you hated Peter, and with good reason."

Everyone nodded.

"Recently, we had several catalysts." Jack made bullet points on the whiteboard as he spoke:

"Victoria tried to get Peter to meet his sons.

"The night of the charity ball, Victoria witnessed a fight between Peter and Andrew.

"John became interested in Sam, but she thought he was dating Melissa.

"Andrew got back together with Melissa and began mixing Ambien in her carafe of whiskey.

"Ara began his campaign for Melissa's affection and was unknowingly assisted by the Ambien cocktail."

Jack paused and looked at Andrew. "Since you are the *good* son, I'm guessing you got the bag of roots for your mother. Why did she say she wanted them?"

"I don't know what you're talking about," he growled.

"Are you talking about the *water hemlock* roots?" Melissa asked with horror.

Jack nodded.

"Victoria buys a salve from me for her arthritis. I've explained to her how dangerous the plant is and told her to never try using it full strength."

Jack paced with his hand on his chin. "She sent Andrew to your house for the bag of roots and suggested he put some Ambien in your whiskey so you wouldn't argue."

"Steven? That can't be true." She looked at him. "Why would you drug me? I almost died."

He didn't say anything, just looked away.

"At least he gave you an alibi," Jack said with a raised eyebrow. "Peter was murdered with those roots while you were staying at Sam's ranch."

"Is that why you told me to go stay with her?"

"Will you shut up?"

"One of John's hairs was left at the murder scene, but since you share DNA, we couldn't get a match without more information."

"One of my hairs?" John asked. "Someone was trying to frame me. I have never even been to Peter's house."

Jack ignored him. "Once Peter was dead, your mother felt free to tell the two of you he was your father and that you would inherit everything. She told you to find his safe, so when Melissa went back home, you got her to tell you where it was by saying you could get the photos back. Correct?"

Stephen said, "Of course not!"

Melissa nodded. "Yes."

"Quit lying, you stupid cow!"

She glared at him. "Did you ever love me?"

"Maybe. Before I saw the pictures of you with that old guy."

Sam squeezed Melissa's hand.

"To continue, I believe John went to Peter's house, opened up the safe, and took everything to his mother's. All of you were angry about the will, especially Victoria, but Andrew, you saw the pictures of Melissa and were furious. You were already drugging her, but that's when your cruelty toward her increased. Correct?"

Victoria started to laugh, "Like anyone would admit to that."

Jack shrugged. "Carrying on, Andrew went to add more Ambien to the carafe and left one picture of each person on the kitchen table. Ara saw the pictures and thought he could make a little extra money. He delivered blackmail letters to Sam, Mark, and Alley that night. Correct?"

"I didn't leave any pictures. That must have been him." He pointed to John.

"Don't try to throw me under the bus! That was all you."

Jack looked at Ara, who paused and cringed, but then nodded. "It was just an experiment."

"The next afternoon," Jack continued with a dangerous glint in his eyes, "Alley was murdered by someone about five-foot-six and left-handed. The murderer tried to make it look like she was attempting blackmail, but Ara's letters had already been delivered. Now, we know the brothers are left-handed, but they are also tall. Who might be shorter and also left-handed, Victoria? Who hated Alley and was angry she got all of Peter's money?"

Victoria's eyes flicked around when she laughed, making her look unstable. The orderly sitting beside her glanced at Dr. Wolf with concern.

John stood up. "Why are you picking on our mom?"

Andrew clenched his fists.

"Shall I continue?"

"Yes," chorused everyone except the brothers and Victoria.

"While we were investigating Alley's death, the twins and Ara disappeared, and Melissa was admitted to the hospital.

When we were cleaning her house up for her return, we found a hair that matched the one in Peter's house and a used condom with a fingerprint."

"You'd better not have been messing with her!" Andrew growled at his brother.

"Aw," Melissa said, "still possessive even after you called me a hopped-up whore."

"And moving on. We locked John up for his own protection, but he would not submit to fingerprinting or a blood test. Since we had DNA and a fingerprint from the condom, we were able to identify Andrew, but we didn't know which twin he was."

"John threatened to tell Sam that he has a brother, and after he was taken into custody, Victoria started worrying about how much Sam knew, so she sent Andrew to kidnap her and bring her to the house. When she got shot, she went back inside for another drink. What she didn't realize was that someone had put Ambien in her bottle, like they did with Melissa." Jack raised an eyebrow at Andrew.

"It wasn't me!" he shouted. "Why would I drug my mom when I was bringing Sam to talk to her?"

Jack looked at John, who said nothing.

"Once we had everyone's DNA and fingerprints, we were able to access a lot more information, so let me tell you what I think happened. Andrew moved here after he burned down his adoptive parents' house, subsequently killing them. There was a warrant out for his arrest, but he changed his name and started a new life in Los Milagros as the local mechanic."

"I didn't kill them. I was framed. When I told my mom about it, she told me to come here."

"His twin brother, John, deserted his army unit while they were deployed. He also came to Los Milagros to hide out, and the brothers decided to share one identity. "Why did you do that?" Jack asked.

"We were both hiding out. We both have automotive training. It just seemed convenient." John shrugged.

"Peter had photos of you. Did he ever try to blackmail you?"

"He did want to meet his sons!" Victoria clasped her hands together.

"I originally thought the photos were showing some underhanded business practices, but then I realized that they showed two different people working at the garage." Jack paused and looked at them, but they didn't speak. "Victoria was in love with Peter as a young girl. When she became pregnant, he offered her a large sum of money if she gave them up for adoption and never spoke of their parentage."

"Can you imagine such a thing?" Victoria waved her arms around in agitation. "What kind of father wants his children to just disappear?"

"The loss of your sons hurt a lot didn't it?" Jack asked with compassion.

Her eyes got a dead look. "It ruined my life."

Jack began to pace again. "I'm not sure what made you decide to kill Peter after all this time. Perhaps it was when you found out he was abusing Melissa or when you saw him punch Andrew."

Victoria stared at Jack. "I didn't kill anyone. Why are you suddenly pointing the finger at me?"

"We found the crushed water hemlock roots in your bedroom, with your fingerprints on the bag."

"I just asked Andrew to get me some for my arthritis." She shrugged.

"Why did you leave John's hair at the scene of the crime? Did you want to frame your own son?"

"You left my hair at a crime scene?" John said angrily. "I knew he was your favorite, but I didn't know you actually hated me."

"I left a lot more clues pointing at the girl and told Andrew to give her an alibi. I was just confusing things."

The room was completely silent as if everyone was holding their breath.

Jack kept his voice soothing. "You had the bad son go to Peter's house to find the will. He finally did what you asked him to."

"About time too." Victoria nodded.

John stared at her with his mouth open, then put his head in his hands.

"When he came back with the pictures and the will, you were all pretty angry, weren't you."

Victoria pounded her fist on the table. "Steaming hot."

"Mama, you shouldn't say anything else," Andrew said, but she was on a roll.

"Don't be ridiculous. You know we were mad. She was trying to steal our inheritance. He should have married me and left his money for our babies. Instead, he married her and left her everything."

"How did she die?"

"She asked me to come up for coffee. I thought we were friends. I thought she was going to tell me that the inheritance belonged to the boys." She shook her head. "Instead, she started hinting that I had something to do with killing Peter. She was asking about poison. I had to make her stop or all of my plans would have been ruined."

"Oh my god," John said, staring at her. "We didn't need the money, mama. We were fine."

"It's your birthright! Your father should have been proud of you. He didn't even want to meet you." Her eyes were on her sons, and a small amount of spittle gathered on the side of her mouth.

Jack had to bite his tongue. "You went up for coffee?"

"She turned to take me to the kitchen, and I put some gloves on and grabbed a cross off the wall and hit her over the head. I wasn't sure she was dead, so I hit her again."

Sam had tears running down her face, and Melissa squeezed her hand hard. Jack's face took on a green tinge and he looked like he might be sick.

"Can you tell me about the photos and the blackmail stuff?"

"I wanted it to look like she was a blackmailer and the evil person she was, so I dumped the photos and the will on top of her and put some blackmail stuff on her table."

"You took them with you when you went for coffee?"

"Just in case. It's good to be prepared."

"So you planned to kill her?"

"I don't know what you mean. I didn't kill anyone." She crossed her arms.

"How did the extra photos end up at Melissa's house?"

"I guess John must have put them there."

"Why are you trying to blame everything on me?"

"You're the one that got them from Peter's, the only one who had time."

"It wasn't me! Andrew was very angry about Melissa's affair with the old man. He probably did it."

"Don't try to drag me into this!"

"Did you intend to kill Melissa with the Ambien cocktail, Andrew?" Jack asked.

"No! I was just trying to keep her a little out of it like mama told me to."

"Now, who's throwing who under the bus?" Victoria cackled.

"Was it also you adding Ambien to your mom's alcohol?"

"No! I already told you. She had me bring Sam to her. She was supposed to be my backup. Why would I want her passed out?"

"So that was John. Why did you try to kill your mother, John?"

"I didn't!"

"See, the bad son," Victoria said sadly.

John sighed and hung his head. "I heard them talking about Sam, and I didn't want them to hurt her. Mom tried to shoot her the last time I went to visit. I wasn't trying to kill anyone; I was just trying to protect Sam.

"I wasn't trying to shoot her; I was trying to shoot you!"

Everyone in the room gasped and John's mouth fell open.

"So, Victoria, you killed two people. Did your boys know what you were doing?"

"No."

"Are you sure?"

"Pretty sure. Did you boys know?"

"Of course not!" said Andrew.

"Did they help you with your plans?"

"Sometimes."

"Did you try to steal our horses when we were camping?"

"That was Andrew."

"Mama!"

"I told him to let them loose so he could kidnap Sam."

"Why was it so important to kidnap her? Couldn't you have gone to the ranch if you wanted to talk to her?"

"I wanted to have the upper hand. I wanted her to grovel."

"Why?"

"She was distracting John and making him disobey his mama. I wanted to make her leave him alone."

John was shaking his head. "I can't believe any of this. She must be having one of her spells, and you tricked her into saying all of this."

"No, I'm pretty sure she knows what she did," Jack said.

"You should stop picking on her and let her talk to a lawyer!"

Victoria just laughed. "Such drama."

"You just admitted to murder," John said. "And you are laughing because?"

She shrugged. "Because it's just a game. You can't win the lottery without buying a ticket. We could have all been very rich, but now I'll go back to the psych ward, and they'll take care of me. Maybe you'll inherit after all, and you can thank your mama. You can come and bust me out!"

Captain Blatt walked over to her wheelchair and read her her rights before she was wheeled back to her room. They could hear her laughter echo down the hall.

Everyone in the room was stunned. Before the deputies took the twins back to jail, John looked at Jack and said, "I'm so sorry. She's my mother. I didn't realize how far she'd gone."

"Poor Alley," Sam said. "She was trying to help."

Mark and Emily had their heads together and said something to Ara before they left.

Dr. Vanzandt and Captain Blatt shook Jack's hand. "Great job, Jack," Byron said. Jack thanked them and smiled weakly. He was exhausted.

Chapter 29

Jack slept the rest of the day. His exhaustion was both physical and emotional. Hearing how and why Alley was murdered was gut-wrenching. He felt guilt too. He should have realized what she was planning and warned her of the danger. He tossed and turned for hours, and when he finally rose, his muscles were stiff. He did some light calisthenics and showered before heading downstairs. He was surprised to smell coffee and hear voices.

"Good morning, Jack!" Sam smiled.

"You made breakfast?"

"I did. You must be starving."

Jack sat at the table. "I could eat a horse. Not Ghost, though!" Jack laughed.

"Hey champ," Mick said, entering the kitchen and joining Jack at the table. "I have a present for the two of you." He placed a thick, file-sized envelope on the table. "I've been doing some research on your families."

"Oh! Thanks, Mick. We got busy, and I forgot to tell you guys I found my dad's journals. I didn't want to read them by myself, so I was waiting for Jack to be here."

"Thank you, both. Let's wait until later, though. I need some time to process before I take on more."

Sam poured everyone a cup of coffee and put a plate with poached eggs on toast and fried potatoes in front of Jack, then dished some out for Mick.

"I did want to give you a little update from yesterday," Mick said.

They both looked at him expectantly.

"Deputy Flores has got the goods on Mark and Emily. Ara has agreed to work with us since he didn't have any direct involvement."

"Any direct involvement in what?" Sam's arm shook as she put another plate in front of Mick. She dished out her own and sat at the table. Jack put his hand on hers and looked up to ensure she was okay.

"Anita followed the three of them from the hospital yesterday and overheard Mark's plan to get into the safety deposit box. We've placed the bank under surveillance and plan to catch Mark in the act. An independent auditing firm has been working on unraveling his embezzlement. Although Emily hasn't really done anything, she has been an accessory after the fact. A jury will have to decide if she is guilty or not."

"I wondered what those two were up to," Sam said. "Ara didn't know anything about it?"

"Not until Mark told him yesterday. He'll be corroborating Anita's tape recording."

"Great work, Mick," Jack said.

The phone rang, and Jack went to answer it. When he came back a few minutes later, he said, "I'm afraid I have to go visit an attorney in Las Rodillas this afternoon. Would you come with me, Sam?"

"Of course. Do we need to leave right away?"

"I'm afraid so."

"Let me just change quick. Mick, the pool party is still on for this afternoon, so we'll meet you back here later."

Mick took his leave, and Jack and Sam were on their way shortly after he left. They were silent during the first part of the trip, then Sam looked at Jack and asked him what the lawyer wanted. "I'm not sure. He said something about Alley's will. I don't know what it could possibly have to do with me unless it's a legal issue to do with the twins."

Sam shuddered. "I hope they don't end up benefiting from what Victoria did. That would just be wrong."

When they entered the hushed offices of Osprey and Gluck, Sam glanced around and whispered, "This sure is fancy. Even the carpet has an attitude."

Jack smiled and approached the receptionist, a young brunette with long, red nails and an inordinate amount of makeup. "Jack Olivares to see Mr. Osprey."

"He'll just be a moment, Doctor," she said, coyly looking up at him through her lashes.

Jack sighed under his breath and went to sit with Sam in the padded chairs lining the wall.

Mr. Osprey came into the waiting room a few minutes later and shook Jack's hand. When he saw that Sam came forward as well, he said, "Your friend can wait here. We have coffee over there." He indicated a small table in the corner next to the reception desk.

"This is Samantha Olivares, my cousin, and she'll be accompanying me."

"I'm afraid that is not permitted."

"Then I'm sorry to have wasted your time. We'll be leaving now." Jack turned toward the door and took two steps before Mr. Osprey stopped him.

"This is highly irregular, but please come with me. Both of you."

They followed him to a spacious office, where he sat behind an enormous desk. Mr. Osprey himself was a large man, both in height and girth. Had he been a smaller man, the desk would have swallowed him. He ran his hand over his nearly bald head. "Let me begin by giving you this letter." He handed Jack a luxurious-looking envelope.

Jack ran his finger along the sealed edge and pulled out a sheet of paper that matched the envelope, unfolded it, and began to read.

Dearest Jack,
It is impossible to know what life might throw at us, how much time we will have together, and where our relationship will take us.

What I do know is that in the short time we have been together, you have helped me experience joy. I have stopped drinking so much and have felt hope. I never thought I would feel cherished again, especially by a man like you. I don't have much, and the saloon is not worth anything, but whatever I have is yours, including my heart.
Love, Alley

Jack swallowed hard and took a deep breath. Otherwise, he was completely still. His eyes were open, but he didn't see the office around him. He was seeing Alley, picturing her bright smile and her warm hug. His eyes were glistening when he passed the letter to Sam.

"Who did you say she is?" Mr. Osprey asked.

"My cousin." Jack's voice cracked. "My only living relative."

Mr. Osprey looked uncomfortable. He moved around in his chair and cleared his throat. "Ms. Carruther's will names me executor but leaves everything to you. When she made the will, it was inconsequential, but she has since inherited everything from her ex-husband's estate. So, you have inherited both their estates."

Jack's eyebrows rose. "Are there any other relatives who were expecting to inherit?"

"I don't believe so."

"All Alley wanted was her family home. She would have finally gotten it."

"Yes. It is a pity." Mr. Osprey frowned.

Jack's jaw clenched.

Sam placed her hand on his arm and said, "It is worse than a pity. It's tragic."

Mr. Osprey looked a little alarmed. "Of course. That was a very poor word choice on my part."

Jack shook his head as if to clear it. "I don't need this inheritance, so if anyone should contest it, please let me know. I appreciate Alley's generosity, but she didn't know about Peter's will either and might want to keep the ranch in her family."

Mr. Osprey folded his arms in front of him. "That is not exactly how it works. As it stands, both wills have to go through probate, so it could be quite some time before funds are released."

"Is there anything you need from me?"

"Not at this time. I will be in touch."

"Thank you, sir." They shook hands. "May I keep the letter?"

"Yes, of course."

Jack took the letter, and he and Sam left the office.

They were quiet on the way home, both lost in their thoughts until Sam said, "I am genuinely surprised. I wouldn't have thought Alley would be so quick to take action on something like a will."

"I don't know what motivated her to do it, if she just happened to be at the lawyer's office or if she made a special trip. I wonder if someone threatened her. Maybe we should ask the police to go back through her things."

"It wouldn't hurt. You two never talked about wills?"

"Not our own. We talked about whether or not Peter would have willed her house back to her."

"I talked to her about that too. Maybe that's what put it in her head."

"Reading her letter today was like seeing a ghost. I wish Mr. Osprey would have given me a little warning."

"For someone who deals with wills all the time, he doesn't seem very…"

"Poor bedside manner?"

"Well, yeah. He should show a little more compassion, don't you think?"

They lapsed back into silence.

Sam was surprised to find Mick waiting for them in the kitchen when they returned.

"Is everything okay?" he asked.

"Yes, did you know about the will?"

He looked a little sheepish. "Captain Blatt and I spoke with the attorney right after Alley's death."

"Why didn't you tell me?" Jack asked. "I probably should have removed myself from the investigation."

"All of the evidence is the same; all you did was piece it all together for us, so we didn't think it would be a problem."

Jack nodded. "I guess that's okay, but it's not really following protocol."

"Are you still up for a quiet pool party?" Sam asked.

"That sounds perfect."

"Monsoon season's coming soon," Mick said. "We'd better enjoy the weather while we can."

"I love the rain!" Melissa said, swirling into the kitchen.

"Melissa! I'm so happy you're here! When did you get discharged?"

"This morning. Mick gave me a ride. And you know what?"

"What?"

"I am full of energy and light." She emptied the pockets of her floaty dress and put a small pile of crystals on the table. "Ara came to the hospital. He brought me my crystals and apologized for everything."

"Have the two of you decided what to do about the baby?"

"Oh, honey, I lost the baby when I was in the hospital." Her face fell a little. "That poisonous concoction I was drinking was too much for his little system. It was very early stages, and perhaps his little soul will return to me in the future. Ara and I are going to work on getting to know each other for real. He asked me out to dinner."

"Are you sure you can trust him?"

"He started off on a dark path, but I believe he really does care about me. We'll take it slow."

Sam smiled at Melissa, then saw Jack out of the corner of her eye. He was sitting at the table by himself, staring off in the distance with a little frown.

She walked over to Mick and leaned in close. "Mick," she whispered in his ear, "could you take Melissa home to put her crystals in a safe place and get a swimsuit, and maybe stop at the store? I'd like to take Jack out for a ride."

"Sure." He stood and approached Melissa. "Let's go for a little ride. We can grab your swimsuit and pick up a few things for the party."

"Okay. Is that okay, Sam?"

Sam smiled and waved, then walked over to Jack and put her hand on his shoulder. "Jack," she said gently. "Jack?"

He looked up quickly, like he was mildly surprised.

"Ghost and Parsnip have been pretty lonely. Are you up for a little ride?"

"Yes. That sounds good."

They walked outside, and Sam hollered, "Roger!"

"The horses, Ms. Sam?"

"Yes, please." Sam smiled. "You always appear like magic."

Jack mounted Parsnip, and when Sam leaped onto Ghost's back, she saw him watching her with a bleak look in his eyes. His whole body seemed to slump. "I'm going to have to return to Albuquerque soon."

"No, Jack! I don't want you to leave."

"It's where my job is. We can see each other on weekends or…"

"When you aren't involved in a case."

Sam stared at him until her eyes started to tear, then nudged Ghost and flew out into the field at a gallop.

Jack hardly had a chance to register Sam's departure because Parsnip took off after Ghost. He was terrified by the speed his gentle horse managed at full gallop, but then he settled into the rhythm and felt the sheer power beneath him. His heart raced as he heard Parsnip's hooves pounding across the range and felt the warm air blowing on his face. When he caught up with Sam at the river bank, she had tears in her eyes. "Sam?"

"I don't want you to go. I've only just found you again. I need you. Can't you apply for the empty position here?"

"It would be a huge demotion for me," he said slowly.

Sam twisted around to look at him. "You can have the money your dad gave me. Is there anything keeping you in Albuquerque besides your job?"

"Not really, and I don't need the money. I guess I've just gotten used to the status."

"Everyone here thinks you're a genius, including me." She smiled sadly.

"I'll look into it." Jack really did love Santo Milagro and enjoyed his stay, but he suspected that he wouldn't be able to stand the lack of professional stimulation. *I would end up resenting her.*

"Thanks, Jack-o." She sniffed.

"That was incredible, by the way, flying across the field."

"It was. Let's do it again!" Sam nudged Ghost with her heels and went flying back across the range.

They raced into the yard laughing, Parsnip hard on Ghost's tail. Jack wasn't quite as in control as he thought, and he promptly fell off Parsnip when she stopped suddenly. He laid on his back, breathing hard, and laughed until tears ran down his face.

Sam leaped off Ghost and ran to where he was lying on the ground. "Are you okay?" she asked, worried.

"I am so okay. I am exactly where I belong."

"On your back in the dirt?"

"In the countryside with my family." *I wish everything could stay like this forever.*

Chapter 30

Mick and Melissa were waiting for them when they returned. Roger had helped Mick remove the pool cover, and Melissa was already floating around in the pool. After they went upstairs to change, Jack carried ice and beer out to the cooler, and Sam carried platters of snacks to the outdoor table.

To Jack's surprise, Byron and Tia showed up as well. Dr. Vanzandt always looked very serious, and he never accepted invitations, but there he was, holding Tia's hand and looking like he had changed somehow. "Byron! Thanks for coming."

"Thank you for having me. You know Tia, right?"

"Actually, we haven't been officially introduced." He shook Tia's hand, "I'm Jack. Nice to meet you."

Tia smiled. "I know who you are, of course. Small town. But it's very nice to officially meet you too."

"I was wondering why you were slacking off, Byron," Jack joked. "Now I know."

"How did you two meet?" Sam asked. "I never even saw you in town, Dr. Vanzandt, except at the meeting at the hospital."

"That is the day we met." Byron smiled at Tia. "I couldn't resist her shop."

"He came in, and the plants went wild." Tia grinned.

"I'm making margaritas," Melissa called out. "Raise your hand if you want one!"

Four hands went up. Roger flexed a muscle and said, "Mick and I are too macho for margaritas."

"That's right," Mick said. "But you can put one of those little umbrellas in my beer if you don't mind."

Everyone laughed and moved toward the barbecue area to get their drinks and nibble on snacks.

They spent the afternoon listening to music, playing in the pool, and visiting. As the sun went down over the wide horizon, the dazzling pinks and oranges lent a tropical glow to the patio.

"I wish we had palm trees," Melissa said.

"Why?" Sam asked.

"Because on nights like these, we might actually feel like we were in Hawaii."

"Who needs Hawaii," Jack said, "when we can live in Santo Milagro? Why don't we light the coals, and we can have a southwestern luau."

"Do we bury a cow?" Sam asked.

"Or a goat?" Melissa asked.

"I remember the day I arrived. I wondered why anyone would want to live here. Now, I wonder why anyone would want to leave," Jack mused.

"I felt much the same way," Byron said. "Staying in town is very different from living out here. This land has its own brand of magic."

"Are you thinking of staying?"

"No, but I may be visiting quite often until I can get my plant princess to relocate."

Tia curled up closer to him and smiled.

They finished off the day with barbecued ribs and coleslaw and Tia's homemade tiramisu. Everyone looked happy and relaxed.

"I need to get some sleep," Jack said. "I have to get up early." He felt guilty putting an end to the festivities.

"You will check into it, right?" Sam asked.

"I will. Give me a hug, and I'll see you again soon."

Sam's eyes started watering again, but she stayed strong and didn't let him see. Mick, Byron, and Tia all took their leave as well. Sam stopped Tia on her way out and said, "Thank you for coming, Tia. I hope you'll come again."

Sam went back outside and sat on the edge of the pool after she heard the cars leave, so she was surprised when Melissa came and handed her a drink, sitting next to her with her feet in the water.

They sat in silence for a while until Melissa said, "Do you want me to stay over tonight?"

"Yes, please." Sam gave a weak smile.

"Good, because I don't have a car." Melissa gave her a good-natured nudge with her elbow. "Let's go in. It's starting to get chilly."

Jack finished packing his bag and sat on his bed with Preciosa. He looked around his room. This really has become home. He thought about how powerful he felt in Albuquerque; his rank had even carried over here. He had attained the status he had always worked for. He had everything he could ever want. Then he thought about his dad. *He got what he worked for too, but there was no love in his life, no true friendship, no sense of community. Do I want that life?* He laid down and tried to sleep, but his thoughts whirled around, and he was restless. Preciosa slept soundly on his stomach, and he smiled at her. He gave up trying at three and went down to make coffee and breakfast for Sam. He tried hard not to think about how much he needed her. She and Santo Milagro had turned his life upside down.

The next morning, Sam was glad Melissa had stayed over. Jack had made breakfast and coffee, but he hadn't left a note. She missed him already, just knowing he was gone.

"You know," Melissa said, "one of the things you probably liked about having Jack here was the company. Not just his company but friends stopping by and getting out of the house. Maybe you should remember that and not go back to being a recluse. Everyone misses you when you aren't around, including me."

Sam thought about that while she sipped her coffee. "You could be right. I'll try not to be a hermit."

"Now I have to get out of here and go open my shop. My customers have probably forgotten about me."

"You are unforgettable! Thank you for staying over last night and for the pep talk."

"I'll see you soon. Stop by the shop if you want."

"How are you getting there?"

"Ara's here to pick me up." She smiled and waved as she skipped out the door.

Sam smiled after her. *It's nice to see her back to herself.* She was genuinely happy for Melissa, but once she was alone again, her spirits plummeted.

Chapter 31

Sam went up to her room and laid on her bed. She didn't sleep or cry; she just laid there. Finally, she got up and strode out to the barn to find Ghost.

"Roger!"

"Yes, Ms. Sam? You want Ghost?"

"Yes. Please."

Sam hugged Ghost when Roger brought her out, and the tears finally came. Roger moved away to leave her with some privacy. "Most people would probably think I'm crazy, but I tell Ghost everything. She's the one being in my life that never changes. She is always here and loves me no matter what."

"I feel that way about Red, Ms. Sam."

She nodded, then leaped onto Ghost's back, neatly jumped the fence, and galloped into the field.

Sam rode for hours every day for the following week.

"Ghost is getting tired, Ms. Sam. You might want to give her a day off every once in a while."

"I know. We don't ride the whole time. I let her graze while I sit and read, or sometimes we go swimming."

"Could I go with you sometime?"

Sam looked at him in surprise. "Yes, I suppose so. You can come riding with us tomorrow if you like. Bring your trunks."

"Thanks!"

"I've been thinking I should start reading my father's journals. Did you know him pretty well?"

Roger's expression fell a little. "He was a great man. I learned a lot from him."

The next day, Sam packed towels and lunch before going to find Roger. They rode to a clearing along a quiet stretch of the river, where the water slowed between two bends. Sam dismounted and let Ghost wander while she laid down a picnic blanket and the lunch basket.

"Do you come here often?" Roger asked.

"I guess I do, lately. It's funny how we form little habits, isn't it."

Roger sat quietly and watched her unpack the picnic basket.

"Why are you watching me?"

"I don't know. Even though you've been around most of my time at the ranch, I don't really feel like I know you."

"I guess that's true. I trust you because my dad trusted you, but I don't really know you either. How did you end up working at the ranch?"

"I grew up in Las Rodillas, and my parents were friends with your dad. When they died, he was the only person who took an interest in me. I was sixteen and not a great student, so he asked if I was interested in working for him. He told me I'd have room and board plus a salary, and I could learn as much as I wanted. It's been ten years, and the ranch is home now."

"Did you know he was seeing Melissa?"

Roger didn't meet her eyes as he nodded.

"They seemed very happy in the photos I saw. I wish he had told me. I feel bad they thought they had to sneak around, that they assumed I would be angry. Maybe I would have been. I don't know."

"You seem like you've changed, Ms. Sam."

"Please, just call me Sam. Maybe I have changed. It's hard to notice it in yourself sometimes." She was silent for a moment. "Enough of this! Let's enjoy the afternoon!" She got up, shucked her boots and jeans, then jumped in the river.

After they got out of the water and ate their lunch, Sam said, "Thank you for spending the afternoon with me, Roger. It was nice to have company for a change."

"My pleasure Ms— I mean, Sam. This is the best afternoon I've had in a long time."

"Let's head back. I think I'm finally ready to face the wall of journals."

There were eleven books, each spanning two to three years. Sam opened the first and began to read. She could hear her father's loving voice in every sentence, and she felt warm and comforted reading his memories of her first years. Reading was slow because she was matching his stories with the pictures in the albums she and Jack had found.

In the fourth book, her father's writing started sounding strained. He sensed that her mother was keeping something from him, and he feared the worst.

> *Today, I accused Erika of having an affair. She was so upset and couldn't believe I would ever think that of her. So we talked about the burden she had been carrying, not her secret, but that of Kaoru. She warned me that if she told me, it would be my burden as well because I couldn't repeat it. I insisted she tell me, and now I wish I hadn't.*

Sam frowned. Her father wrote about a secret but didn't say what it was.

Jack was back on campus, resuming his chaotic role as Chief Medical Examiner. He not only created policy and oversaw the entire state system, he also carried his own caseload and consulted with his staff of medical examiners and pathologists. He kept so busy that he rarely had time to think about his personal life. He pushed thoughts of Sam and Santo Milagro into a dusty corner of his brain and concentrated on catching up. His problems occurred once he was off work. He didn't want to go out on the town with his colleagues.

He spent his time either home alone or going through his father's things. Both activities made him think of Sam. *I wonder what she's doing now. Does she miss me? It's not fair to have to give up my whole life to move there.*

That evening Sam sat down with the journals again.

> *Kaoru's secret is eating at me. I think about it every time our families are together, and it is interfering with my relationship with my brother. I told Erika that Kaoru needs to be honest with him. I can't keep her secret. Now it is causing a rift between Erika and me, but how can she expect me to keep such a secret? How can I not tell my brother that his son is not his? And how could his wife deceive him this way? Loyalty has always been important in our family, and he would not forgive me for keeping this a secret.*

Sam sat staring at the page. Jack was not an Olivares by blood? Could that be true? She read on.

> *Our wives are both pregnant, and they are so excited. They went out shopping together, and Martin and I were preparing the barbecue. I wasn't sure I should interfere when Kaoru was pregnant, but I felt like he needed to know. Rock and a hard place. I knew Erika would feel like I betrayed her trust as well, but I had to tell him.*

"Oh no! He didn't!"

> *We each had a couple of beers, and I told him what Erika had confided in me. I told him it was third hand information so not to take it as gospel. I suggested he talk to her and find out the truth. Our wives both died that day. I have wished over and over again I hadn't said anything.*

230

I betrayed Erika's trust and tarnished Kaoru's name, and she doesn't even have a chance to explain. I feel lower than low right now.

Sam cringed. She felt her father's pain at that moment. *You try to do what's best, and it backfires. You can't undo it.*

Martin is so angry. He is angry at God and at the world. He is angry at me. I should have listened to Erika and kept her counsel. After the funeral, he looked into the timing and spoke to Kaoru's parents, and found out the truth. Jack's father was a Brazilian man working illegally in Japan. He got Kaoru pregnant and disappeared. I think she was happy with Martin. They had a good marriage. But because I had to tell him her secret, poor Jack suffered for it. Jack and Sam both suffered for it because they were torn apart right after they lost their mothers, and it was my fault.

Sam sat there in shock. She didn't know what to think. At first, she hadn't remembered Jack. Then she was excited to have one remaining relative. She loved him. He was so like her in many ways but complimented her in others. And now he had left her like everyone else important to her had, and she found out they weren't actually related. Does it matter if we aren't related?

Sam stopped reading the journals for two days and went back to riding during the afternoon. Her feelings for Jack were more complicated than she had thought. But perhaps her feelings didn't matter since he left and hadn't even called. I need to put those thoughts away and finish reading the journals.

She got up the next morning and grabbed the fourth journal on her way to the kitchen. She got the coffee brewing and sat down with the book.

I have lost everyone but my precious Samantha, and I know her world has come crashing down as well. I need to take better care of both of us since it's just the two of us. I don't know what to do to make things better. She has turned into a quiet, serious child, and she watches me constantly.

Sam went to pour a cup of coffee and thought about her father's feelings of guilt. She wished she could remember that period of her life, but maybe it was better she couldn't. She retrieved book five and began reading.

Mother came back from Martin's house today. He allows her to visit on the condition she doesn't discuss him or his household with me. I wonder if he will ever let go of his anger. Mother broke the rules and told me Jack is something of a prodigy. He is several years ahead in school and plans to be a doctor. Martin, rather than be proud of him, treats him as if he's an obligation. There is no love in that household, she told me, and I know it's my fault.

Oh, Dad. What a terrible burden you carried, and poor Jack. She continued reading until he began to mention Melissa, then she wondered if she should read that part.

It was mid-afternoon, so Sam drove into town to see Melissa. Her shop was dimly lit with tinkling music playing softly in the background. A lump rose in Sam's throat as she remembered Jack's allergic reaction.

Melissa floated over to her and gave her a hug. "Hey, sis! It's been a while."

"Yes, too long. You look like you're doing well."

"I am! Ara and I are talking about getting married, and I seem to have regained the positivity and light that were missing for so long."

"I'm glad." Sam smiled softly. "I wanted to ask you something."

232

"Yes?"

"I'm reading my father's journals, and I have gotten to the part where he mentions you. I wasn't sure if I should read it. Would you rather I didn't? Should I give those to you instead?"

"Sam, I loved your dad very much, but he's gone, and I need to move forward. My life spiraled out of control after he died, and I don't want to revisit that. You can read the journals if you like, but I can't. I know how we felt about each other, and that's enough."

"I hope I'm lucky enough to find a love like that someday."

"You will, sis. The cards told me." Melissa gave her another hug.

Sam left before her emotions got the better of her. She made one more stop before she went home. She wanted to visit Tia's tropical garden. The deep gong of a bell sounded as she stepped into the lush, rich-smelling shop.

"Do you need some time alone?" came Tia's soft, melodious voice.

"Yes, please." She found the hidden stool and sat for a long time, letting the plants absorb her sadness and uncertainty. Tia somehow knew when to reappear. She pulled out another hidden stool and sat across from Sam.

"I don't know what to do," Sam said with a stuffy nose.

"Finish your task, and you will know. Take him with you. He likes you best." She handed her a large purple and blue plant.

"I don't usually keep plants in the house because my cat eats them."

"He will like this one. And don't worry about its care; just water it when it droops and talk to it every day."

"Thank you, Tia."

"You're welcome." She smiled. "Please come and visit any time."

Sam took the plant home and set it on the kitchen table while she fixed herself a sandwich. When she was done, she was surprised to see Chiquito and Preciosa curled around the pot, purring, and she wondered if Tia might be more mystical than Melissa.

233

Grabbing the last two journals, she continued to read.

It's funny the paths our lives take, for better or worse. Sam is off at college, and I have been lonely. Today, I went for a ride and found Melissa picking flowers on the river bank. She had been crying, and I sat with her and asked her why. She was missing Sam too, and we talked for a long time before I asked her if she'd like to have dinner with me.

Sam stopped reading and looked at her companions. The plant seemed to be leaning in her direction, and Chiquito licked one of its leaves. "We don't know if our new friend is poisonous," she said, "so don't go trying to eat him." Chiquito just looked at her and laid back down.

"Tia said to talk to you," she told the plant. "You sure are beautiful. Please don't die. I don't have much experience with plants." She stroked its leaves and went back to reading.

Melissa and I have been spending every evening together. We've gotten into a routine. We have dinner, then watch TV or read and talk about what we're watching or reading. This evening we were watching ballroom dancing, and I let slip that Erika and I had taken lessons. That led to Melissa asking if I could teach her, and I felt the first tremor of desire in over ten years when I held her in my arms. Perhaps I shouldn't see her any more, as Sam would likely disapprove.

Sam thought about her father's words. Would she have disapproved? Probably, but it would have been wrong. Her dad deserved happiness too. She continued reading their love story, which spanned the four years she was at school. Then she returned home, brokenhearted and had no inkling of the strife behind the scenes.

Sam has come home, and I am worried about how she might react to our relationship. For us, the past four years have been a progression, but it will be a shock for Sam. We have talked about getting married, but I don't know if I can do it. I want to take care of her, but the memory of my Erika remains strong. I wish I had someone to talk about it with. I would like to talk to Sam about it, but I am afraid to rock our foundation.

"I know how you felt, papa. I wish I had someone to talk to about Jack. What is it with our family? It's all about trust, loyalty, guilt, and betrayal, isn't it? And we never talk about any of it."

There was more about Sam and Melissa in the journal, but nothing earth-shattering until the entry about Martin.

Martin wrote to me today and asked if he could come talk to me. I am so happy he has finally broken his silence. My heart has been heavy all of these years, and I miss him. We were always so close. I know it broke Mother's heart as well, watching him wallow in anger and pain.

"Oh, papa. How terrible that must have been."

Martin arrived today without Jack. He was not friendly, but he was humble. He said the business was not doing well and asked me if he could borrow money. This is not a good time for me, but if it will help him and possibly mend our families, I will give him what he asks. Since Samantha is home from school now, her head full of business ideas, I will have to make sure I get things caught up.

"Why didn't you just tell me? Why did you have to struggle alone with all these secrets?" Sam cried out. His last entry was painful to read.

I'm not going to make it much longer. I've had one heart attack, and I will have another. Sam, if you read this, I love you more than life itself. You have been the apple of my eye, and I wish your mother could have been with us to guide you and watch you grow. I did my best and am sorry I couldn't do better. If you are reading this, you probably know about Melissa. She loved me, but she always loved you more. Please look after her. She has a sweet, soft heart without the wisdom to take care of it. I know you love her as I do, and trust you will care for her.

I love you and am so proud of you. Dad."

Sam just sat there staring at the page. *He knew he was going to die.* She felt like she couldn't move. She couldn't think. She sat there for a long time. She suddenly felt an intense need to get away—to escape her thoughts, her loneliness, her routine. She picked up Cathy's card from her desk and remembered her words about creating her own adventure.

Two weeks later, Jack showed up at the ranch for a visit. He was excited to see Sam. He had missed her. He had decided to stay in Albuquerque, but he wanted to spend time with Sam when he could get away. He was prepared for a difficult conversation.

When he let himself in the house, it was very still. He called out and was surprised that the cats didn't greet him. A letter with his name on it and an open journal sat on the kitchen table.

He read the journal entry first since it was open, and sat down hard. He read it several times, his life with his father finally making sense, and his father's last words becoming more meaningful. He sat at the table for a long time, eyeing Sam's letter but afraid to read it. He wondered where she was. His hands trembled when, at last, he opened her letter.

Dearest Jack,

I understand that asking you to uproot your life was unreasonable. I found the marked entry in my father's journal. I don't want it to affect your decision one way or the other, so I'm leaving it here for you to process on your own terms if you decide to visit.

I was so happy when you showed up in town. Having family is wonderful, and even if we live in different places and we're not technically related, you and Melissa are my family. You always will be.

But my reasons for wanting you to stay were more complicated than that. I saw my life and this land through your eyes and enjoyed our adventures. My boring, lonely life became active and social. I was having fun. I looked forward to getting up and having breakfast with you and seeing what the new day would bring.

Someone told me recently that I need to make my own adventures, so that is what I'm doing. Melissa is cat-sitting, and Roger is looking after the ranch. Stay as long as you like, and I will see you again one day.

Love, Sam

Jack thought about Sam and how she made him feel. Everyone had their own reasons for why they wanted to be with someone else. *I have always had a carefully scheduled, loveless existence. All I do is work and socialize with people I don't care about. Sam and the people I met here gave me love and a sense of community.* "She doesn't realize that we both want the same things," he said aloud.

"Then why did you leave?" Roger startled him.

"How long have you been standing there? I didn't hear you come in."

"Just for a second."

"Do you know where she went?"

"Not exactly, but I think she needs her little adventure."

Jack nodded. "Do you have any idea when she'll be back?"

Roger shook his head.

Jack looked at him silently, then extended his hand and shook Roger's. "Thank you."

"Hopefully, we'll meet again."

He turned and walked outside, climbed back inside his Portofino and drove away in a plume of dust.

Alice Kanaka has been reading everything she could get her hands on since she could hold a book and writing stories aboutthe world around her. Her youth was a series of moves across the United States, accompanied by her sibling sidekick and her books.

After studying abroad in England and Spain and a short stint working for Club Med, Alice packed her bag once more and went to teach in Japan. Her story continues along the same vein, adding languages, kid sand cats into the mix. Open one of her mysteries to see the world through her eyes. You won't be disappointed.

HTTPS://AliceKanaka.com

If you'd like to see more of Alice's adventures, make sure to check out her **travel blog!**

https://ExploringWithAlice.com

Sign up for Alice's mailing list to get notifications and to be entered in a monthly raffle!

Coming Soon:
The Cardinal, the Fat Boy & the Flamingo

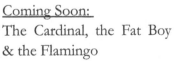

Made in USA - Kendallville, IN
10543_9798986310510
05.27.2022 1303